A REEL CATCH

LORRAINE BARTLETT

COPYRIGHT

For more information on Lorraine's books, check out her website: http://www.LorraineBartlett.com

Other Books By Lorraine Bartlett

THE LOTUS BAY MYSTERIES
Panty Raid: A Tori Cannon-Kathy Grant Mini Mystery
With Baited Breath
Christmas At Swans Nest
A Reel Catch

THE VICTORIA SQUARE MYSTERIES
A Crafty Killing
The Walled Flower
One Hot Murder
Dead, Bath and Beyond
Yule Be Dead
Recipes To Die For

LIFE ON VICTORIA SQUARE
Carving Out A Path
A Basket Full of Bargains
The Broken Teacup
It's Tutu Much

TALES FROM BLYTHE COVE MANOR
A Dream Weekend
A Final Gift
An Unexpected Visitor

TALES OF TELENIA
Threshold
Journey
Treachery

SHORT STORIES
Blue Christmas
Prisoner of Love
Love Heals
We're So Sorry, Uncle Albert
An Unconditional Love

ACKNOWLEDGMENTS

My thanks to Mare Fairchild for walking me through high school library procedures. And my thanks also go to Mary Kennedy, my friend, and cheerleader. She stood on the sidelines cheering me on when I had writer's block and she and her husband, Alan, helped me hash out an important plot point. If you haven't read Mary's cozy mystery and young adult books—you're missing out on a treat! (MaryKennedy.net) Thanks also go to my proofreaders: Linda Kuzminczuk, Debbie Lyons, and Pam Priest.

Cover by Wicked Smart Designs.

*T*he sky above was an opaque white, but farther to the north, over Lake Ontario, it was crystal blue, meaning colder air was on its way from Canada. Tori Cannon and her BFF, Kathy Grant, were bundled up on that raw April day. Loppers and saws in hand, they trudged through the spotty lawn that was just starting to green up, heading for the untidy tangle of willows and brush at the side of Kathy's property that bumped up to the marshy south end of Lotus Bay.

"I hate lawn work," Tori grumbled as they neared the edge of the lot near the bay bridge.

"I'm not fond of it either, but I helped you tidy up your yard last year, girlfriend. You *owe* me."

Truer words were never spoken.

That said, they'd decided that Tori was to woman the tools and Kathy would haul the brush to the burn pile since that was the harder, more boring of the tasks at hand. Kathy really was a doll.

"Give me some direction," Tori said, looking at the mess before her.

"Just start hacking away at the branches—then we can go at the trunks with the saw."

"We're never going to finish this in one day."

"I know, but if we don't start—it'll never get done."

Tori nodded, opened the loppers, and began to chop off branches right, left, and center. "Anissa should be doing this, not me. She's strong, with arms like a weightlifter."

"That's because she lifts weights," Kathy commented about their contractor friend, who'd been Tori's childhood compadre. "And I'm not about to pay for stuff when I can get you to do it for free."

Tori savagely chopped off yet another limb. "She's inside where it's nice and warm and we're outside freezing our butts off."

"The heat in my house is set at sixty degrees. I seriously doubt she'll break a sweat."

"Yeah, well, the wind isn't whistling around her ears, either," Tori said, viciously hacking off another branch. In reality, she didn't mind the work, especially since Kathy had done so much to help shape up the Cannon Compound the summer before, cleaning, painting, and helping Tori dispose of the flotsam and jetsam of her grandparents' collection of broken and useless junk. Still, she felt she had to protest; Kathy would expect it, and she wasn't about to let her best friend down.

"I'm going to haul these branches to the burn pile," Kathy said, gathering up as many skinny limbs as she could muster, and started dragging the wood away.

Tori continued nipping the branches close to the sapling's trunk. She'd soon need to attack the bottom of the trees with the saw and wished she had kneepads. Once she knelt on the newly greening grass, she knew the dampness was sure to seep into her jeans, and then she'd feel even colder. Still, if she kept moving, kept attacking the branches, she might soon be warm enough to take off her jacket, though not her hat.

Kathy returned and the women worked at the worst of the junk trees and suckers for the better part of an hour before Tori's back began to protest. Maybe they could take a coffee break for fifteen or twenty minutes before coming back to give the most untidy part of the yard another go. They'd cleared an almost six-foot square space, getting closer to the water's edge when Tori saw what looked like a soaked hunk of dark cloth in kind of a hump among the spent cattails.

"What's that?" she asked, pointing.

Kathy squinted. "Probably a jacket somebody lost when fishing last fall."

"Maybe it got too warm to wear during duck season and somebody accidentally dropped it in the water."

"Maybe," Kathy agreed, sounding anything but sure.

"We should probably get an oar from my boathouse and haul it ashore. I mean, if you want to clean up the area, we've got to get all the crap out of the water, too."

"Yeah. I think I counted at least fifteen of those little Styrofoam cups you and the Bayside Marina across the bridge sell bait in."

"I know the cups aren't biodegradable, but I plan to stop using them as soon as I run out."

"I should hope so," Kathy said in rather a threatening tone.

Of course, the fact that there wasn't much money coming in and Tori's Gramps had stocked a couple of caseloads of the offensive cups had a lot to do with her decision to keep using them. She wasn't exactly rolling in dough after a winter spent substitute teaching kids who thought their teacher's absence meant a free period. And, generally, they were right. Yet Tori had put together her own curriculum for classes from kindergarten to high school senior—which mostly consisted of age-appropriate discussions of world events. So far, the school districts she'd worked for hadn't censored her, which she accepted as tacit approval. And Tori regularly patrolled the bay bridge and retrieved the cups from the water and disposed of them appropriately. It was the least she could do.

"Haul all the rest of this stuff to the burn pile, and I'll go get an oar," Tori said, tossed the loppers to the ground, and headed for home. She stopped at the boathouse first, then grabbed her red and white polka-dot waterproof wellies, just in case she'd have to wade into the bay.

By the time she returned, Kathy had removed the majority of debris and was working with the saw on yet another tree trunk.

"Stand aside!" Tori called in a commanding voice. Kathy glared at her but got up to comply.

Tori stood close to the water and poked at the soggy fabric with the tip of the oar, but couldn't get the wood under the material.

"Is it stuck on something? A log maybe?" Kathy suggested.

"No, it feels—" Tori paused. "Heavy."

"Heavy how?" Kathy asked, sounding concerned.

Tori poked the oar at the wad of fabric, wishing she'd thought to bring her waterproof gloves, too. "Like ... there might be something in it."

"Uh-oh," Kathy said, and took a step back.

"It can't be a body," Tori said, trying to put some teacher's authority into her voice. "I mean, it doesn't stink to high heaven."

Kathy sniffed the air as though to test that theory.

Tori continued to jab the fabric with the oar, wondering if they should just call it a day for yard/marsh cleanup, knowing Kathy—often acknowledged as a taskmaster—would nix that idea. She was just going to have to muster a little bravery and grab the coat, haul it out of the ice-cold water, toss it in the trash, and get on with the job.

Yeah, that's what she'd do.

Tossing the oar aside, she put her heavy-duty gardening gloves back on and took a step forward.

"Wait," Kathy called. "You don't want to fall in. I'll hold onto the back of your coat ... just in case."

Kathy moved to stand behind Tori, grabbing her jacket, and shuffling behind her as Tori stepped close to the marshy edge of the water. Bending down, she grabbed the fabric, and a bubble of gas rippled through the water. She pulled it while Kathy dug in her heels, hanging onto the back of her jacket.

Intent on her work, Tori kept her focus on the dirty coat— that is until Kathy screamed, and let go of her jacket, and she went careening—face first—into the icy, murky water. Then it was Tori's turn to scream—once she came up for air, struggling to right herself before her wellies completely filled with water. "What did you do that for?"

Kathy had grabbed the oar, holding it out for Tori to grab onto. She did, and Kathy pulled her back onto dry—well, damp—land.

Furious, Tori waved her arms like a wet dog, sending a shower of droplets over her friend, who backed away. She peeled off her gloves and was attempting to remove her jacket when she noticed the look of anguish on her best friend's face. "What?" she nearly barked.

Kathy pointed toward the water.

Tori turned but saw only the brackish water and the sodden fabric.

And then her breath caught in her throat.

There, at the end of a floating sleeve, was a not-so-fleshy hand floating in the water.

KATHY KNEW THE DRILL. After all, she'd been interrogated by the Sheriff's Department on more than one occasion following the terrible events of the previous summer. The bad guys hadn't yet gone to trial, so there was still that horror to come.

What she minded most was the suspicion law enforcement leveled at one when it came to reporting a dead body.

"Detective Osborn," she said, unable to keep the testiness from her voice, "The guy in the water has obviously been in soak for quite a while, so it's not like we killed him."

Osborn had been the detective in charge of the Michael Jackson homicide the year before. He'd been a sour SOB then and his personality had not undergone any improvement, although he seemed to have lost the beer belly and gotten a decent haircut. Maybe he had an upcoming court appearance and wanted to look good. Kathy couldn't imagine any woman actually being attracted to the man. But then he was middle-aged, and she still had more than a decade to go to get to that point in life.

"So you say."

"Are you crazy?" Anissa Jackson asked, giving the detective the fisheye. "There's a reason black folk like me don't like to talk to white cops like you—" she began even more testily than Kathy.

Kathy waved her hands in the air as though to erase Anissa's words. "Let's not go there," she placated. "It was Tori and *I* who found the jacket in the water—with the guy still in it."

A still-shivering Tori stood nearby. Despite the fact she'd changed clothes and donned warm shoes, hat, scarf, and boots, she complained that she couldn't seem to get warm. What she needed was to be inside with a lap robe, a cat, and a big mug of cocoa. "We figured he must have fallen overboard while hunting or fishing last fall. Or maybe crashed through the ice on his snowmobile."

"A very good theory," Osborn said, "except for one thing. Nobody around here has been reported as missing."

"Well, then I'm stumped," Kathy said wrapping her arms around herself in an effort to keep warm. She was ready for cocoa and a lap robe, too. "Is it really necessary that we stand around in the cold while you guys do whatever it is you do?"

Osborn frowned. "I suppose not. But I'm not done questioning you."

"Fine. We'll go back into my house and when you're ready, we'll be available to talk."

"Very well." He turned, heading back toward the medical examiner's team that had arrived from Rochester and was about to pull the body from the water. It wasn't something Kathy wanted to witness.

"Come on, ladies. Let's go back inside."

"You don't have to convince me," Tori said.

The three women trudged back up the small rise to the large house, past the big sign that had been erected just the week before. The name, Swans Nest, Kathy's about-to-open bed and breakfast, was raised from the chiseled background of the pressure-treated wood and filled in with gold leaf. The image of a mama swan sitting on a nest was situated above it, and a temporary vinyl banner attached to it promised OPENING SOON.

They climbed the steps to the newly replaced front porch, and Kathy opened the heavy oak front door that had been restored to its former glory. Anissa was responsible for a lot of the repairs and refurbishments, but Kathy had invested months of sweat equity as well.

Upon entering the house, Anissa closed the door and she and Tori followed their hostess into the kitchen, where Kathy immediately put the electric kettle on, taking out cups, spoons, and cocoa powder.

"You're going to make hot chocolate with water?" Anissa protested.

"I made it that way all winter and you never complained."

"That's because—" But she didn't seem to have an answer. "Then why's it so chocolatey?"

"Because I add chocolate chips."

"Are you gonna make it that way for your guests?"

"Probably not. The idea is for them to come here to be pampered. The three of us merely need to warm up."

"I'm all for that," Tori announced and took a seat at the marble-topped island. She seemed to shudder once again and blew onto her still-gloved hands to warm them.

Anissa joined her childhood friend at the island. "Got any cookies?"

"Have I ever not?" Kathy asked, pointedly.

Anissa shot Tori a smug look. She was the ultimate cookie monster.

Kathy scooped half a dozen sunflower seed cookies from the big glass jar on the back counter, placed them on a plate, and set it in front of her friends. Neither wasted time grabbing one—although Tori did at least remove one of her gloves first.

Anissa took a bite, chewed, smiled in approval, then swallowed. "Damn, they're good. Another new recipe?"

Kathy nodded, pleased at her friend's reaction. "I need to have an array of options to offer my brides."

Kathy was gambling that she would be able to throw bridal showers, and possibly host weddings and receptions, at Swans Nest. She'd been gathering recipes and testing them on Anissa and Tori all winter. Catering would be a big part of her business...she hoped.

"So what do you think the story is with that dead guy?" Tori asked.

"Seems weird that a body washes up when nobody's been reported missing," Anissa commented before taking another bite of cookie.

"Who do you think he could be?" Kathy asked.

"He could've come from Canada," Tori offered, watching as Kathy spooned cocoa mix into the mugs. "I mean, he was wearing a plaid coat."

"You think only Canadians wear plaid jackets?" Anissa asked.

Tori shrugged. "So do the Scots."

Anissa frowned. "That's an awfully long way to float."

"Yeah, around fifty miles," Tori said. "But think of how those waves crash up at the Point."

"Point nothing—your breakwall," Kathy said.

Tori nodded. "With a wind from the north, anything's possible."

"I'm sure the detective will put out a call. I mean, just because nobody has disappeared on Lotus Bay doesn't mean the dead guy wasn't a missing person. There's a reason Ontario's called a Great Lake."

"Luckily we're not going to have to worry about this guy," Anissa said and reached for another cookie.

"Oh, no? What if they want us to look at his face? Besides the normal putrefaction of flesh, you don't know what else could have been nibbling on him all these months."

"You mean like fish and turtles and stuff?" Kathy asked.

Again Tori nodded.

"I certainly don't want to look at a putrefied dead guy," Anissa announced, glanced at her cookie, and decided to put it down.

"Osborn can't *make* us do that, can he?" Kathy asked, aghast.

Tori shrugged. "Maybe."

The kettle began to boil and Kathy poured the hot water into the mugs, stirring each of them before adding a heaping table-spoon of chocolate chips to each mug, again stirring until they'd melted and thickened the liquid. She passed the mugs around.

Anissa blew on her cocoa to cool it. "How long do you think it will be before Osborn knocks on your door?"

As if on cue, the bell rang.

"Not long?" Tori suggested.

Kathy left the kitchen to answer it. She came back less than a minute later with Detective Osborn in tow. "Would you like some cocoa?"

"No, ma'am. I just wanted to make sure I have all your personal information."

"Couldn't you just look it up in your files from last year?" Anissa asked and Tori gave her a nudge to cool it.

"We're more than happy to cooperate," Kathy said sincerely.

Osborn took down their full names, phone numbers, and addresses.

"What's going to happen to the body?" Kathy asked.

"It'll be autopsied to try to ascertain the cause of death, and then go into the cooler for a time in hopes someone will identify it and assume responsibility."

"And if that doesn't happen?"

"The county will have to bear the expense of burial."

"Poor man," Tori said. "I mean—it was a man, wasn't it?"

"Apparently," Osborn agreed. He stuffed his notebook into his coat pocket. "If you ladies will excuse me. I'll be in touch." He turned for the hall and the front door.

"Aren't you gonna say thank you?" Anissa called after him.

Osborn pivoted. "What for?"

"For being good citizens and reporting the body."

For a moment, Kathy thought Osborn might explode. But then he answered through gritted teeth. "Thank you."

Kathy saw him out and returned to the kitchen to find her friends again munching cookies and sipping cocoa.

"Did you have to tease him?" she asked Anissa.

"I didn't *have* to—I just wanted to."

"You could get us *all* in trouble."

"For what?"

"I don't know. Disrespecting authority?"

"I predict the detective won't bother. The guy drowned. End of story."

"You hope," Tori said.

The three of them looked at one another.

Kathy knew that she sure *hoped* that would be the last they heard about dead plaid guy. And yet ... the tight feeling in her stomach told her otherwise.

echnically, Cannon Bait and Tackle was open for the season, but the day had been so raw and nobody had come around, so Tori hadn't bothered to even open that morning. But when she got back from Swans Nest, she saw a strange car on the lot and a man dressed in a black raincoat, what her grandfather had called a porkpie hat, and smoking a cigarette, looking at The Lotus Inn, giving it a thorough going over.

"Can I help you?" Tori asked.

The man turned. "Looking for the owner of this fine establishment."

"That would be me." Tori offered her hand. "Tori Cannon."

"Rick Shepherd." They shook hands and then he handed her a business card: Shepherd Enterprises Ltd.

"What can I do for you, Mr. Shepherd?"

"Call me Rick. I'm scouting the area for development opportunities. Your little motel has seen happier days."

"It's been closed for a decade, but I have plans to resurrect it in the not-too-distant future."

"Then isn't it lucky I just happened to come by?"

Lucky? She doubted that. It wasn't exactly a secret that she hoped to reopen The Lotus Lodge and that it was a distinct lack of capital that kept her from doing so. She'd scraped by, financially, during the winter—and that was mostly because of substitute teaching. She was counting on a good summer season to get her on track to save a little money toward refurbishing the seven-room motel. She had equity in the place but wasn't in a position to pay back a substantial loan should the fishing season turn to crap due to weather or some other unforeseen problem. "What did you have it mind?" she asked.

Shepherd took a last drag on his cigarette, tossed the butt on the ground, and stomped on it. "Ideally, to buy the entire enterprise."

Tori stared at the offending butt, then raised her gaze to stare at Shepherd. "This business has been in my family for almost fifty years. I intend to make that a century."

"Would you be open to a partnership deal?"

Tori shrugged. "I guess that would depend on the terms."

"I'm a busy man. I wouldn't have time to run such an operation, but I'd consider keeping you on for that responsibility."

Tori merely looked at him. *Oh, would you?*

"I'm sure we could hammer out an agreement."

"You haven't even properly examined the property." And she wasn't sure she wanted to take a stranger on a tour—not while she was on her own on site. However Kathy and Anissa were right across the street—just a phone call away.

"Why don't I call my contractor? She could be here in a matter of minutes."

"If I were to invest in the property, I'd want to bring in my own people to do the work."

She nodded—but they were nowhere near an agreement so that point was moot. She would have to know a heck of a lot more about Rick Shepherd before she would even consider doing business with him.

"Just a moment." Tori turned, pulled her cell phone from her pocket, and called Anissa. "Can you drop what you're doing and come over to the compound? There's a guy here who wants to invest in The Lotus Lodge."

"You're kidding? Be right there. Hey, Kath—you won't believe this," Anissa said, and then the connection was broken.

"When was the motel originally built?" Shepherd asked, taking in the shabby façade and missing stucco.

"I'm not certain, but I could look it up."

"And you say it's been a decade since it was in use?"

"My grandmother ran it—singlehandedly," Tori said with some pride. "But eventually it became too much for her."

"I'm seeing this as a two-to-three person seasonal operation. But with a bit of decent marketing, it could evolve to year-round, at least for a few of the units—on weekends."

He'd been thinking along the same lines as Tori. And how had he found out about The Lotus Lodge?

"Hey, Tori," Anissa called as she approached, and right behind her was Kathy. Good. Tori could handle herself in just about any situation, but Shepherd was a big, burly man, and Tori's hackles had been raised, although she wasn't exactly quite sure why. Having back-up by two of her BFFs was comforting.

"Mr. Shepherd, I'd like you to meet my contractor, Anissa Jackson. Anissa, this is Rick Shepherd."

"My pleasure, Ms. Jackson. It's not often I meet a lady contractor."

"Well, then you ought to get out more often," Anissa said and laughed, but Tori heard the undercurrent of annoyance in her friend's voice.

"Just what is your expertise, Ms. Jackson?"

Anissa stood tall and Tori was glad her friend still wore a tool belt around her waist. It gave her a level of authority that Tori wished she possessed.

"My current project is the restoration of the Swans Nest property across the road. And what's *your* claim to fame?"

Shepherd laughed. "I own forty-seven hospitality properties in Central and Western New York. Restaurants, B and Bs, and franchised motels. I'm on the lookout for other properties and I'm drawn to The Lotus Lodge."

"How did you hear about it?" Anissa asked, and Tori's ears perked up. Yeah, she'd like to know the answer to that question, too.

"I like to take rides around the state. I saw the for-sale sign on this place late last summer and cursed the fact I didn't act on it back then. It was taken off the market before I got a chance to bid on it."

If Tori's grandfather hadn't won the Mega Millions Lottery the previous summer, he would have jumped at the opportunity to sell the place off to the highest bidder. It was only the fact that Tori's grandmother's best friend—and now likely at some future date her step-grandmother, Irene Timmons—had wanted to see Tori carry on the family business that Tori was able to buy the property for one dollar and now struggled to keep the bait and tackle part of the operation alive. There was potential in the property. Resurrecting The Lotus Lodge was just one possible source of income. Anissa had suggested, and on more than one occasion, that the upper level of the boathouse could be converted into a high-end rental, and that appealed to Tori, too. The only thing that stopped her from doing any of that was a lack of capital. Was it worth seriously considering Shepherd's offer?

"What kind of investment are you talking about, Mr. Shepherd?" Kathy asked.

"And you are?" he asked, and not too kindly.

"Kathy Grant. I own the Swans Nest Inn across the road."

"Oh, yes. I've studied your website. It would be great for The

Lotus Lodge to offer a better value for more cost-conscience clientele to your high-end establishment, especially in as rural a spot as Lotus Bay."

"I have *not* published my rates online, so I don't see how you can say that I—" Kathy began, but Shepherd cut her off.

"We have a different demographic in mind, Ms. Grant. You want to cater to the wedding crowd. I propose to cater to families and sportsmen and give them a much different guest experience than you."

Yeah, but the truth was that The Lotus Lodge might never be able to cater to a year-round audience—despite the possibility of ice-fishing clientele.

"You've given me a lot to think about, Mr. Shepherd," Tori said.

"Call me Rick," he insisted with what Tori thought of as a smarmy kind of smile.

"Rick."

He glanced at his watch. "I've got an appointment with a restauranteur in Lotus Point in ten minutes, but I'll be in touch. It was nice meeting you, Ms. Cannon."

"And you, Mr. Shepherd."

"Rick," he insisted once again.

"Rick."

He nodded toward the three women. "Ladies."

They watched as he headed for his black Mercedes, started the engine, backed up, and pulled out of the lot. No one spoke until he was out on the highway.

"So, what do you think?" Anissa asked Tori.

"I don't know. I would have to see his proposal—in writing—before I could consider anything."

"You wouldn't really let somebody else call the shots on The Lotus Lodge, would you?" Kathy asked, her tone conveying her disapproval.

Tori let out a frustrated breath. "I really don't know."

AFTER SHEPHERD'S DEPARTURE, Kathy and Anissa went back to Swans Nest to concentrate on work inside the house, and Tori returned to the bungalow to study her spreadsheet to try to figure out what she should buy to stock the bait shop—and worry about how she'd pay for it.

A couple of hours later, the women gathered back in Tori's kitchen and shared a frozen pizza—not great, but cheap and filling since it was doctored with extra mozzarella and the addition of sliced banana peppers, which were Kathy's favorite topping.

"What do we want to do now?" Kathy asked her friends after the one leftover slice had been wrapped and put in the fridge. "Want to watch TV?"

"Boring!" Anissa asserted.

"A DVD?" Kathy suggested.

"We've watched everything we've got a gazillion times," Tori said.

Kathy frowned. "Cross the road and get stinking drunk?"

"Now you're talking," Anissa said, although no matter how many times they'd visited The Bay Bar, none of them had ever left drunk. Tipsy maybe, but never drunk

Shrugging into their jackets, they headed across the road for the only hot spot on the south end of Lotus Bay. As it was still quite early in the "season," there were probably no more than a dozen or so patrons in the place and the three women took seats at the bar nearest the kitchen and away from the regular clientele. They didn't really fit in, but nobody bothered them and they got a chance to connect with their friend and the bar's cook and co-owner, Noreen.

Paul Darcy, Noreen's husband and the bartender, strolled up to the trio. "Hey, ladies—same old, same old?" he asked.

"You got it," Anissa answered. That meant a gin and tonic for Kathy, a Margarita for Tori, and a beer for Anissa.

"Coming right up. Noreen—the girls are here," Paul hollered in the direction of the saloon doors that separated the kitchen from the bar.

"Be there in a minute!"

The jukebox was quiet that night, as a cluster of guys at one end of the room watched a basketball game, while another had their eyes glued to another TV and the Yankees game.

"I saw the Sheriff's cruisers at your place today, Kath," Paul said and the well gin bottle gurgled over a tall glass filled with ice. Since they were regulars—and Noreen's friends—he was always a bit more generous with their pours.

"Yeah, Tori found another dead guy," Kathy said, then her gaze darted to Anissa. Tori had found Anissa's father's body stuffed into one of The Lotus Lodge's ground-floor units the year before, but Anissa didn't seem to take offense. "Some poor guy drowned. Detective Osborne said nobody had been reported missing, so Tori thinks he might be a Canuck."

"Poor sod," Paul said and turned to pour Anissa's favorite brew from one of the brass taps.

"He'd been in the water quite a while," Tori piped up and then shuddered.

Paul retrieved the Margarita mix, poured it into a cocktail shaker, added the tequila, and then dipped the lip of an appropriate glass into salt before pouring the concoction. Finally, he laid out napkins before each of them and delivered the drinks. "Let me know if you need anything else."

"Thanks," the women chorused. Paul ambled back down the bar to check in on the basketball game.

Noreen pushed through from the kitchen with a heavy china

plate piled with piping hot mozzarella sticks and a ramekin filled with what looked like marinara sauce. "Hope you're hungry," she said, setting the plate down in front of Tori. "Dig in."

"Aw, you didn't have to do that," Kathy said.

"Shut up," Anissa said, and reached for one of the golden bundles, then immediately dropped it. "Wow—that's hot."

"That's God punishing you for telling me to shut up," Kathy said with amusement.

"They're straight out of the fryer," Noreen said and reached under the bar to grab a pile of paper napkins. "They'll cool off fast enough." Grabbing one of the napkins, she wrapped it around the end of one of the sticks, dropping it into the sauce to coat it, and then took a bite. "Mmm. Mighty good."

Anissa took a napkin and did the same. "Why is it your mouth can take temps higher than your fingers?"

"Because we've gulped far too many hot cups of coffee over the years," Kathy said.

"I'll say," Tori agreed, even though they all knew she preferred tea.

"You girls had a busy day," Noreen commented.

"*Too* busy," Tori agreed and took a slug of her Margarita.

"Besides the visits from the cops?"

"Tori got propositioned," Anissa said and laughed.

Noreen poured herself a glass of ginger ale from the well trigger. "Oh yeah?"

"Do you know a guy by the name of Rick Shepherd?"

Noreen's eyes narrowed. "I've heard of him."

"And?" Kathy prompted.

Noreen frowned. "Let's just say he has his sticky fingers in a lot of pots around here. Don't tell me; he wants to buy the bait shop," she stated.

"Not exactly," Tori said. "The Lotus Lodge. I told him no."

"And when you said so, he offered to be your partner?"

Tori nodded. "What do you think about that?"

Noreen took a sip of her drink and shrugged. "There's no denying that the businesses he invests in do well, but the original owners sometimes—maybe always—feel like they've sold their souls."

Kathy glanced at her friend, but Tori's expression was impassive.

"How much control are you willing to give up on your property?" Noreen asked.

Tori looked thoughtful. "I don't know. All I know is...I don't have the money to reopen the Lodge and it might never be a possibility for me to swing it on my own."

Noreen nodded. "We felt that way a few years back when we were trying to get a loan. Nobody would talk to us. Then we had a really good summer. Maybe the bait shop will have a better summer this year. You girls have sure dolled up the property."

"All except The Lotus Lodge, which still looks like an eyesore," Tori grumbled.

"We could paint it," Anissa suggested. "Everything looks better with a fresh coat of paint."

"What about Herb? Wouldn't he loan you some money to fix the place up?" Noreen asked.

"It was hard enough getting him to let me have it."

"What's he been spending his big lottery bucks on?" Noreen asked, her tone neutral.

"As far as I know, just a new truck and his condo. He complained about how much it cost to furnish it. Irene sent me some pictures. I don't think he spent a fortune."

Noreen shrugged. "Men." She picked up another mozzarella stick and plunged it into the sauce, then took a bite. She chewed and swallowed. "Dig in. They're not scalding anymore."

Kathy and Tori each grabbed a stick. A cheer went up from

the guys watching the basketball game. They were happy, but the women clustered at the bar all shared the same resigned expressions.

Finally, Noreen shrugged her shoulders as if to shake off the blues. "Summer's coming. Everything will look brighter when the days are hot and the dark closes in late. It always does."

Kathy felt that way, too. Her dream would come true the day Swans Nest opened. Unfortunately, it looked like Tori's dream might take a lot longer to happen.

3

*K*athy was up before dawn, which wasn't all that unusual, but Tori hadn't stirred. After four days of substitute teaching, and then a day of yard work, she deserved to sleep in late. But Kathy often awoke in the wee hours and her big mistake was to start thinking about her B and B and everything that needed to be done before opening day. When that happened, it was the end of sleep for that night.

She'd had two cups of coffee and half an everything bagel (courtesy of Tom's Grocery, and leaving the other half for Tori) before she set off across the darkened road to Swans Nest. She never failed to feel a surge of love and pride when she unlocked the front door and stepped inside. And she gave a silent thanks to her deceased grandparents and their generosity in leaving her the money that paid for the majority of the renovations to the once-decrepit building. And she marveled at the skill Anissa possessed that had restored the once-abandoned house to all its former glory.

Turning on the hall light, she locked the door behind her and headed toward the beautiful new kitchen. It was a dream come true for any wanna-be caterer. She started the next part of her day by making yet another pot of coffee and then sat down at the kitchen counter to review the list of tasks she needed to accomplish. Happily, that inventory grew smaller and smaller as her opening day approached and she delighted in crossing off more and more of the tasks.

It was almost nine when the kitchen phone rang. It was probably Tori, who'd slept late and wanted to assure Kathy she'd be over soon. So Kathy was surprised to hear another voice on the other end of the line

"Hi, Kath. It's Noreen."

"Oh, hi. What's up?"

"Did you get your certificate of occupancy yet?"

"Yeah, on Thursday. Why?"

"Both my rooms are booked and I've got a couple looking for a place to spend the night."

"What about Don Newton? He's got a couple of rooms over his bait shop."

"He won't be reopening until May first."

"Technically, I'm not open."

"I know—but you were going to do a dry run soon anyway. You wouldn't have to feed them. Just give them a place to sleep."

"I don't know," Kathy said as the hairs on the back of her neck prickled.

"They're willing to pay seventy-five bucks, which is more than we charge. They've got a wedding reception to go to at the American Legion."

"Do you know these people?"

"They're friends of the people we're renting to, and they've been staying with us for at least five years. They'll vouch for them."

Seventy-five bucks was a lot less than Kathy intended to charge the people who would visit her inn. Then again, they weren't expecting a gourmet breakfast. And seventy-five bucks would give her a tiny influx of cash at a time when she was hurting financially.

"Well, okay. What time are they going to arrive?"

"It probably won't be until late this afternoon. Have you got your credit card account established?"

"Yeah."

"Good. I'll have them call you and you can run it through your setup."

"Okay."

"Great. The guy who needs the room is Jack Ruffino. I'll give him your number. And thanks, doll. This will be a boost for both of us."

If you say so, Kathy thought.

"Talk to you later."

"Yeah. Bye," Kathy said, hung up the phone and frowned. A pre-dry run dry run? That sounded okay in theory, but that meant she'd have to abandon her list of things to do for the rest of the morning and wash the sheets and clean the room and bathroom instead.

Kathy downed the rest of her coffee and reached for the phone, punching in the number.

"Cannon's Bait and Tackle. Can I help you?" Tori answered.

"It's me," Kathy said.

"I was just on my way over."

"Don't bother. My day just took an unforeseen detour."

"What do you mean?"

"Noreen wants me to put up her overflow."

"You mean rent out a room? But you're not ready."

"All they need is a bed, and I've got one."

"Are you sure you want to do this?" Tori asked, sounding concerned.

"No, but Noreen is a friend."

"Yeah," Tori agreed. "Okay, I've got stuff I can do over here. Like updating both of our websites."

"That's better than cleaning a toilet," Kathy said wryly.

"Are you coming back for lunch?"

"Sure. See you then," Kathy said and ended the call, setting the receiver back on its wall cradle. She blew out a breath. "I'm not ready," she declared, but that was irrelevant. Ready or not, she was committed.

Now, where had she stashed the box that contained the four-hundred count Egyptian cotton sheets?

TORI HUNG UP THE PHONE, still rather stunned that Kathy was going to jump the gun and welcome her first guests before having a dry run. But that was her decision to make.

A glance at the clock told Tori that she had a couple of hours to kill...and she really did need to add photos, captions, and check hers and Kathy's website links. But before she could log on, a knock came at the bungalow's front door.

Tori got up and looked out the window that overlooked the parking area outside the little squat house and recognized the man who stood before her front door. They'd never been formally introduced, but she knew his face: Avery Simons. What in the world could he possibly want? She opened the door to greet Lucinda Bloomfield's property manager. Lucinda was the richest woman in the county and owned an elaborate estate up the hill on Resort Road.

"Hello, Mr. Simons."

He touched the bill of his baseball cap, which said LOTUS BAY YACHT CLUB. "Ms. Cannon." He raised his right hand and offered her a plain white envelope.

Tori took it from him but wondered what she was supposed to do.

"If you could please read it. I'd like to take your answer back to Ms. Bloomfield."

Tori ran her finger under the flap and then tore open the envelope. Inside was a hand-written note.

Dear Ms. Cannon,

I would be very pleased if you could join me for tea this afternoon at 2 pm at my home at the top of Resort Road.

It was signed: Lucinda Bloomfield.

Tori's brow furrowed. What in the world could Lucinda Bloomfield possibly have in mind by inviting her to tea? Then again, she'd never find out unless she agreed to go.

Simons waited.

"Yes. Please tell Ms. Bloomfield that I accept her invitation and I'll see her at two o'clock."

Again, Simons tipped his hat. "Thank you."

Without another word, the man turned and headed back to his pristine white Ford pickup truck, got inside, started the engine, pulled out of the compound's lot, and turned north on Resort Road.

Now, why on earth would Lucinda Bloomfield want to see Tori? She supposed she'd find out at two o'clock.

ª

KATHY TOOK in the pretty guest room and frowned. Something was wrong. The wallpaper—the reproduction of a vintage hydrangea pattern—had been a bear to hang because she'd bought it on eBay for a song, but Anissa had somehow performed a miracle and had gotten it to stretch to fill the entire room. Kathy had decided to name her guest rooms after flowers, but despite it being her favorite, this one had defied being called anything but Floral. It sounded dumb, even to Kathy. She'd have to come up with something better before opening day.

The bed looked absolutely gorgeous. The new, freshly washed sheets, a snow-white coverlet, and a light gray counterpane at the foot of the bed, looked lovely, but she hadn't put all the decorative items out on the flat surfaces. She basked in the noticeable care she had taken to pull the room together. Painstakingly washed and starched doilies were ready to be put in place, but Kathy was hesitant to use too many, worried she might overdo it and instead of a nostalgic comfortable feeling it might impart a dated ambiance. It would be a delicate balance.

Since the couple who'd arrive later that afternoon were only expecting a bed to sleep in—and weren't paying top dollar for the experience—she figured she could wait to fully decorate the room.

Moving to the bathroom, she straightened the towels on the burnished nickel rack. She'd originally wanted to go with oak, but Anissa convinced her that wet towels draped across them would damage the wood. The nickel matched the tub and pedestal sink's faucets, looking quaint, and would require less maintenance.

As she surveyed the suite, Kathy frowned. This wasn't the way she had planned her pre-opening dry run. She, Tori, and Anissa were to be the guinea pigs. She had her first breakfast all planned. She'd already picked out the linens she'd use in the refurbished dining room. How she'd serve the food and drink, and on what mismatched china and silverware.

But worst of all, she worried about the caliber of the guests Noreen had steered her way. They weren't the barkeep's regular customers. Noreen's accommodations were bare bones at best. Was Kathy worried that these people might not be up to the standard that she expected to accommodate, and what kind of a terrible person did that make her?

She wasn't sure she wanted to know the answer to that.

Giving the coverlet one last tug to make sure it was perfectly straight, she exited the room, leaving the door open—welcoming—for her first guests. She just wished she felt more comfortable about their arrival.

A loud buzz sounded from the utility closet that held the oversized washer and dryer, and Kathy was happy she'd let Anissa talk her into putting them on the second floor instead of the basement. She pulled the still warm sheets from the drum and tossed them on the top of the machine, then she turned to test the temperature on her iron—still hot—and heard a voice calling her from the bottom of the stairs.

"Kath?"

It was Anissa.

"Upstairs."

She listened as the sound of footsteps bounded up the pine staircase and seconds later Anissa joined her, not even out of breath. She looked from the ironing board to the pillowcase Kathy had just smoothed over the ironing board and frowned.

"You're going to iron your sheets?"

"Just the pillowcases and the upper portion of the top sheet. I want it to look pretty for my guests."

"I thought Tori and I weren't going to stay for the night until at least next week."

"Change of plans," Kathy said and squirted some spray starch onto the soft material which was lace trimmed. Her female guests were sure to fall in love with them—as she had.

"Whatever," Anissa said. "Can you give me a hand with—"

"Sorry," Kathy interrupted. "I've got guests arriving sometime this afternoon."

"Guests?"

Kathy told her about Noreen's phone call. "Are you sure you want to do this?" Anissa asked skeptically.

She wasn't. "Of course," she bluffed. "They're giving me seventy-five bucks, which I can use to pay my Visa bill at the end of the month."

Anissa frowned. "Do you need help making the bed or something?"

"No, their room is all set. I thought as long as I was washing sheets, I'd get started on The Daisy Room."

"Good," Anissa said and sounded relieved. "I've got a bunch of small stuff I can do that'll keep me occupied for most of the day. Like finishing the trim in the Lilac bathroom and staining it to match the rest of it."

Kathy's cell phone rang. She pulled it out of her pocket, saw that it was Tori calling, and answered it. "Hey, Tor, what's up?"

"You're going to have to fend for yourself at lunchtime."

"How come?"

"I've been invited out."

Kathy stabbed the speaker icon so that Anissa could hear. "Say that again."

"I've been asked to lunch. Or rather, I've had an invitation to afternoon tea."

"Who around here serves afternoon tea?" Anissa asked.

"Lucinda Bloomfield."

"What?" both Kathy and Anissa asked in unison—and disbelief.

"Why would she do that?" Anissa asked. She was always suspicious of anything Lucinda Bloomfield did. The woman had badgered her father to sell his property, but since his death and since Anissa moved in, Lucinda hadn't mentioned it again.

"I don't know. But I'll tell you all the juicy details when I get back."

"What time are you going?"

"Two."

"That gives you almost three hours to get ready."

"And it's going to take me that long to iron a dress and do my hair. Do you think I should wear heels?"

"Are you planning on dating her?" Anissa asked.

"Don't be silly," Tori said, I just don't want her looking down at me."

"Now, Tor, has she ever really done that?" Kathy admonished.

"Considering I've only spoken to her twice, how would I know?"

"You watch your back, girl, you hear?" Anissa warned.

"She's not going to shoot me."

"Knives can be just as dangerous."

"Don't be ridiculous," Kathy said. "I've got a can of tuna and some bread in the freezer. I can make lunch for Anissa and me."

"Great."

"Now pay close attention to everything that woman says because we want a full report," Anissa ordered.

"Yes, ma'am," Tori said, but Kathy could hear the amusement in her tone. "See you later."

"You better believe it," Anissa said.

Kathy tapped the end-call icon. "Well, that was unexpected."

"What in the world could that evil woman possibly have to say to Tori?"

Kathy shrugged. "Let's be friends?"

Anissa glowered and shook her head. "I'm going out on the back porch to cut that trim."

"And I'm going to continue to iron. As soon as I'm done, I'll come down and make the tuna."

"You don't have to feed me."

"No, but if I do, you might hang around longer and maybe help me move that sectional in the basement game room."

"Girl, don't tell me you're going to rearrange that area a third time."

"Who's counting?"

"Me," Anissa said flatly, but Kathy knew she was game to help out. Anissa had never said "no" to any of Kathy's requests—and because of that, Kathy needed a way to show her appreciation to her friend.

And something Tori had said earlier gave her an idea of just what that something might be.

4

———

*T*ori arrived at the Bloomfield estate at precisely two o'clock, parking her truck outside the front door. She'd donned her prettiest—and if truth be told, only decent—dress and had actually put on some make-up to meet with the illustrious Ms. Bloomfield.

She pressed the doorbell and from somewhere inside heard the Westminster chimes echoing. Nothing happened for long seconds and she glanced around, looking through the sidelights that surrounded the home's great oak door. Finally, she saw a dark shape approach. The door swung open and a tall, gray-haired man in a gray suit and a bow tie stood before her.

"Ms. Cannon?" he inquired.

"Yes," she said, feeling a little intimidated.

"Please enter." He stood aside for her to do so, then closed the door behind her.

Tori found herself standing in a large foyer, its floor of black-veined, white marble. Cove molding surrounded the ceiling, and a grand staircase was the focal point off to her right, its balusters dark with age and polished to a gleam.

"May I take your coat?"

"Oh. Yes, thank you." Tori shrugged out of the sleeves and handed it over. The man hung it in a large closet under the stairs and turned back to her. His face seemed familiar, but she couldn't place where she'd seen him. The hardware store? A bait customer? Eventually, it would come to her.

"If you'll follow me, please," he said and led her through a corridor into a large living room that overlooked the water. What a magnificent view of the burn side of the bay Lucinda would enjoy come fall when leaves changed color and seemed as though aflame. And one could see all the way to Lotus Point, too.

"Great view," Tori said.

Lucinda had been partaking said view and turned at the sound of Tori's voice.

"Ms. Cannon. Welcome to my home."

"Call me Tori."

"And I'm Lucinda." She gestured to a small linen-clad table that had been set up in front of the large floor-to-ceiling windows and French doors that led to a large empty deck. The table was set with elegant ivory and gold-rimmed china, silver cutlery, and a vase of fresh, peach-colored roses that complimented Lucinda's silk blouse. "Please take a seat."

Tori took the chair facing north—the one with the better view. Lucinda sat opposite her. "Will you please bring the tea, Collins?"

"Yes, Madam," the man—butler Tori guessed—said in an accent that was distinctly American, and leaned forward in a slight bow. Tori was surprised he didn't click his heels as well. Her gaze wandered around the beautiful living room which she knew had been featured in at least three nation-wide magazines, including *Architectural Digest*. A great fireplace with a big white mantle dominated the east side of the room with a crackling fire on that raw April day.

"You have a beautiful home."

Lucinda nodded. "Thank you."

Now, what could Tori say? She found herself fidgeting. "I ... I was surprised to get your invitation this morning."

"It was long overdue."

Why?

Collins reappeared with a silver teapot. "Shall I pour, Madam?"

"Yes, please."

Tori watched as the butler first poured tea into her cup, and then that of his mistress.

"Shall I bring out the sandwiches?"

"In five minutes," Lucinda said. "Thank you."

Again, Collins nodded before taking off in the direction of what Tori assumed to be the kitchen. She was dying to ask how anyone in Ward County found a butler, but she didn't want to look like a rube. Lucinda obviously had the dough to pay for one.

"From what you said last summer, I assumed you would have been working on getting The Lotus Lodge up and running once again."

Tori managed the ghost of a smile, picked up the small pitcher and added some cream to her tea, then picked up her spoon and stirred it. "We wanted to get the bait shop back in the black before we tackled the lodge."

"We?" Lucinda inquired.

"My friend, Kathy, and me. She helped me spruce up the compound last summer, and now I'm helping her—as much as possible—to open her B and B."

"Ah, yes. Kathryn Grant of Swans Nest Inn. The property has certainly undergone a spectacular renovation."

"Yes, your neighbor, Anissa Jackson, has been the contractor in charge," Tori said, rubbing it in just a little bit.

Lucinda nodded. "Ms. Jackson's home has undergone a major renovation, as well. It looks wonderful." By her tone, it sounded as if Lucinda had forgiven the Jacksons for the time when the property was an eyesore.

Lucinda picked up the delicate cup before her and sipped her tea. Tori did likewise. Now what could they talk about? And when would Lucinda introduce the reason for the apparently spur-of-the-moment invitation.

It was Lucinda who broke the quiet.

"I understand it was you who found a man's body in the bay," Lucinda said.

Tori nearly spewed her tea at the change of subject. "Yes," she said and coughed. "Me and Kathy."

"Most unfortunate," Lucinda said with a shake of her head.

"Do you have any idea on who it could have been?" Tori asked.

Lucinda's expression was bland. "Why would you ask that?"

"I've been here less than a year. You've been here your whole life."

"*Nearly* my whole life," Lucinda agreed but didn't answer the question.

Collins arrived with a three-tiered silver cake plate and set it on the table. On the bottom level were delicate sandwiches—cucumber and egg salad by the look of it. The second level held four scones, and on the top petit fours and ripe, plump choco-late-covered strawberries. Everything sat on dainty, individual paper doilies, looking like something out of one of the maga-zines Kathy subscribed to. Collins set a pair of silver tongs, on the table. "Will there be anything else, Madam?"

Lucinda smiled. "I'll call if we need anything. Thank you, Collins."

He nodded and Tori watched him leave. Again, Lucinda picked up her cup and sipped her tea. Tori shook her linen napkin over her lap and wondered if she should pick up the tongs or wait to be invited to do so.

She waited.

"Please help yourself," Lucinda encouraged with a nod.

Emboldened, Tori chose one each of the little finger sandwiches, and a scone—raisin and walnut, she guessed. Butter and jam were already on the table in matching ramekins. She split her scone and slathered it with some of the soft butter, then applied a thin layer of jam. She took a bite. Whoa—just as good as what Kathy made.

Lucinda chose one triangular sandwich and a strawberry. Eating like a bird was probably how she kept her fantastic figure. She was said to be in her mid-forties, but she sure didn't look it. Had she undergone plastic surgery or did she just take very good care of herself?

"I understand you had a visit from Rick Shepherd yesterday," Lucinda said.

A crumb caught in Tori's throat, and she began to cough. She groped for her teacup, taking a healthy swig.

"Oh, my—are you all right?" Lucinda asked.

"Yes," Tori said and coughed again. "Thank you. How do you know about that?"

"I hear things," Lucinda said enigmatically.

Tori didn't doubt it.

"I assume he wanted to buy your property."

"It's not for sale."

"Then he must have offered to be your partner."

Tori frowned. "How did you know?"

"That's the way he operates. He's well known in these parts," she said by way of an explanation. "Have you made a decision?"

Tori wondered if she should answer that question. She hesitated, then said, "We only spoke the one time. I would have to see a written proposal before I could make a decision."

Lucinda nodded and bit into her strawberry. She chewed slowly and swallowed before speaking again. "If you do receive a proposal, I hope you'll consider partnering with me before accepting whatever Mr. Shepherd offers."

"You?" Tori asked aghast, glad she hadn't been about to swallow and end up choking once more.

"Why yes. I *am* a businesswoman."

"I knew you had rental properties, but—"

Lucinda nodded. "Among other enterprises."

"Such as?"

Lucinda's eyes narrowed at the impertinent question, but she sighed and answered. "I own stakes in several restaurants in the county and beyond, as well as a couple of inns. There's an untapped market here on Lotus Bay for lower-end accommodations."

"Lower end?" Tori asked, offended.

"Yes," Lucinda said matter-of-factly. "I understand you were considering refurbishing and going with a retro vibe for The Lotus Lodge. I believe that could be very successful. You could also finish off the upper level of your boathouse and offer that as additional rental property."

How could she possibly know all that? Did she have Tori's home bugged?

Tori swallowed. "What kind of an arrangement did you have in mind?"

"A silent partnership."

"What would that entail?"

"I would advance you the capital to make the improvements necessary to get The Lotus Lodge up and running, and to hire the necessary personnel to ensure the venture operates smoothly."

"And what would you get out of the deal?"

"A portion of the profits."

"What number were you thinking?"

It was Lucinda's turn to hesitate. "Fifty percent."

Tori's eyes widened. Did the woman really expect her to do all the work and then give up that much of the profit? She let out a breath.

"Of course, everything is negotiable," Lucinda added. "And you might find my terms are far better than Mr. Shepherd's."

Oh yeah? If his conditions were in the same ballpark, The Lotus Lodge would stay shuttered indefinitely.

Tori looked down at the cup of cooling tea. "You've given me a lot to think about." And she couldn't wait to tell Kathy and Anissa about it, either.

"A BUTLER?" Anissa repeated, taken aback.

Tori nodded. After she'd returned from the Bloomfield estate, she'd changed back into jeans and a sweatshirt before joining Kathy and Anissa at Swans Nest. "The house is gorgeous, and the view is breathtaking."

"I'm more interested in what Lucinda had to say." Kathy put the kettle on, presumably for a pot of tea. Tori always found comfort in a cup or mug of tea. "Did Lucinda reveal her reason for the invitation?"

"Oh, yeah," Tori said sourly. "She knew all about Rick Shepherd's offer of partnership for reopening The Lotus Lodge. She'd like to cut him out. But get this; she wants fifty percent of the profits."

Kathy wasn't at all shocked at the notion, and it seemed that Anissa wasn't, either.

"How could she know about Shepherd's offer?" Tori asked. "I haven't told anyone but you guys, and you haven't told anyone, either."

"No," Kathy said with authority. "Although we did talk about Shepherd at the bar with Noreen."

"But there was nobody nearby."

"Maybe she told Paul and he told one—or a bunch—of the customers. You know how liquor loosens the tongue," Anissa said sagely.

Tori sighed. "I guess you're right. I mean, we didn't swear her to secrecy."

"I wouldn't put it past old Lucinda to regularly plant a spy at the bar," Anissa said sourly.

"I sure didn't see Avery Simons the other night."

"No, but she has a lot of tenants in this county—hell, probably right around here. Maybe she gives one or more of them perks if they come up with some good gossip."

That was a distinct possibility.

"I want to hear more about the house," Kathy said eagerly.

"Then you should try to look it up online. I can't possibly describe it to your satisfaction."

"Maybe I will."

"I want to hear more about this butler," Anissa said, her dark eyes widening.

"He looked familiar, but I couldn't place where I've seen him."

"A local guy?"

"Why not?" Kathy asked. "There are schools here in the US and abroad where you can get trained as a gentleman's gentleman. I even considered taking a course."

"There's no such thing as a woman butler," Anissa protested.

"Valet," Kathy corrected, "and there most certainly is. Although these days, the job is geared more toward running a household—with staff."

"So why didn't you take the course?" Tori asked.

Kathy smiled and looked around her gleaming new kitchen. "Another opportunity presented itself."

"Let's get back to Tori's opportunity," Anissa said. "Do you *really* want to take money from either of these sleazy people?"

"I don't think Lucinda is sleazy," Kathy said with authority.

"From what we've heard, she ain't no better than a slumlord," Anissa reminded them.

"She said she has business interests in several restaurants and inns in the area," Tori said.

"Probably desperate people grasping at anything to keep their livelihoods intact."

"Maybe," Tori said as the kettle began to boil furiously.

"I wouldn't worry about it until you see something in writing," Kathy advised. "Until then, it's all pie in the sky."

"Of course, there is somebody else who's got big bucks and could easily bankroll the project," Anissa said.

"Who's that? Don Newton?"

"No. Your grandpa."

"Ha!" Tori said and gave her friend an eye roll. "Never in a million years."

"Why would you think Don Newton would have the money?" Kathy asked.

Tori shrugged. "He's nice. And, as my main competition, he makes a very, very good living."

The electric kettle clicked off and Kathy picked it up and scalded the teapot, tossing the water into the sink and stuffing a couple of tea bags into it. She replaced the lid and settled a quilted cozy on it. "You could broach the subject with your grandfather," she suggested.

Tori shook her head. "Not a chance." And yet, it had been she who had paid for the winning lottery ticket that had turned her grandfather from a failed bait seller into a multimillionaire. She must have thought about it many times, but had never mentioned it to Kathy. That would be bad karma, not that Kathy was sure Tori even *believed* in karma.

"I don't suppose you're even going to want to think about supper until late tonight."

"I didn't eat much—in fact, hardly anything. Got any cookies?"

"I baked a fresh batch just this afternoon," Kathy said and reached for the cookie jar on the counter behind her, placing it on the island where Tori and Anissa sat. "Have a cup of tea. It'll make you feel better," Kathy encouraged.

With all Tori had on her mind, Kathy wasn't at all sure she believed that.

5

*I*t was almost six when the bell rang and Kathy opened Swans Nest's big oak door to find standing before her a man with a scraggly beard and a woman with long bleached blonde hair, a nose ring, and acrylic nails long enough to dig a trench. Both were dressed in black leather jackets, black denim pants, and black boots, looking like the worst stereotypes of bad-ass bikers. They were much younger than she'd anticipated—early twenties, not at all The Bay Bar's usual demographic.

"You must be The Ruffinos."

The woman laughed. "He's Ruffino. I'm Cass Merritt."

Kathy wasn't a prude. Plenty of unmarried guests would bed down at Swans Nest during her tenure as its owner/protector—a very *long* tenure, she hoped. She pasted on a smile. "Come on in and I'll show you around."

They stepped inside and both scoped out the restored entryway. Cass laughed. "Looks like somewhere my grandma would like to stay."

"Maybe *her* grandma," Jack said with a smirk.

Kathy felt like reopening the door and ushering them right

out it. Instead, she reminded herself that she wasn't always going to like the people who walked through the entrance and she may as well learn that lesson as soon as possible.

"I'm sorry I can't offer you breakfast in the morning, but I'm not really open for business yet and don't have everything set up." Especially not for seventy-five bucks.

"Yeah, Noreen told us that. Don't worry. We'll catch a donut or something on the way home tomorrow morning."

"Yeah, there's a McDonalds up on Route 104—I love an Egg McMuffin any time of the day or night," Cass piped up.

"So where's the room?" Jack asked.

"Upstairs on the right; number three." She wasn't about to tell them the room's name and suffer another round of ridicule. "Let's get you checked in and then you can go right on up."

"Yeah, I need to change for the wedding," Cass said, indicating the little black suitcase on wheels that had accompanied her into Swans Nest.

Kathy stepped behind a podium in the front parlor that would act as her reception desk. She pushed an old-fashioned ledger in front of Jack, offering him a pen. "Please sign in."

He shrugged and scribbled something—she wasn't able to read it. "Your address and license plate number, too, please."

"What do you need that for?"

"It's an industry standard," she said. It was—for all the motels she'd ever worked in. Under ordinary circumstances, she would have already had that information before her B and B guests showed up. She wasn't sure Noreen had taken down that information and wanted to make sure she could add them to her database for future marketing purposes.

"And your credit card?" she asked.

Jack pulled out a wallet on a chain from his back pocket and dug out the grimy card, handing it to her. She swiped it through her little machine, holding her breath until the transaction was approved, then let out a breath and smiled once again.

"Check out time is eleven o'clock."

"Don't worry, we'll be long gone by then," Jack said and accepted the old-fashioned skeleton key that Kathy offered him.

"I hope you'll enjoy your stay at Swans Nest. I understand you're going to a wedding reception. Do you have any idea what time you'll be coming in tonight?"

"Whenever."

"Oh. The doors are locked at eleven. But if you come in later than that, you can call me and I'll come over and open it for you."

"You don't live here, too?" Cass asked.

"Not yet. I've got a place across the road, so it will only take me a minute to get here when you return later tonight. Please let me know if you need anything."

Jack nodded. "There's towels upstairs?"

"Yes, in your bathroom. If you need more, there's a linen closet next to your room."

He nodded toward the stairs. "Come on." He started off without offering to help Cass with her suitcase.

Kathy watched them go. She had a bad feeling about them and hoped it was just a touch of indigestion.

JACK AND CASS didn't stay long, and when Kathy heard the roar of the big black Harley take off, she resisted the temptation to go check on room three, locked the inn's door, and headed across the road for the Cannon Compound.

Kathy found Tori sitting at the kitchen table, reading one of her decorating magazines. The aroma of baked chicken filled the room.

"Did your guests finally arrive and then depart for the evening?"

Kathy nodded. "I think I'm going to rethink the whole door-locking situation. As long as I'm not living on site, I need to be able to lock and unlock the front door remotely."

"There's an app for that."

"Yeah, so Anissa said. And I was too cheap to go for it, but I think it's a necessity. I'm going to go online and see if I can order one after supper."

"Good idea."

Kathy opened the fridge and pulled out the already opened bottle of cheap Chardonnay. It tasted like shoe-polish remover, but that was all they had in the house. "Join me in a glass?"

Tori giggled. "I don't think there's room for both of us."

"Another one of your Gramps's jokes?"

Tori smiled. "You got it."

Kathy poured the wine, giving one of the glasses to Tori. "When do we eat?"

"In about half an hour. I didn't want to start the chicken too soon in case you were any later."

"Okay, I'll get some frozen veggies going in a minute, but I need this first." Kathy took her first sip and grimaced. Shoe polish remover all right.

Tori didn't seem to be in a hurry to drink her wine. "What were they like?"

"My guests? About what you could expect; typical Bay Bar customers—except they're young. They said my B and B looks like something their great grandma might like."

Tori frowned. "Oh dear. Are you worried?"

Kathy nodded. "I don't want to think badly of people, but...." She shook her head. "I need to stop thinking about it—or I'll drive myself crazy."

"Good idea," Tori agreed. "Anything else new?"

Kathy shook her head, took another sip of her wine and shuddered. She pushed her glass away. "Let's never get this brand of wine again."

"You got it!"

Kathy sighed. Now what could they talk about? And then it came to her. "While I was ironing earlier today, I got to thinking how Anissa has been so good to both of us—charging us less than market value for her labor, etcetera. I'd like to do something to thank her. What do you think?"

Tori shrugged. "Off the top of my head?"

Kathy nodded.

"Business cards?"

Kathy frowned. "Not nearly enough. She could have been making a lot more money these last six months working for people other than us."

"Yeah, but they don't know about her; hence, business cards."

"You're thinking twentieth century. What she needs is a dynamite website. Then people who've heard about her could just Google her name and find her online."

"You're forgetting we live in rural New York. I'm pretty sure that around here, pinning a card on the bulletin boards at Tom's Grocery and the hardware store might be just as good."

"You did a fantastic job setting up the Swans Nest and Cannon Bait and Tackle sites. Would you be willing to do the web design?"

"Sure," Tori said.

"How much would it cost to set up a website?" Kathy asked.

Again Tori shrugged. "Maybe a hundred bucks, depending on how long you pay for the domain name and host server."

"I think that's the perfect gift for an entrepreneur like Anissa."

"Maybe, maybe not. You don't chart the website hits on a

spreadsheet and compare them week to week. I do," Tori said, sounding discouraged.

"I do, too. And we're offseason. Interest in our sites is bound to explode as we move into summer."

"From your lips to God's ears," Tori muttered.

"We could split the cost for cards *and* a website."

"Yeah, we could," Tori reluctantly agreed.

"I've been taking pictures of Swans Nest's revival since day one. We'll have no problem putting together a portfolio of photos to chronicle her accomplishments," Kathy said.

"Yeah," Tori agreed, seeming to warm to the idea. "We need an idea for a theme—or at least a logo."

"And what would we call the business?"

"Anissa Jackson contractor dot com works for me."

"Sounds rather pedestrian," Kathy commented.

"Yeah, but if people know her name, it could be an easy Google search to find her."

"That's true. Okay, let's start working on it. How about tonight?"

"We could at least pick some pictures and write out the copy. Then during the next few days, I could round up the domain and server, but the security certificate is going to double that hundred dollar quote."

"We'll charge it to overhead."

"I just hope we have some income to pay for it."

"I got seventy-five bucks from my guests."

"And by early next month a couple more boats will be in my slips," Tori said.

"Then things are definitely picking up for us. I'm optimistic about the summer."

"Which is officially almost two months away," Tori pointed out.

"Spoilsport."

"I'm just being realistic."

Kathy studied her friend's face. "You're brooding about your tea with Lucinda."

"Yeah, I guess I am. I'm wondering what I should say to Gramps about it—or if I should even mention it."

"There's no reason to tell him anything until you know what your options are."

Tori nodded.

Kathy got up and spilled her wine down the sink. "I guess I'll get those veggies going. Do you want corn or peas?"

"Surprise me," Tori said, but there was no hint of joy in her voice. As she thought about the people—guests she reminded herself—who'd return to her B and B and stay there alone in her painstakingly renovated house, Kathy couldn't say she blamed her.

6

*B*oth Tori and Kathy were glad of the distraction of pulling together the elements for Anissa's website and worked far longer on it than they'd anticipated, During the evening, they heard bikers coming to and leaving The Bay Bar, but Kathy got no call to open Swans Nest's door for her guests.

Eyes drooping with fatigue, Tori went to bed around midnight, leaving Kathy to sit up in the living room's recliner waiting for the call to open the inn. Meanwhile, Tori had dozed off and must have slept for at least an hour when the call finally came. She heard Kathy talking, and then the kitchen door close. She rolled over and went back to sleep. Several times during the night when she'd awoken, she noticed the lights in the living room were still on, but then she'd dozed off again.

It was still dark out when, still in her jammies and with a bad case of bedhead, Tori staggered into the kitchen, taking in the aroma of freshly brewed coffee. The room was empty, but she found Kathy, already showered and dressed for the day, standing at the window in the darkened laundry room, binoculars in hand, staring across the road at Swans Nest.

"What the heck are you doing?"

Kathy didn't bother to look back. "Keeping watch."

Tori laughed. "You're like a parent waiting for a naughty teenager who stayed out all night."

"Just the opposite of that. Swans Nest is my baby and I want to make sure it's safe and sound."

"You know, when you find out nothing bad has happened, you're going to feel awfully foolish in the light of day."

"So be it."

"Come on into the kitchen and have a cup of coffee. You'll be able to hear when that guy's motorcycle takes off. It'll be loud enough to wake the dead."

Tori wandered back into the kitchen and put the kettle on for a pot of tea. She could drink coffee, but she preferred not to. That morning it would be English breakfast tea. She favored black teas—and thought it funny that it was Kathy who had gotten her into the tea-drinking habit back in college, but who now drank more coffee.

Kathy set the binoculars on the kitchen table and took a seat, then immediately got up again and began pacing the kitchen floor.

"Are you going to be this nervous every time you have a guest?" Tori asked.

"Maybe for the first hundred or so," Kathy admitted. "But I suppose I'll eventually get used to it. I'll feel better once I have enough money and can add my own living quarters at the back of the main house."

"That's a few years down the line," Tori muttered, taking from the cupboard one of the old Lotus Lodge mugs her grandmother had commissioned more than a decade ago, before staring at the kettle as though daring it to hurry and boil.

"Why don't you go get dressed? I'll make us both a nice breakfast. By the time you take a shower, the tea will be stewed —just the way you like it."

"Okay, but only because you might tear your hair out while waiting for your guests to leave."

It didn't take Tori more than ten minutes to get washed and dressed, and she found Kathy just sliding a vegetable omelet onto a plate as she reentered the kitchen. As though on cue, two slices of toast popped up from the toaster.

"Here you go," Kathy said, putting the plate down on the table in front of Tori's usual spot.

She sat down and grabbed the pepper shaker. Salt made you retain water, but pepper was just...peppy! Tori picked up her fork, ready to cut a piece off the end of the eggy semi-circle when the sound of a motorcycle roaring to life cut through the virtual silence on Lotus Bay and they heard it thunder even louder when it took off.

Abandoning their breakfasts, the women flew out the home's door and hurried across the road.

Kathy reached for her keys, but they were unnecessary: the front door was unlocked. "I told them—I *told* them to make sure to lock the door when they left."

"What does it matter? The house has been empty less than a minute," Tori said reasonably.

The light in the stairwell and entryway shone brightly, and Tori knew Anissa had set them on a timer. "You take the parlor, I'll take the library," Kathy said, her voice tight with anxiety.

Tori shrugged and turned to her left, switching on the lights as she went. Everything looked in perfect condition. She met Kathy in the hall. "Nothing wrong in there."

"You check out the dining room, I'll do the kitchen."

Tori couldn't see that anything had been disturbed in the dining room, either. All the pretty dishes, cups and saucers were in their usual places in the china cabinet and on the sideboard along the east wall.

She soon joined Kathy in the kitchen, which wasn't in such

pristine condition, as evidenced by the empty half-gallon milk container—some of which had been spilled on the granite counter—along with the two gummy glasses, and crumbs from the now-empty cookie jar.

"Somebody had quite a snack," Tori said unnecessarily.

Kathy shot her a sour look.

"The price of overhead?" Tori suggested.

"Let's go upstairs," Kathy said, turned, and headed toward the staircase at a fast clip.

She charged into the bedroom to the far left, switching on the light. "Oh no!" she wailed and stooped to pick up a pile of towels. From the look of them, they were heavy with water.

Tori looked around the room. The bedclothes were on the floor in a heap, but that wasn't the worst of it. Holes were punched into the walls—a bunch of them—and the globed sconces on either side of the bed were both smashed. Someone had stepped in said glass as evidenced by the bloodied foot-prints, washcloths, and splatters on the pretty hooked rug that sat beside the left side of the bed.

"What the heck went on in here?" Tori asked, taking in the destruction.

"My room—my beautiful room—is ruined," Kathy literally cried, her voice breaking with emotion.

"I'm sure we can fix it. Just a little drywall, some new globes for the lights, and some OxiClean."

Kathy shook her head. "That wallpaper is discontinued. Anissa had to be careful to make sure what we had would cover the room. We'll have to steam it off and start all over again. And this rug. The bloodstains might have come out if we'd found them when fresh, but they're hours old." Silent tears ran down Kathy's cheeks as she gazed around the once-pretty room.

Tori didn't know what to say.

Kathy let out a long, shuddering breath. "I knew it was a mistake to take in guests before I was ready. I knew it—but—"

"You wanted to help out Noreen. I'm sure she had no idea anything like this could happen."

It was Kathy's turn to say nothing.

"Come on. I'll help you clean up. We'll get these sheets in the washer and when it's a decent hour, we'll call Anissa to see what she can do to pull things back together."

Kathy nodded. "But first, I need to document the destruction." She took out her cell phone and tapped the camera icon. Once she photographed all the damage, Kathy threw the wet towels into the tub, shook out the obviously soiled sheets, then gathered them up and left the room. Tori looked for broken glass but found the biggest chunks in the wastebasket in the bathroom. No doubt Kathy would want to pretreat the bloodied washcloths before she did another load.

She heard the washer start pumping water and pulled out her phone, wondering if it was too early to call Noreen—probably. She didn't quit work until after ten most nights but was usually back in the kitchen between eight and ten each morning to get things ready for their lunch and happy hour crowds. She'd call later...and say what? The people you sent to stay at Kathy's B and B trashed the place and it's going to take real money to fix it. She would probably sound like a tattletale. She'd ask Kathy what she wanted to do and then ... somehow they'd fix this. They had to. Kathy was supposed to open Swans Nest in less than two weeks.

❦

ANISSA STUDIED the piece of paper before her, wincing. "Not counting the cost of the wallpaper, five hundred to a grand."

Kathy hung her head, but she didn't cry. She was determined *not* to cry. "When can you start work on it?"

"I can give you today—but tomorrow I've got a laminate floor, a toilet, and a vanity and sink to install over in a rental property in Warton. I scheduled three days for the job, but I've also got a couple of windows to replace in a cottage up at Lotus Point before the weekend."

Great. Anissa had been hungry for other jobs all winter, with not much more than the projects Kathy could provide, and now the work was piling up. Kathy supposed she understood. It was inconvenient to do repair and cosmetic fixes when the weather didn't cooperate. But Swans Nest was scheduled to open in exactly twelve days. She had two confirmed bookings and one of them was meant to be in this room.

"What if ... what if you repaired the walls? I could paint instead of wallpapering them. Maybe put up a border from the hardware store in Warton under the crown molding to dress the room a little until we can buy and then schedule the time to re-wallpaper."

"That would work. Fixing the holes is going to take some time. The joint compound has to cure between patching and sanding. The floor could take even more time. I can rip up the boards, but I don't know if I have enough stock to repair them and finding it could be a problem. It's not a modern-standard size. Then they have to be sanded, stained, and get a couple of coats of poly. I can do that in the evenings and next weekend—if I don't get any other paying jobs. But if someone calls me, I really *need* to take the job."

"I know you do. I can't tell you how grateful I am for everything you've done on the house—and I know you haven't charged me what you're worth—"

"You've said thank you enough. You've fed me, and you and Tori have entertained me. We're square as far as I'm concerned.

Besides, I've been taking lots of photos. One day I'm going to have a website and this job will be my big portfolio piece."

Kathy nodded, thinking about the site she and Tori were already planning. She was about to say thank you once again, but Anissa gave her one of those *no-you-don't* looks, and Kathy managed a smile. "Okay, why don't you start working on the walls. Meanwhile, I have some detective work to do. I need to find the bastards who ruined my room and make them cough up for the damage."

Anissa smiled, shaking her head. "I'm sure glad it ain't me in your sights."

Despite her bravado, Kathy wasn't at all sure she would be able to track down the destructive duo who had done so much damage to her fledgling inn. But if she could, she was determined to extract payment.

She had to.

7

*T*he bait business was not exactly lucrative in early April, Tori decided. She'd had a spate of customers earlier that morning. Diehard fishermen who weren't afraid of choppy water, cold winds blowing across the lake from Canada, and a little drizzle. Most of them fished off the bay bridge, but a few of them rented her aluminum boats and motors and went trolling.

Since she hadn't had a customer in almost two hours, Tori was contemplating closing for the day when she heard a car pull into the gravel parking lot. She decided to wait a few more minutes before shutting down the little heater that kept the shop heated to a tolerable sixty degrees.

Tori waited and waited, but no one came into the shop or down to the dock. Her interest piqued, Tori got up, left the building and headed for the parking lot and saw with alarm that the door to her home was open.

She didn't dare go inside. Her Gramps had left his shotgun behind when he'd moved to Florida some six months before. She kept it in her bedroom closet, unloaded, but there was a box of shells right next to it.

Tori withdrew her cell phone from her pocket and was about to call 911 when a somewhat familiar and unwelcome voice hailed her from within.

"Where the heck have you been?"

"Amber?" Tori asked, annoyed.

A woman, just about her own age, was suddenly visible behind the storm door. "Where the heck have you been?" she repeated.

Tori advanced, wrenching the door open and storming inside. "How did you get into my house?"

"I have a key," Amber said and brandished it, a sneer plastered across her face.

Tori reached to grab it, but Amber pulled her hand back. "Uh-uh-uh!"

Tori glared at her cousin. They'd never been close as children, and it had been several years since she'd even seen the woman. "What do you want?"

"I just came to see what Gramps *gave* you."

"I bought the business and the property from him," Tori asserted.

"Yeah, for a buck," Amber jeered. "He won millions of dollars, and you're the only one who got anything out of it."

Tori said nothing. She had worked hard the previous summer to bring Cannon's Bait and Tackle back from the brink of insolvency. And she had no say in what their grandfather did with his lottery winnings. He'd once mentioned setting up some kind of a trust for certain family members, but he hadn't given her specifics and she hadn't asked.

"What did you expect? You haven't seen Gramps for years. You never even called."

Amber glanced around the shabby kitchen. "This place is still a dump, but at least it's not a pig pen anymore."

Tori's cheeks grew hot with anger. Yes, their grandmother

had been a packrat, but the house had never been dirty—just terribly cluttered. Tori figured she'd eventually update the kitchen, but there was no money for that. And as long as the appliances still worked, what was the point?

"Where did you get the key to *my* house?" Tori demanded.

"Mom and Dad."

"Do they know you have it?"

Amber shrugged. "It doesn't matter. The whole family is angry with you *and* Gramps. This place should have gone to his children first."

"Your mother and my dad had plenty of opportunities to become part of the business. They declined. You didn't even come to grandma's funeral."

"I had to work."

"You couldn't have taken a day off or called in sick?" Tori demanded.

Again, Amber shrugged.

"What made you decide to come all the way out here today?"

"I saw your name in a news story online. You sure make a habit out of finding dead guys. Maybe that's why you can't keep a man.

Tori fumed in silence.

Amber turned toward the living room, but Tori raced to block her.

"Get out of my house or I'll call the police," Tori said —no bluff.

Amber scowled. "Fine. But I'll be back. Count on it." And she pocketed the key, pushed past Tori, and exited the kitchen.

Tori stood behind the storm door and watched as her cousin got in her car, started the engine, and then burned rubber— sending clods of dirt and gravel into the air as she peeled out of the compound's parking lot.

Tori found her hands were shaking as she pulled out her

phone and stabbed at a name on her contacts list. "Anissa, how fast can you install a couple of new locks?"

ANISSA TURNED the last screw on the spring latch for the shiny new polished nickel lock on Tori's front door. She'd already installed a deadbolt lock, but somehow Tori still felt uneasy.

Anissa stood. "That should do it. Why didn't you think to change the locks before this?"

"It never occurred to me that anyone would violate my home," she said. "Especially a family member." Tori held out a duplicate set of keys.

"What's that for?"

"You."

"You're giving me a set of keys to your house?"

"I trust you. I can't say the same for most of the rest of my family."

Anissa shook her head. "No. I wouldn't feel right about it."

Tori stuffed the keys back in her jeans pocket. At the very least, she needed to give Kathy a new set.

"How long do you think your cousin was nosing around the place before you got here?"

"Five or ten minutes. I bought new locks for the bait shop, and the boathouse, too. I suppose I should think about replacing the locks on The Lotus Lodge as well. I wouldn't want somebody to access the rooms and trash them."

"Honey, if someone is determined to get inside, locks won't keep them out," Anissa said.

That statement didn't make Tori feel any better about her sense of violation.

"Are you going to tell your Gramps about this?" Anissa asked.

She shrugged. "It might sound like sour grapes."

"On whose part? You or your cousin?"

"Me."

"There's probably a reason he didn't give money to any of your other relatives. From what you've said, they kind of abandoned him and your grandma. I wouldn't feel any loyalty to people like that, either."

Although Anissa and her brother, James, had both inherited their late father's house, James had no problem with Anissa living there. He'd come out to have a look at the updates she'd made to the outside of the home, and they had an agreement that once she was on a better financial footing, she could buy him out for less than half the appraised value of the home. He was a good guy—an oral surgeon with a very successful practice —and he only wanted the best for his sister.

Since Amber had blatantly trespassed on her property, Tori couldn't say the same for her family and felt infinite sadness. Did her aunt and uncle—and her own parents—feel the same anger as Amber? They rarely called her, and she didn't think to contact them much, either.

The truth was, Tori had felt much closer to her grandma and grandpa than her own parents and that had always felt *wrong*. Shouldn't she have a stronger bond with the people responsible for her birth? And yet ... she didn't. She'd only ever felt connected to Lotus Bay—to this place and the two people who had made her feel loved and valued. Especially her grandma, who had loved her unconditionally. *Unconditionally*. And after she—and Kathy—had worked so hard to resurrect the dying business, her grandfather had gifted her with the house—home —she'd always loved.

Anissa packed up her tools. "You're good to go."

Tori smiled. "More like stay—and hopefully safe."

"If your cousin returns, she might not be happy to find she can't come and go in as she pleases."

"Too bad. Because if she trespasses again, I *will* call the Sheriff's Department."

"That might make things worse."

Tori shrugged. "I don't need mean-spirited people like Amber in my life." She smiled. "Not when I have you and Kathy around."

Anissa's brown eyes seemed to twinkle. "You are one lucky woman."

Tori's grin widened. "Yeah. I am."

TORI WAS POKING AROUND in the refrigerator, trying to work up some enthusiasm for making their evening meal when a rattle at the door, and then a sharp knock sounded. She opened the door to a tired and dispirited looking Kathy.

"What's with locking up the place when you're here?" Kathy asked and hung up her jacket on a hook by the door. Earlier, Tori had called to tell Kathy about Amber's visit.

"After what happened this morning, I just felt safer." She reached in her jeans pocket and pulled out the new set of keys, handing them to Kathy. "Here. I meant to come over to your house, but then I remembered I hadn't closed the shop, and then I got distracted—"

Kathy held up a hand to cut off the rest of the explanation. Instead, she made a beeline for the table, taking her usual seat. Pulling out her own set of keys, she picked out one and began the process of extracting it from her ring.

"What do you want for supper?"

"I'm too tired to cook. Why don't we do a Herb Cannon special; scrambled eggs and toast."

Tori shrugged. She wasn't interested in anything more elaborate, either. She took her own seat. "What did you find out about your trashy guests?"

"Not much."

"What do you mean?"

"There's no record of them. It turns out the credit card they used was stolen. It initially went through—until the real owner was alerted to the charge—which I didn't hear about until I started poking around."

"What about the license plate on their motorcycle?"

"I never saw it myself. What they wrote in my register was totally bogus."

Tori's stomach did a flip-flop. "Geeze, Kath, I'm so sorry."

"No sorrier than me." She shook her head and began taking the second key from the ring. "It's totally my fault. I should have never let them stay."

"Yeah, but didn't Noreen say she could vouch for them?"

"No, she said her *guests* could vouch for them. Thanks to this unfortunate experience, I've learned a valuable lesson early on: to never accept a guest I don't personally vet."

"What are you going to say to Noreen?"

"Nothing. She would never have steered them my way if she thought they were deadbeats."

"Not only deadbeats but vandals."

"Yeah, that, too," Kathy admitted. She seemed to shake herself. "But I can't dwell on that. I have to move forward. I have guests coming in far-too-short a timeframe. I need to be ready."

"And you will be," Tori reiterated.

Tori made their dinner with an eye to the clock. It was almost time to make her weekly call to her grandfather.

Since she had cooked, it was Kathy's turn to clean up and Tori left the kitchen and headed for her bedroom where she'd make her call. She'd installed a small wingback chair that had seen happier days, but since her cat, Daisy, was napping on it, she sat on the edge of her bed, scrolled through her phone's contacts, and tapped her grandfather's number. He answered it on the second ring.

"Hello?"

"Hey, Gramps, it's Tori."

"Right on time," Herb said, sounding pleased. "What's up in your neck of the woods?"

"Oh, not a whole lot," she fibbed. "The weather's still raw, and there haven't been many customers at the bait shop, but that'll change come Memorial Day."

"It always does," Herb said.

"How are things in sunny Florida?"

"Hot. I didn't realize I'd be frying so early in the spring."

"You're a long way from western New York, Gramps."

"Yeah, and I was surprised that your cousin Amber tracked me down."

Tori closed her eyes and grimaced. "Did she?"

"Uh-huh. And she seemed to be on a fishing expedition."

"Not for marlin."

"No. She was as sweet as pie and even asked if she could come down here to visit us."

"And what did you tell her?" Tori asked, deliberately keeping her tone neutral.

"That I don't have a guest room," he said grimly.

Tori couldn't help but smile. "She came to visit me, too. In fact, I was out in the shop at the time, but she had a key and I found her rummaging around in the house."

"A key? She must have got it from her mother. Did she steal anything from you?" Herb asked, his voice hard.

"Not that I could see."

"I probably shouldn't say this, but I never was fond of that girl. She's got a 'tude. Always has." Tori pictured her grandfather shaking his head.

"I noticed that, too. She seemed very unhappy that you let me buy the bait shop."

"I'll bet."

"I changed the locks, but Anissa said a determined person will find a way to get inside if they really want to."

"That's true. Do you think she'll be back?"

"I hope not. I mean...I really don't think I have anything she might want."

"But she might want to deprive you of what you've already got," Herb said tartly.

It wasn't a pleasant thought.

He changed the subject. "What's this about you and Kathy finding a dead guy on Kathy's property?"

Tori cringed. "Uh, you heard about that?"

"You're not the only person on the bay who calls us, you know."

It had to have been one of Irene's friends. Herb wasn't known to be a chatterbox when it came to making calls.

"So what's the story?" he pressed.

"They think he drowned. Maybe a fisherman or a hunter. He'd been in the water a long time."

"Are you all right?"

"Finding him was pretty nasty, but we're okay," she assured him, which gave her an opportunity to tell him about Kathy's problems with Swans Nest, but not mentioning her encounter with Rick Shepherd. She could guess what his reaction might be —and she didn't want to discuss it.

"I miss you, Gramps. Will you come back up to visit this summer?"

"How can I? You moved into my old bedroom. Kathy's got

your dad's old room, and you made the other bedroom into an office."

"I will always make room for you, Gramps."

"I know it, honey. Let me think on it. Irene wants to see her grandkids, so maybe we will come and visit once the weather warms up."

"There will always be a place for you here on Lotus Bay," Tori promised—and she meant it.

8

*I*t was still dark out when Tori awoke the next morning. She'd gotten used to the phone ringing at just after five in the morning, alerting her as to where she'd be substitute teaching on any given day. She averaged three or four days a week and had even gotten a couple of one, two, and even one four-week gig when a teacher came down with the flu or was out for surgery. But despite waking in anticipation of gainful employment, the phone hadn't rung on that Monday morning. By six, Tori was in the kitchen, boiling water for a pot of tea, had fed her own and Kathy's cats, and was contemplating what to have for breakfast when a sleepy-eyed Kathy joined her.

"No work today?"

"No," Tori said, "which means I'm yours all day. We can strip wallpaper, wash walls, or anything else you need help with."

"And I'll be eternally grateful," Kathy said. She said that a lot and Tori had no doubt of it. The truth was, Kathy had been living rent-free in the guest room of the little bungalow on the Cannon Compound, while Tori supported the two of them via substitute teaching. That sounded pretty generous until Tori factored in the work Kathy did around the place, which was spotless, and the laundry was never piled up, either. And despite working for eight or more hours a day at Swans Nest, Kathy often managed to have a tasty meal on the table for the two of them—and many times, Anissa, too.

"You're not opening the shop?"

"If I was teaching, I wouldn't anyway. Weekdays are dead this time of year. Don across the bridge can pick up the slack."

Kathy nodded, but her head was hanging and she looked whipped as she measured ground coffee, dumping it in the maker's basket. Tori watched as Kathy filled the pot with water and poured it into the maker's reservoir.

"Don't worry, Kath, we'll have that room ready and pretty in time for you to open the inn."

"I hope so."

The kettle, which had reached a boil, clicked off. "Now for the most important decision of the day," Tori said, changing the subject.

"And that is?"

"What to eat for breakfast, of course."

WHEN TWO DETERMINED women work together, there is no end to what they can accomplish, and by late afternoon, Kathy and Tori had stripped the wallpaper from the entire damaged room and scrubbed the walls. Afterward, they headed east to Warton to buy the paint and—hopefully—a pretty border to gussy up the now rather boring guest room.

Tori pulled her pickup into one of the parking spaces in front of Reynold's Hardware, slammed the gearshift into park and yanked the key from the ignition. "Can your credit card take another charge?" she asked.

"I sure hope so," Kathy said, but her tone conveyed her concern.

"If there's a problem, I can get it."

"Absolutely not. I already owe you the moon."

"I don't think so. And let's not even talk about it. You've got a looming deadline and we're going to meet it."

Kathy allowed herself a smile. "Yeah. I'm crossing my fingers we will."

They entered the store and were immediately welcomed by the establishment's mascot, a rather fat tabby cat.

"Hello, Winston," Kathy said and bent down to give the cat a scratch between his ears.

"Whoa—and it's our favorite customer," said Tammy, the cashier. It had been more than a couple of months since the fifty-something salesclerk had dyed her hair, as evidenced by the inch or more of white on either side of her part, but she wasn't entirely without glam. Her fingernails were polished a bright red, and she wore a silver chain with some kind of an odd-shaped pendant of dainty flowers. "What are you here for today?" she asked Kathy.

"A gallon of paint and a couple of rolls of wallpaper border," Kathy said.

"Well, you know where they are. Just shout if you want assistance. Either Gary or I can help you with anything you need."

"Got it," Kathy said, and she and Tori headed toward the paint and wallpaper section.

Choosing the paint was easy. Kathy already knew she wanted a warm ivory. Unfortunately, the wallpaper border choices weren't as expansive. But after pondering the limited stock on hand, Kathy and Tori agreed on a design featuring yellow roses on an arbor that would do in the short term. They brought Kathy's choices up to the register and Tammy rang them up.

Kathy presented her credit card and—thank goodness—the charge went through.

Tammy handed her the receipt and bagged the rolls of wallpaper border.

"That's a pretty necklace you're wearing," Tori said.

Tammy fingered the pendant. "Cute, huh? It's broken china."

"Get out," Tori said.

"Oh, I've seen them before—in a museum gift shop," Kathy volunteered.

"Really?" Tori asked.

"I got this at the Strawberry Festival last summer. One of the vendors was selling them anywhere from twenty to seventy bucks."

"Really?" Tori repeated thoughtfully.

"Hey, I heard about you guys finding a body in the bay. Hell, just about everybody in the area did," Tammy said, changing the subject.

"Yeah," Kathy admitted, feeling glum.

"What's the word on the street?" Tori asked.

Tammy shrugged. "Some of my customers said they haven't seen Mark Charles in a while."

"He was nobody I'm familiar with," Tori said, but then until recently, Kathy knew Tori hadn't been a part of the scenery since she was a tween.

"He kept to himself for the most part. But he would come into the village every few weeks to stock up on groceries and hit the pharmacy. He lived over on Falcon Island year-round."

"And nobody missed him?" Tori asked.

Tammy shrugged. "Lots of people around here are snowbirds. I've been thinking about trying it myself. If I never had to snow blow my driveway again, I would die a very happy woman."

Kathy felt her pain. She hadn't employed a guy to plow the

front of Swans Nest, but she would have to if she hoped to entice customers for certain weekends, like New Year's, Valentine's Day, and St. Patrick's Day visits during the long, cold winter. And, of course, if she could add President's Day and Easter weekends in the mix, too—all the better. The place would have to have clear parking. Paul and Noreen employed someone to keep their lot clear. Maybe she'd ask them...but not any time soon.

"What else do you know about this Mark Charles?" Tori asked.

Tammy shrugged. "Not much. He was real quiet—almost a hermit. He always wore sunglasses and a ball cap pulled down over his eyes. He kind of skulked."

"Did he come in here often?" Kathy asked.

Tammy shook her head. "He'd trade in his propane tanks. Always paid cash for everything." She frowned.

"Is that suspicious?" Kathy asked.

"Used to be everybody paid in cash. These days—not so much. People even charge two or three bucks for stuff. It used to be we had a ten-dollar minimum. Not anymore." Tammy shook her head, then looked Tori in the eye. "Did you see the guy's face?"

"No!" she said emphatically. "Considering he'd been in the water so long, I'm not even sure he *had* a face."

"What *did* you see?" Tammy asked with keen interest.

Tori hadn't really spoken about it. Would she now, just to exorcize the memory once and for all? "I only saw the body's hand." She shuddered. "There was still some flesh on the bones —and the sight made me feel sick."

"Oh yeah?" Tammy asked eagerly.

"We really need to get going," Kathy said tersely, grabbing the bag of merchandise from the sales counter. "Talk to you later."

"Bye, girls," Tammy said and gave a cheerful wave.

Tori and Kathy headed back to the front lot and got back in Tori's truck, but Tori didn't immediately start the engine.

"Are you okay?" Kathy asked.

Tori forced a smile. "My Gramps asked me the same question."

"And?" Kathy demanded.

Tori shrugged. "Pretty much."

"Which doesn't sound like a yes to me," Kathy said.

Tori clenched the truck's steering wheel. "Tammy at least had a probable name for the dead guy."

"Which meant nothing to either of us."

"But it did to her, and maybe it will to others," Tori pointed out.

"It's not really our business."

"How can you say that? We *found* the dead guy."

"Yes, but he has no connection to us."

"We may know other people who knew the guy."

"Such as?" Kathy demanded.

"I don't know. Maybe Paul and Noreen."

"A hermit doesn't go to a bar."

"He might. Who says he has to go to a bar to associate with other people? Maybe he went to drown his sorrows."

"It's a lot cheaper to buy your booze from the liquor store and drink alone," Kathy pointed out.

"You're right," Tori agreed. She turned the key in the ignition, stepped on the brake, and slid the gearshift to reverse, then steered the car westward. "I'm just surprised you aren't more interested. I mean, we found him on *your* property."

"If I thought he'd been murdered, I might feel differently. The guy drowned. End of story. I have a bed and breakfast to get up and running and have less than two weeks to do it. That has to be my priority. I'm sorry if that sounds cold and unfeeling, but that's where I am."

Tori kept her eyes on the road. Kathy knew she had a point. Still, she knew Tori couldn't help but feel some kind of responsibility toward the guy. Officially, apparently no one had reported the dead guy as missing. If there was no DNA or dental match, he'd remain that way.

Still, she hoped *somebody* had cared for the man.

Nobody deserved to die without that.

9

*T*ori pulled the truck up to her usual parking spot in the Cannon lot, shifted to park and killed the engine.

"I'm going to take the paint over to my house and get things set up so we can start work first thing in the morning," Kathy said.

"We can begin tonight if you want."

Kathy shook her head. "It's been a long day. We both deserve a few hours off. Besides, the light will stink. It'll be better if we can work in full daylight."

Tori nodded and the women exited the truck, with Kathy heading across the way to her house and Tori unlocking the door to her home and letting herself in. As she hung up her coat, her stomach growled. She switched on the kitchen light and headed for the fridge. There wasn't much in there, and the cupboard was pretty much bare as well. Damn. They'd just returned from the village and had been only a few blocks from Tom's Grocery; they should have gone inside and stocked up on a few items. It was edging toward six o'clock and she didn't feel inclined to get back into the truck and make a return trip to

Warton. It looked like supper was going to be scrambled eggs once again.

Tori heard the sound of a vehicle pull up outside the house, looked out the window and saw Anissa get out of her truck. She opened the door. "Hey."

"Hey, yourself."

Tori retreated into the kitchen to lean against the counter as Anissa entered the house.

"What a day," Anissa said.

"Did you have problems with your bathroom rehab?"

"I worked my butt off and got the entire job finished in just one day."

"Didn't you say you'd scheduled three days to do it?"

"I like to give myself some leeway. I figured it would take two days, but to save a few bucks, my client did the demo herself and the job went as smooth as silk. Unless something else comes up, I'll be able to help Kathy with her wrecked bedroom tomorrow."

"We stripped the wallpaper and it's ready to paint."

Anissa shook her head. "I've still got drywall work to do. With all that dust, you might want to wait a day or two to start painting."

Tori frowned. Kathy wasn't going to be happy about that.

Speak of the devil; the door handle rattled and Kathy entered.

"Hey, Kath," Anissa greeted.

"Hi."

"Anissa has good news. Her job ended early and she can get back to work on your room."

"Great," Kathy said, but there wasn't much joy in her tone.

"Only you can't paint if I'm doing drywall work."

"Crap!" Kathy groused.

"Are you ladies hungry?" Anissa asked.

"Our cupboards are pretty bare," Tori said.

"Let's head over to The Bay Bar and get something to eat," Anissa suggested.

The tense set to Kathy's jaw telegraphed her reluctance to face the possibility of confronting Noreen. Logically, they all knew Noreen hadn't been to blame for the trouble Kathy's first guests had caused, but Tori suspected Kathy's grief and anger was a little too raw to acknowledge it.

"No, thanks," she said, turning away.

"Want us to bring you back something?" Anissa inquired.

"No, thanks," Kathy reiterated.

Anissa turned to look at Tori. "How about you?"

"Do you mind?" Tori asked Kathy.

Kathy shook her head. "You go ahead. I have some work I need to get done on the computer."

"Okay," Tori said, but she felt guilty just the same. She grabbed her coat from the peg. "Lock the door after us, just in case Amber shows up again."

"Will do," Kathy said.

The door closed behind them and Kathy locked and bolted it.

"That's a cold sound," Anissa commented, and the women headed across the road to The Bay Bar.

It was early, so the place wasn't exactly full, and Tori and Anissa took seats at the bar.

"Where's your partner in crime?" Paul asked and laughed.

The ladies didn't.

Paul frowned at their lack of enthusiasm. "The usual?"

"Sure," Anissa said.

Paul looked toward the kitchen. "Noreen—the girls are here. At least two of them are."

"Coming!"

Paul drew a beer for Anissa and made Tori's Margarita,

setting a couple of Genesee Beer coasters before them and plopping down their drinks.

"Thanks," Tori said.

"Yeah, thanks," Anissa echoed, but neither was quick to pick up their glasses.

"Give me a holler if you need anything else," Paul said and wandered down the bar to watch a rerun of a close-captioned basketball game.

The jukebox belted out a Faith Hill tune that Tori vaguely recognized—not that she knew enough of the words to sing along—and she stared into the depths of her margarita.

"Should we drink to something?" Anissa asked.

"Kathy's guest room, because boy does it need some goodwill."

They clinked glasses just as Noreen pushed through the saloon doors that separated the kitchen from the bar room.

"Haven't seen you girls in a couple of days. Where've you been hiding?"

"Swans Nest," Tori said.

"And where's Kath?" Noreen asked, grabbing a glass, filled it with ice and, just like always, poured herself ginger ale from the well trigger.

"She's at home nursing a stomachache," Tori said.

"Aw, that's too bad. Did she take something for it?"

Tori shook her head.

"Gee, and I wanted to ask how she made out with her first guests."

Tori and Anissa gave each other sideways glances.

"Is something wrong?" Noreen asked.

"Nothing a grand won't take care of," Anissa muttered and took a sip of her beer.

Noreen's eyebrows rose. "What happened?"

"Well, we have no real proof it was them who trashed Kathy's prettiest room—" Tori said.

"Except for DNA evidence," Anissa mumbled.

"Since we tossed the bloodied towels, washcloths, and semen-stained sheets into the washer, I doubt we even have that, now," Tori said and shrugged.

"Blood and—and—?" Noreen stammered.

"She did take pictures," Tori volunteered, even though they were virtually useless.

"I can fix the floor and the walls," Anissa said.

"Kath and I are going to paint what we can," Tori added.

"It might not be perfect in time for Kathy to open," Anissa admitted, "but we'll do our best."

"Will insurance pay for it?" Noreen asked, her voice rising just a bit.

Tori shook her head. "Swans Nest wasn't officially open."

"Why didn't she tell me about this?" Noreen asked, obviously distressed.

"It's not your fault," Tori said. "Kathy doesn't blame you."

Much.

"But I sent those people to her," Noreen said, her eyes filling with tears.

"Kathy tried to track them down, but they gave her bogus information. In fact, the credit card they used was ... stolen," Tori said.

"Oh, no," Noreen practically wailed.

Tori looked away. She wanted to be angry—or at least annoyed with Noreen, but seeing how upset she was at learning Kathy's troubles, she felt vexed at causing the poor woman's angst.

"I've got to make this right." Without another word, Noreen plunked down her glass. "I'm going to call the guest who said they could vouch for those deadbeats and if they won't come clean, then they will be banned from the bar forever." And with that, she marched back into the kitchen.

Tori turned to Anissa. "Do you think she can get them to cough up the vandals' real names?"

"Not a chance."

Tori took a sip from her salt-rimmed glass and hoped Anissa was wrong.

Anissa looked toward the doors to the kitchen. "Um, seeing as how Noreen didn't take the news all that well, do you think she's up to cooking us a couple of burgers?"

Tori frowned. "Maybe not."

Anissa's stomach growled. "Think we can bum some pretzels off Paul until we find out?"

"We can but ask."

Anissa raised a hand and got Paul's attention. He sauntered back down the bar.

"What can I get you, ladies?"

"Got any pretzels or chips?"

He shook his head. "Ran out last night. My distributor shows up on Thursday to restock."

Anissa shrugged, and her stomach growled loudly once more.

"Where's Noreen?" Paul asked.

"I think she went to make a call," Tori said innocently.

Paul shrugged and meandered back down the bar to watch the tube.

"Maybe we should drink up and go somewhere else."

"There's always McDonald's," Tori agreed, and that's where they ended up. They ate in and ordered a burger and fries to go for Kathy.

When they returned to the Cannon Compound, a not-too-pleased Kathy was waiting for them in the kitchen and seemed itching for a fight.

"After you left the bar, I got a call from Noreen. You *told* her?" she accused.

"Well, she asked about you and—"

"You lied, telling her I had a stomachache."

"Well, it wasn't far from the truth. Here," Tori said, brandishing the bag. "Peace offering?"

Kathy grimaced but took the bag from her. She unwrapped the burger and placed it and the fries on a plate then set the microwave for thirty-five seconds.

"What else did Noreen tell you?" Anissa asked.

"That she wasn't yet able to contact her guests to find out about the vandals, but said she wouldn't rest until she made things right. I believe her."

"Does that mean Anissa and I are off the hook?" Tori asked.

The microwave gave a *beep, beep, beep*, and Kathy retrieved her dinner. "Only because I'm starved."

Tori and Anissa exchanged guilty looks. It was Anissa who broke the quiet.

"I need to go home and check my landline's answering machine to see if anyone needs my services." Since cell towers weren't always nearby in rural New York, and coverage was spotty, Anissa didn't use her cell phone as her main means of communication with her customers.

"Okay," Kathy said, taking out her dinner plate and then settling at her usual spot at the kitchen table. "Come on by for breakfast tomorrow and then we'll all head over to my inn."

"Will do," Anissa said. "See ya!"

"Bye," Tori said as their friend headed out the door. Kathy's mouth was full so she merely waved.

Tori locked and bolted the door after the contractor. She faced her friend. "I hope I get some gainful employment tomorrow, but if not—I'm at your beck and call."

Kathy swallowed before answering. "And I thank you."

"You're welcome."

Kathy sprinkled a small pile of salt onto her plate and then dipped a French fry into it. "But if we can't paint, I'm not sure I have anything for you to do."

"Then I'll put out my OPEN flag and hope I get a few bait customers."

Kathy nodded and took another bite of her burger, chewing but obviously not enjoying the taste sensation.

Tori looked away, feeling dispirited. If the school district didn't call and Kathy couldn't use her, she would open the bait shop. But sitting in the barely warm concrete block building during April was not enticing. Tori still had work to do on Anissa's website and she could play with that if she brought her laptop into the shop. She would rather play house at Kathy's B and B than suffer chilblains in her toes. And the truth was, they needed the money from her substitute teaching to keep afloat.

Until Swans Nest opened and until the weather warmed, and fishermen and women returned in droves, they needed the income.

It felt awful to be so desperate.

10

*T*he phone hadn't rung before six, so when Tori awoke and looked at the red numerals on her bedside clock that read 6:02, she knew that she would not be gainfully employed for yet another day.

Hauling herself out of bed, she shuffled into the kitchen to put the kettle on for a pot of tea. Kathy would be up soon, too, so she also got a pot of coffee going. And, of course, as soon as the cats heard her stir, they'd assembled in the kitchen near their food bowls, patiently waiting for their next handout, which often would not meet their demanding expectations.

"You could at least try the food I give you every morning," she said tersely. The cats merely looked at her with practiced disdain.

Sure enough, all three cats sniffed the gourmet tuna and egg medley, turned up their noses, and walked away. And yet, by the time dinnertime rolled around—when it was Kathy's turn to feed the pride—the bowls would be licked clean.

The kitchen seemed barren and lonely on that cold spring day, so Tori hit the on switch on the battered old radio her grandfather had left behind when he'd moved to the Sunshine

State. It was tuned to the local soft rock station in Rochester, which played a mix of contemporary tunes and oldies from the 1990s to present day. Except...they seemed to be in love with, and played on an almost excessive basis—a tune that was almost ready to collect Social Security—"Brown Eyed Girl." Who even knew what the heck the mentioned transistor radio even was— and yet it was supposed to be a "contemporary" tune?

The coffeemaker and kettle seemed to race to see which would finish first, and that day it was the hot water, so Tori made her pot of tea.

With her pink bathrobe cord knotted at her waist, Kathy staggered into the kitchen with classic bedhead, rubbing the sleep from her eyes. "Did they call?"

"No," Tori said wistfully. "I guess none of the Ward County teachers are under the weather today."

Kathy frowned, then looked in the direction of the radio with its crappy little speakers. "Not 'Brown Eyed Girl' again."

"I swear, they have it in rotation at least every two hours," Tori declared. "What do you want for breakfast?"

"I'll find something in the freezer," Kathy said. And why not? It was stocked full of her baking experiments. She'd been testing recipes for months. There was no way the two of them could eat all that bounty, so she'd been sharing her culinary efforts with Anissa and the Darcys, too. Available on any given day were muffins, scones, cupcakes, and cookies to choose from. On that morning, Kathy retrieved two plastic-bagged muffins. "Is lemon poppy seed okay with you?"

"Always," Tori said and poured coffee into Kathy's favorite mug. She would wait a few minutes for the tea to steep before she poured it into a mug for herself.

Kathy plunked down at the kitchen table and accepted her coffee with thanks. Tori picked her favorite mug—Johnson Brothers Rose Chintz—as a reporter from one of the local TV stations, who moonlighted mornings, came on to share the weather and road report. Sometimes they gave a recap of the latest local news, too. So, after finding out that the next few days would be fair, and that there was a slowdown on Route 590, the reporter turned to the news of the day.

"And the body recovered last week on Lotus Bay has been positively identified as Charles Mark—a man who was reported missing almost twenty-five years ago. But in a bizarre twist, he was also known as Mark Charles, a Ward County resident who lived on Lotus Bay. It's a strange turn of events. Why did this man disappear two and a half decades before, only to reappear with a similar name? The Ward County Sheriff's Department hasn't indicated his death was suspicious."

Tori turned down the sound. "Well, that's good," she said then frowned. "But doesn't it seem odd that someone would leave the area under unusual circumstances, and reappear years later using a different, but similar name?"

"Yeah, that does seem weird," Kathy agreed and took a sip of her coffee.

"And it sounds like Tammy was right about the dead guy's identity."

"Do you think others suspected the same?" Kathy asked.

"Maybe. But, honestly, although I've been here for ten months, I'm more familiar with my bait shop customers than my neighbors." She bit her lip. "I'm going to get on the computer to see if I can find a more complete report."

"You do that," Kathy said and got up from her chair. "I need to get sustenance."

Tori retreated to the makeshift office and fired up her computer. Moments later, her online search hit pay dirt. "Kath, come here," she called.

Moments later, Kathy stood behind her, nibbling her muffin and gazing at the computer screen. She read the story headline:

"Ward County Downing Victim Identified." She leaned in closer to take in the details.

Although the body was badly decomposed, it was identified as Charles Mark, a man who disappeared some twenty-five years before. That said, he was also identified as Mark Charles, a man who had lived on Falcon Island for at least two years.

"Yeah. How did they get two different names for one set of DNA?" Tori asked.

They read further into the story where the answer was forthcoming.

It seemed that both men were registered into the state's criminal and missing persons database. Charles Mark had been declared a missing person decades before and, despite what Detective Osborn had initially told them, Mark Charles hadn't exactly been reported as missing some five months before by a neighbor, but by the owner of the house Charles had been renting when eviction procedures started. Police said a database cross-reference had matched the two identities.

Kathy shrugged and took another bite of her muffin, chewed, and swallowed. "Now that they've identified him, we can get on with our lives. Which reminds me; I'm waiting for a box of sample soaps to come. Have we even looked in the mailbox lately?"

"I hadn't thought about it. Since I'm dressed, I'll go see."

"Great." And Kathy picked up her cup for another swig of coffee.

Tori trudged through the damp gravel parking lot to the newer, rural mailbox, wishing she had put on a jacket. Kathy had installed the mailbox soon after she'd officially moved in as a kind of house-warming gift. It was big enough for boxes of stuff they ordered, and Kathy's decorating magazines no longer got mangled. But the most interesting piece of mail they'd neglected to collect the day before was for Tori, not Kathy: A bulky envelope with a return address of Shepherd Enterprises Ltd.

Tori didn't wait to get back to the house, tore it open, and scanned the cover letter.

Dear Ms. Cannon,

Thank you for speaking with me late last week. I'm sorry I couldn't give you more details about the exciting plans I have for your property and businesses, but if you'll look through my proposal, I'm sure you'll be as enthusiastic as me at the possibilities.

Feel free to give me a call and we can discuss our future together in more detail.

Sincerely,

Rick

Tori glanced through the eleven-page document, which was part-sales pitch, part-legalese. She'd study the document, all right. But her inner red-alert claxon had gone off and she wondered if she should consider the pages as possibly toxic.

"Anything for me?" Kathy called and began peeling the paper surround from yet another of her jumbo homemade muffins.

Tori handed her the lone magazine.

"Oh, goody—something fun to read tonight."

"If you're not too tired."

"What have you got there?"

Tori flopped down on the chair opposite Kathy. "Rick Shepherd's proposal for The Lotus Lodge."

Kathy frowned. "You don't sound happy."

"I haven't read it all, of course, but it looks like if we went into business together, *I'd* be the silent partner. He even wants to knock down this house. Where would I live?"

"Even worse, where would I live?" Kathy asked. "I'm already squatting." She pushed Tori's plate closer. "Eat."

"I think I've lost my appetite."

"You don't *have* to go into partnership with him," Kathy said reasonably and pulled the top off her muffin.

"Without a partner, I don't think I could ever afford to upgrade the business and reopen The Lotus Lodge."

"Maybe you should show the contract to Lucinda Bloomfield. Maybe she'd give you better terms."

"I don't know. I'm not sure I want her to know everything I've got going."

"That's the most important part of being a business partner," Kathy pointed out.

"And why you're smart to stick to the decision not to have one?" Tori questioned.

"I don't know. I'm not in the same situation as you. It might be that I'd want a partner someday. I'm not kidding myself; managing an inn is already a lot of work—and I haven't even opened yet."

"Are you regretting the whole idea of running a B and B?" Tori asked, concerned.

"No, but this setback with the crappy guests has given me a lot to think about."

There was no time to consider Shepherd's proposal because Anissa's battered old truck pulled up outside the house. She got out, walked up to the door, and knocked before entering. "Hey, ladies, got an extra cup of coffee available?"

"You know where the cups are," Tori said and nodded in the direction of the appropriate cabinet. Anissa had started the day so many times at the Cannon Compound that she really needed no invitation to join them.

"Have a muffin," Kathy said and pointed to the counter where another two muffins sat. "Zap it in the microwave for thirty seconds, and it'll taste like it just came out of the oven."

Anissa got herself a plate, nuked the muffin while she

doctored her coffee, and then sat down at the table, not bothering to take off her sweat jacket.

"What are you going to work on today over at the house?" Kathy asked.

"Sorry, Kath, but I got another job. But both of you might be interested in what it entails."

"That sounds like a bit of a mystery," Tori said, pushing the proposal aside and unwrapping her own muffin.

Anissa sported what could only be called a shit-eating grin. "Not so much."

"Spill it," Kathy ordered.

Anissa held out her hands in submission. "Well, it seems that your dead guy was renting a house on Falcon Island."

"That we knew," Tori said authoritatively. She'd told Anissa about hers and Kathy's conversation at the hardware store the evening before during their fast-food supper. "And?" Tori asked.

"When Mark Charles dropped out of sight and didn't pay his rent for several months, the owners began an eviction process. They live out of state, but a neighbor told them about me and it just so happens that they called me to clear out the place."

"But what about the cops?" Tori asked.

"Apparently, they've already been through the place, but I'm betting they aren't as sharp as you two gals. I wouldn't be surprised if you find something they overlooked."

"Or is it that you're looking for two unpaid helpers to clear out the place?" Tori asked wryly.

Anissa smiled. "Maybe. Are you going to refuse the opportunity?"

"Heck no!" Tori declared.

Anissa turned to Kathy. "And what about you?"

"After all the work you've done to bring my pitiful wreck of a house back to being a welcoming home I can be proud of—and for far less than you deserve to be paid—how could I say no?"

Anissa smiled. "I was hoping you'd be game because the owners want the place cleared in only two days."

"Wow," Tori exclaimed, "that seems unreasonable."

"It is. But I need the work," Anissa said honestly.

"Then we are at your beck and call," Kathy said. "Or at least I am."

"Since the school district didn't call—I'm all yours, too," Tori said.

Anissa smiled, but then her lips flattened into a frown. "There's just one problem. They can't deliver a Dumpster to the island because the bridge to it won't take the weight. So we're responsible for getting everything to the dump ourselves."

"Then it's a good thing you and I have pickups," Tori said.

"And it's a good thing the dead guy didn't choose to live on one of the other two islands that *don't* have a bridge, otherwise we'd be hiring a boat to get the stuff out."

"When do we start?" Kathy asked.

Anissa smiled. "As soon as we finish breakfast."

11

*I*t was another cold day on Lotus Bay, especially with the stiff wind blowing from the north across Lake Ontario. Tori and Kathy piled into the pickup at just after seven, turned onto Old Ridge Road until they came to the T in the road, heading down Lake Bluff Road for several miles with only the radio as a diversion.

Nearing the island, Tori drove her truck across the bridge and onto the rutted road, looking for number forty-seven.

"It sure is dark around here," Kathy commented.

"Wait until the trees are fully leafed out—then it'll be even darker."

"So what's the point of living on one of these islands?" Kathy asked.

"Beats me."

It turned out they didn't have to identify the house by its number, as they spotted Anissa's truck sitting in a grassy area not far from a rustic cabin that looked like it had seen better days.

"About time you malingerers got here," Anissa called and tossed a big black garbage bag into the back of her truck.

"We were only ten minutes behind you," Tori exclaimed and

eyed the pile of trash already in the back of the battered blue pickup.

"More like twenty," Anissa groused.

"I thought Kath and I were supposed to go through the stuff to look for clues," Tori protested.

"Believe me, you weren't going to find any clues in old beer, tuna, and baked bean cans. This is stuff that's going to be recycled. You gals can go through the paper and other crap to see what you can find, but first, can you help me get the kitchen furniture out?"

"Furniture?" Kathy asked, perking up.

"Most of its crap, but there are a couple of pieces in other parts of the house you might like to think about refinishing."

"Can we just take anything?" Tori asked uncertainly. It seemed so...crass, digging through a dead man's things and taking what they liked.

"Yes. Otherwise, it's destined for the landfill. Whatever we can keep out and repurpose is better for the environment," Anissa commented, handing the women pairs of heavy-duty leather gloves. "Come on, let's get to work."

Tori didn't know what she was expecting to find inside the cabin—but for some reason, she wasn't prepared for the gargantuan amount of trash that was piled in the kitchen. Thanks to the improved weather, things had started to rot and the stench was unbelievable.

"Here, take a mask. You're gonna need 'em," Anissa advised.

Anissa had already taken out several large bags of trash, but it hadn't made a dent in the mess.

"Are there likely to be mice in here?" Kathy asked, sounding squeamish.

"Uh-huh," Anissa said. "Tori and I will scare them away."

"I don't like mice, either," Tori protested.

"You who handles worms and other disgusting bait all day long?" Anissa inquired.

"I wear gloves."

"And you're wearing them now, too."

They each took a bag and began shoving trash into them. Nothing looked to be of particular value on the floor or counters and soon the three of them had the majority of trash cleared, much sooner than Tori had anticipated.

"Now what?" Kathy asked.

"Tori, you start going through the drawers, and Kath, you take that cupboard over there," Anissa said and wrenched open the cabinet under the sink.

Tori pulled open the nearest drawer, which was filled with tarnished silverware. "Kath, take a look at this."

Kathy abandoned her cabinet and hurried over. Tori handed her a serving spoon. "Wow, this is very close to the cutlery I bought at the auction last month."

"That's what I thought." Of course Tori remembered it. She'd helped Kathy polish over two hundred pieces of the set.

"Can I have it?" Kathy asked Anissa.

"Sure. Stow it in a box and put it outside so it doesn't get mixed up with the trash."

Kathy took over emptying the drawer and Tori went to the cabinet Kathy had abandoned. In it were a mix-and-match stack of chipped plates. The patterns were pretty, but they were worthless as is. But then Tori remembered the broken china pendant Tammy at the hardware store had worn. What if she could learn to make similar jewelry? Maybe it would sell in the bait shop. Lots of women came in with their husbands and boyfriends. She shrugged. Maybe she'd just appropriate these chipped dishes... just in case.

Other finds included a grimy milk glass vase and compote found under the sink, and equally filthy depression glassware in pink and green, all of which was saved from being chipped by virtue of it having resided in the back of several cabinets. Kathy claimed that, too. Anissa wasn't interested in appropriating anything; her only motive was to get the job done as quickly as possible.

The meager items worth saving weren't the kind of things a man like Mark Charles would have owned anyway, but Tori figured they had been part of the rental house. But Anissa was told "everything must go," so there was no guilt in taking what they pleased.

By the time they finished clearing the kitchen—with plenty of visible mouse poop but no sign of a live mouse, Tori was happy to note—it was after nine, and the backs of both pickups were full. "We'd better head for the dump."

"I can keep going," Kathy volunteered.

"Okay," Anissa said, pulling off her gloves. "We might be gone as long as an hour."

"There are still plenty of trash bags I can fill. Maybe by the time you get back, I'll have enough bags ready to fill at least one of the trucks."

Tori gave her friend a skeptical look. Her back was aching, and sitting in the truck for the better part of an hour was preferable to more bending and stooping. But Tori wasn't fooled. She knew Kathy intended to scope out the rest of the house looking for hidden treasure—and didn't for a moment blame her friend for wanting to snoop unobserved.

KATHY LISTENED as the two pickups roared down the road and suddenly found the quiet rather eerie. She wasn't usually the nervous type but found herself locking the back door before she ventured into the living room. It, too, had piles of trash and dirty clothes. Mr. Charles (or Marks) hadn't been a neatnik. With a trash bag in hand, Kathy began picking up the dirty clothes, paper, and plastic plates and cups. A dusty stereo sat in the corner, surrounded by scratched and cracked CD cases. Most of them were bootleg copies by heavy metal bands—not her taste in music—but she managed to turn the thing on and tune in the soft rock station in Rochester to keep her company while she tidied.

The living room furniture was a mix of yard-sale finds and some filthy upholstered pieces, including a rickety recliner, a beat-up wooden coffee table, and a number of greasy, dust-caked tray tables in various degrees of destruction. Nothing to do but toss them out the door to be loaded on the next batch of detritus destined for the dump.

Kathy took a moment to stand in the middle of that mess to think. Now, where would a slob keep his important papers? Probably the bedroom. Maybe in a drawer or under the bed.

She again thought about the possibility of mice and shuddered. Well, she was a big girl, and if she screamed loud enough, she'd probably terrify the mouse (or mice) as much as she'd be frightened at seeing it or them.

Gathering her courage, Kathy kicked her way through the mess and headed for the bedroom. No doubt the cops would have already thought about the best places for a man who'd been in hiding to secret his treasures. Shoe boxes and plastic grocery bags were probably as secure as anything the man could have chosen.

The bedroom wasn't as messy as the rest of the house, but the sheets on the bed were positively gray. There were signs a dog had been in residence at one point, thanks to the large grimy-and-hairy bed that Kathy found stuffed in a closet. She hadn't seen any other signs, but then maybe the dog had eaten dry food. If it had only consumed canned food, Anissa might have tossed those empty cans in with the rest of the recycling.

If Charles—or Marks—had had a dog when he'd disappeared that second and final time, what happened to it? Would the neighbors know?

A small dresser drawer contained an odd collection of yellow pill bottles—maybe fifty or more—standing in neat rows, all of them stripped of their prescription labels. The collection wasn't complete, for there was room for at least one more bottle. Had the deputies taken one for analysis? The caps weren't child-proof, and Kathy had no problem opening one, surprised to find it was filled with nothing more than small white dried beans.

What the heck?

Had Mark Charles been a gardener? That didn't make sense. Seed packets never came with the amount of beans that the pill bottles contained. Had the guy been using the bottles as some kind of accounting system? Kathy had read romances where cops put a bullet in a jar for every time they had sex. If Mark Charles used a similar accounting system, he was one horny guy indeed.

Kathy took a picture with her cell phone, and then into a trash bag they all went, along with the clothes in the other drawers. Nothing unusual there but brown-streaked underwear and sweat-stained T-shirts.

Stacks of yellowed newspapers were piled beside the bed. Kathy remembered seeing a YouTube video where a hoarder had hidden money between the pages of newsprint. Could Mark-Charles have done that, too? Was it worth her time to look?

Kathy pulled out her phone and set a timer for ten minutes. She'd give the task that long and then she'd abandon it for more positive purging.

A dusty straight-back kitchen chair sat in the corner of the room. She grabbed it and plunked down, picking up the first newspaper and shaking it. The middle fell out—not the way to do it. She picked up the stray sheets and plucked another section. This time, she held the folded sheets by the corner and shook. Nothing fell out, but it didn't fall apart, either.

It was obvious that the deputies hadn't gone through the papers, since the farther down the stack she went, the older the news. Kathy had almost gone through the entire pile—covering more than a year of stale journalism—when the timer app sounded. "I'm done," she announced to the empty room, but there were only a few more papers left to go through. "Oh, what the heck," she said and shook out the next few on the pile. With one section left to check, she hit pay dirt. A piece of paper fell to the floor. She picked it up and looked at what appeared to be a list of names and telephone numbers with a couple of them starred. On the back side was some kind of memorandum with the county's official seal at the top of the page. It was smudged with dirt and as Kathy skimmed over the six or seven paragraphs she involuntarily yawned. It would seem the phone numbers and names meant more to its former owner. And what the heck could those names and numbers represent? And why had Mark Charles hidden it away?

Setting the paper aside, Kathy took the pile of newsprint out to the kitchen. Anissa would want to recycle that, too. Back in the bedroom, she found a brown paper sack that was filled with yet more papers. It took less time to go through them; most were store and money order receipts. But one piece was bigger than the others: a yellowing envelope. Kathy set the bag on the chair she'd abandoned and picked up the envelope. It wasn't sealed, but the flap had been tucked inside. Pulling it back, she saw a discolored Valentine. The faded pink heart had probably once been red and sat on a dirt-speckled background. In the middle of the heart were lines that looked like notebook paper, and printed on the front were the words *You're cute. I mean* really *cute!* Kathy opened the card and her gaze was drawn to the girlish script written at the bottom of the card.

Charlie,
Luv you always!
Lucinda.

12

*A*fter dropping off their cargos at the dump and the recycling center, Tori followed Anissa's pickup back to Falcon Island. Kathy must have been very busy during the hour or more they'd been gone, for bags of trash were lined up outside the cabin. Kathy sure knew how to clean and organize. But there was something a lot more important on Tori's mind.

"Hey, Anissa—are we going to take a lunch break any time soon?"

"Lunch?" She repeated the word as though she'd never heard it before.

"Yeah, you know. You sit down and consume food—and maybe a drink." A margarita sure sounded good about then, but not while there was still so much work to do.

Anissa frowned. "We going back to your place?"

"No. I don't have much in the fridge. Cunningham's Cove is right down the road a ways. They serve sandwiches as well as dinners."

"That'd be cutting into my profit," Anissa grumbled.

"I didn't ask for you to pay for us," Tori said pointedly.

"Are you trying to make me sound like a cheapskate?"

"No!"

Anissa's stomach took that opportunity to growl.

"And you're hungry, too!" Tori accused. "Besides, they have a working bathroom and this dump," she jerked a thumb over her shoulder, "doesn't."

Anissa nodded sheepishly. "Yeah, I guess you're right. Let's get Kath and go. But we should try to be back here within the hour."

"The sun doesn't go down until almost eight o'clock. We've got plenty of hours left to work today."

"All right. Why don't I go down and grab a table and you and Kath catch up with me?"

"We'll only be a minute behind," Tori promised, and headed for the house, while Anissa got in the truck, revved the engine and backed out of the lot once again.

Tori yanked open the cabin's screen door, but found the main door locked. "Kath?"

Kathy arrived a few seconds later, hanging onto a big black plastic bag filled with yet more trash, and let her friend in. "Sorry, I was in the bedroom."

"How's it going?"

"Except for the furniture, I've got the bedroom nearly cleared out. And what 'til you see what I found."

"Can you save it for a bit? Anissa went to Cunningham's to get us a table for lunch."

"Oh, yeah?" Kathy said and whipped out her phone to check the time. "I didn't realize it was so late. Let me grab my purse, then I want to douse my hands in sanitizer. This place is filthy."

Tori pulled the door shut behind them and they headed for the pickup. She started the engine and pulled back out onto the dirt road. "So what did you find?"

"I may as well wait until we're at the restaurant so I can show Anissa, too."

"Whatever," Tori said, even if curiosity began to niggle at her brain.

While Kathy massaged a huge dollop of sanitizer between her fingers, Tori kept her gaze intent on the road. She turned right, heading for the restaurant. Only a smattering of cars dotted the small dirt and gravel lot across the road from what looked like a little cottage with colorful neon beer signs glowing in the front windows. Looks were deceiving because most of the restaurant was situated away from the bar and on the lower level. It was so dark inside it took long seconds before Tori's eyes could adjust. She looked past the big fish tank on the left and didn't see Anissa at the bar or the few tables that overlooked the marina.

"Your friend is downstairs," said the female bartender.

"Thanks," Tori said. She turned to Kathy. "I'll meet you downstairs. I gotta visit the little girl's room."

Kathy nodded and walked past the bar and over to the steps leading down. By the time Tori joined her friends downstairs, they were both perusing the menu. She took a seat and grabbed the one in front of her place setting.

"What's the special?"

"Soup and half a sandwich—tuna or egg salad."

"I think we've had enough egg salad to last a lifetime," Anissa said pointedly. Tori's grandfather, Herb, was famous for making it and seemed to eat it just about every day for lunch.

"What's the soup?" Tori asked. Cunningham's always had two soups on offer, and they were *good*.

"Vegetable beef or cream of Brussels sprouts."

"Oh, that sounds disgusting," Tori said with a frown.

"I'm trying it. I'm open to anything that isn't made with bugs as an ingredient," Kathy said and folded her menu shut.

"Me, too," Anissa said, and she, too, pushed her menu aside.

"All right. Where's the waitress?"

"Waiter. He said he'd be right back with some water."

And sure enough, a young, sandy-haired guy with a sweating plastic pitcher arrived at their table. "Have we decided what we want?" he asked as he filled their glasses.

"We're going to make it easy on the chef. Three tuna half sandwiches and soup," Kathy said.

"Great. I'll put your order in. Help yourself to the soup," he said, nodding toward the salad bar where two covered, heated tureens steamed away.

Anissa got up, heading for the salad bar, but Tori turned to Kathy. "You said you had something to tell us."

"Show *and* tell you."

"I'm intrigued, but I'm also starved," Tori said and got up to get her soup. Kathy soon followed and a minute later they were breaking into oyster cracker packets and taking their first sample of Brussels sprouts soup.

"Hey, this isn't half bad," Anissa said as the others plunged their spoons into the creamy green glop.

"I'm shocked," Tori said. "I actually like it."

"I knew I would," Kathy said confidently, dipping her spoon into her bowl once again.

"So tell us your exciting news," Tori said and bit into one of her oyster crackers.

"News?" Anissa asked. "Did you find something in the house?"

"I sure did—and it's sure to be explosive."

"Well, don't blow the place up until after we get our sandwiches," Tori advised as Kathy reached for her purse and took out her cell phone. She tapped on the gallery button, made a few swipes and handed Tori the phone.

"Look at this?"

Tori's brow furrowed. "What's that?"

"Pill bottles filled with dried beans."

"What?" Anissa said and stopped spooning up her soup.

"Lots of them. I found them in a dresser drawer."

"Why would anyone save beans?"

Kathy told them her theory.

"Nobody that guy's age was getting laid on such a regular basis," Anissa said.

"My point exactly," Kathy said.

"Where did he get all those yellow pill bottles?" Tori asked. "Scouring people's recycle bins?"

"Tammy at the hardware store said he came into Warton on a regular basis—and she specifically mentioned that he went to the drugstore."

"Big deal," Anissa said.

"Not one of those bottles had a label—just the shards of sticky paper left behind from pulling them off,"

"Weird—but not necessarily suspicious," Tori said and ate some more soup.

"But that's not the *pièce de résistance*." Kathy replaced her phone and took out an envelope. "Take a gander." She passed it to Tori, who pulled the card from the envelope.

Tori glanced at the wording on the front before opening it. She took in the signature and her eyes widened. "Shut up!"

"What? What?" Anissa demanded, making a grab for the card, which Tori easily surrendered. She glanced at the signature inside, but her eyes merely narrowed. She looked up at her companions, brows furrowed. "So?"

"So—how many women in Ward County are named Lucinda?" Kathy asked. "I'm betting only one."

Anissa passed the card back to her. "Yeah, and this thing is decades old. The fact that Lucinda Bloomfield knew the dead guy back in the day has absolutely no bearing on the present, let alone his death."

"But how can you be sure?" Kathy demanded.

"I don't like that woman," Anissa said, and with reason. Lucinda had harassed Anissa's father to sell his property so that she could get water access to moor her forty-foot yacht and he'd refused. But since Anissa had taken over the property, the two women hadn't spoken more than once or twice. "But the fact she knew this guy years ago—before he disappeared the first time—doesn't mean a thing. Hell, I declared my love to at least five guys when I was in high school—and I'll bet you did, too."

Kathy frowned and glanced at Tori. The truth was, Tori had been an awkward tomboy and it wasn't until college that she'd had a real date. And since then, she hadn't exactly been batting a thousand when it came to successful relationships, which was why she was thirty and still had a female roommate.

"Did you find anything else worth mentioning?" Tori asked.

"Just a list of names and telephone numbers. It was hidden in an old newspaper."

"How'd you ever find that?" Anissa asked.

"I shook them all looking for money."

"Say what?" Anissa asked.

Kathy explained.

"Isn't something like that exactly what the cops should have been looking for?" Tori asked.

"You'd think. But it could be entirely innocent, too."

"Then why was it hidden?"

Kathy shrugged.

"So, what are you going to do about these developments?" Anissa asked and took another spoonful of soup.

"Me?" Kathy asked.

"Yeah, you!"

Kathy said nothing, but then her gaze swung to Tori.

"Don't look at me like that."

"The card would seem to be an important piece of evidence, and you've got an in with Lucinda," Kathy stated.

"In what way?" Tori asked.

"She wants to be your business partner."

"And I don't know that I *want* a business partner."

"You don't have to actually *tell* her that. Play coy."

"And say what?"

"That you'd need to see a proposal in writing. And then you can ask her about her relationship with Mark Charles, or Charles Marks—whoever he was."

"Are you out of your mind?"

"Not at all," Kathy said. "In case you forgot, we found that dead guy on *my* property."

"It isn't all that unique an experience," Tori said, but then shot a look at Anissa, whose father had been found murdered on the Cannon Compound. Thankfully, she didn't seem to take offense.

"Just yesterday you told me your priority was Swans Nest—not Mark Charles."

"That was yesterday," Kathy asserted.

Tori shook her head and turned her attention back to her cup of green goop, which was rapidly cooling.

The only sound they heard for the next minute or two was of spoons scraping the sides of china. It was Anissa who finally broke the quiet. She turned her attention to Kathy.

"Are you going to call Detective Osborn and tell him about your finds?"

She shrugged. "I guess I'll have to."

"I still don't see how the card is relevant," Tori said.

"That's up to the detective to decide," Kathy said authoritatively.

Probably so, Tori decided. But for some reason, she didn't

want Lucinda Bloomfield to have a part in the man's death. How would she even know the man she'd had a relationship with had returned to Lotus Bay? But then, Lucinda seemed to know *everything* that went on in the area—including Tori's businesses. She had no reason to trust the county's richest woman who lived up on the hill above Resort Road, and yet for some reason ... she wanted to.

13

*I*t didn't take as long to clear the cabin as Kathy anticipated. Tori and Anissa had taken what they hoped was their last trip to the dump while Kathy stayed behind to assess the items they'd saved. Among them were a couple of tables they agreed they could refinish and try to sell on Craig's List, the cutlery, Tori's box of chipped and broken dishes, and a box of assorted odds and ends. It sure wasn't much to show for a whole lifetime.

Kathy heard the sound of an engine and looked out the front window to see a car pull up next door. A woman, who might have been in her early fifties, got out, closed the car door, and moved to stand before the cabin. Seeing Kathy, she waved.

Kathy moved to the door and went outside. "Hi," the woman called. "I'm Diane Brewster. I live next door."

"I'm Kathy Grant. I'm here to help Contractor Anissa Jackson clear out the house."

"From the looks of it, you pulled it off pretty quick."

"There were three of us working on it all day."

The woman shook her head, taking in the cabin. "This used

to be such a pretty little house—until it became a rental. Do you mind if I come inside and take a look?"

"Sure." Kathy led the way and they paused in the kitchen.

Diane's frown was tinged with sorrow. "Oh, what a mess," she said, taking in the grimy walls, the broken cabinets, and the ruined floor.

"How long was this house a rental?" Kathy asked.

"Ten years. It hasn't been pleasant to live next door to the squalor. We thought about moving several times."

"Were you the one who called Anissa to clean up the place?"

"I told the owner about her. I heard she was the one bringing that decrepit house at the south end of the bay back to life and turning it into a B and B."

Kathy tried not to look sheepish but didn't entirely succeed. "That's my house."

"Oh, well, it's something to be proud of—now."

"Thanks. We've put a lot of hard work into it."

Diane indicated the kitchen. "Maybe the owner will hire her to fix up this place just enough so they can dump it."

"Anissa does beautiful work," Kathy was proud to say. But there were other things on her mind. "Did you know Mark Charles well?"

Diane shook her head. "We didn't speak often—and when we did, it was about his dog," she said none too kindly.

"I saw a dog bed stuffed in one of the closets. Was it a nuisance?"

"Yes, barking all day and half the night. He left the poor thing tied up out in back year-round. I called animal control several times, but they said as long as it had water and shelter, there was nothing they could do. When Mark disappeared, I came over and got the dog. He's been ours ever since, and he's a totally different animal now. Friendly, happy, and finally living a good life. He's currently at my sister's house while her husband is out of town—supposedly protecting her, but I suspect he's just being spoiled. I'm worried Jill might not give him back."

Kathy smiled. She liked hearing happy endings to animal abuse stories. They seemed all too rare in poverty-ridden Ward County.

"What else did you know about Mark?"

"You mean Charlie Marks?" Diane asked.

Kathy nodded.

Diane shrugged. "Only that he disappeared a long time ago. The Mark I knew kept to himself. I suspect he didn't want anyone to know he'd come back to the area."

"But why?"

She shrugged. "We figure he must have done something criminal. He didn't seem like a model citizen. He had a shifty look to him—wouldn't look you in the eye. We were glad that he kept to himself."

Kathy nodded. "What kind of work did he do?"

Again, Diane shrugged. "Odd jobs, I'd guess. He didn't seem to have a schedule of any kind. He'd toss a rusty old mower into the back of his truck a couple of times a week. We figured he mowed lawns for some of the people in the area. He might have done other work for people, but not anybody around here."

Maybe that list she'd found wasn't all that unique after all. It could have just been the names of Mark's customers.

Diane gazed around at the filthy walls caked with some kind of dark debris. "Do you mind if I have a quick look around the rest of the place? Then I need to get home and get supper started."

"Sure thing."

Kathy walked behind Diane, who kept shaking her head while taking in the shambles of what had once probably been a pretty little home.

They circled back to the kitchen. "It was nice meeting you, Kathy. When does your inn open?"

"The first week in May. I'll be updating my website with pictures as soon as we get the rooms decorated. I'd appreciate it if you'd tell people about Swans Nest."

"Living on the water, we get loads of visitors—*too* many of them. I'd love to be able to refer them to you. I've even heard The Lotus Lodge might reopen."

"It's a possibility. I'm a friend of the new owner."

"Great. I want to turn my spare bedroom into an office. The sooner there're more guest rooms in the area, the better." Diane gave a wave. "See ya."

Kathy closed the door behind her and went back to the living room. No sooner had Diane gone home than Anissa's truck rattled to a halt in what served as the cabin's driveway. She came inside the house.

"Where's Tori?" Kathy asked.

"Home. I told her I could pack up the last of the stuff and bring you back. As a thank you, I want to take you two over to The Bay Bar for supper—that is if Noreen is up to cooking tonight."

Kathy frowned.

"You two are friends," Anissa pointed out. "You're going to have to face her sooner rather than later."

"You're right. Okay, let's get this stuff packed up and get out of here."

Anissa picked up the box of cracked and broken dishes. "Why didn't these go to the dump?"

Kathy shrugged. "I dunno. Tori wants them for some reason."

Into the back of the truck they went with the other pitiful items.

Five minutes later, they were bumping down Lake Bluff

Road. During the ride, Kathy told Anissa what Diane had said about Mark Charles's job situation and about upgrading the cabin.

"I wouldn't mind giving that little house some TLC. Then again, I've been thinking of investing my profits into rental properties. Maybe it's something I could buy as is."

"I don't think Diane would be happy to hear it would remain a rental."

"I'd do my due diligence and vet prospective renters. No landlord wants someone like Mark Charles messing up their property so that they have to continually fix or replace everything."

Kathy had no doubt that Anissa would make a great landlord.

Upon arriving at the Cannon Compound, they dropped off the stuff they'd collected at the cabin, stowing everything in one of The Lotus Lodge's empty rooms, and then Anissa headed for home to clean up before she collected Kathy and Tori to join her for dinner.

Kathy watched as the truck steered north up Resort Road. It was then she wondered what a refined woman like Lucinda Bloomfield had ever seen in someone like Charles Mark.

IT WAS TOO EARLY for The Bay Bar to be hopping when Tori, Kathy, and Anissa crossed the highway that separated it from the Cannon Compound and entered. It was cozy inside, with the lights dimmed, and a smattering of customers chowing down on burgers and fries, the aroma lingering in the air.

"Noreen," Paul called, "the girls are here."

"Be right there."

But Paul didn't immediately gravitate toward the women,

who settled in their usual seats at the bar, turning his back on them instead of immediately fixing their usual drinks.

The women looked at each other.

"Is it just me, or are we getting the cold shoulder?" Anissa asked.

"I'm not feeling particularly warm," Tori said.

"Maybe I shouldn't have come," Kathy said.

"It's not your fault someone they steered toward your inn trashed it," Anissa said.

Kathy didn't look quite convinced.

They sat in silence, waiting for Noreen to join them, just looking at one another. Finally, the swinging doors to the kitchen opened. Noreen seemed to hesitate before plastering on a fake-looking smile and plunging forward. "Hey there," she said, her voice sounding just a little shaky.

"Happy Tuesday," Anissa said.

"Tuesday?" Noreen asked, sounding a little dazed.

"Yeah, the second day of the week," Anissa said. "We'd toast to it, but...we don't seem to have drinks."

Noreen looked nervously at her husband, but he had his attention focused on one of the TVs bolted to the walls. "I—I can make them."

They watched as Noreen pulled out glasses, filling one with ice, and making Kathy's drink first. Were Noreen's hands actually shaking?

"Did you hear they identified the dead guy Tori found," Anissa said.

Noreen's gaze didn't lift from the top of the bar. "Did they?" She shoved Kathy's glass before her—not bothering to place a cocktail napkin under it. It was also missing its lime garnish.

Tori frowned. The Bay Bar had to be teeming with gossip. It seemed impossible that neither Noreen nor Paul could have escaped the chatter. "Yeah, and we spent the day cleaning out his rental place," she said.

Noreen finally looked up, her eyes widening. "You—what?"

"The owners hired me to clear it out so they can sell it," Anissa explained.

"What a dump," Tori muttered.

Noreen looked away, grabbing a pilsner glass and pouring a draft. She hurriedly placed it on the bar before Anissa, slopping some on the old oak top. "Sorry," she said, sounding nervous.

At last, she scooped some ice into a chrome shaker, measured no-name tequila into it, then poured in some green liquid from an unlabeled bottle, shook it several times, then dumped it into a glass. She'd forgotten to run the lip of the glass with a piece of lime and dip it into salt. It wasn't going to be at all satisfactory.

"I—I need to get back in the kitchen," Noreen said rather briskly, which was unlike her. In a male-dominated establishment such as The Bay Bar, she was usually starved for a little girl talk.

They watched her pass through the swinging door, retreating to the kitchen.

"Did we somehow offend her?" Tori asked.

"Only by you finding the dead guy," Anissa guessed.

"Do you think she knew him?" Tori asked.

Kathy shook her head. "Noreen told me she's only been a part of the bar for the past five or six years."

"She might not have known Charlie Marks, but she could have known Mark Charles," Anissa pointed out.

Tori picked up her glass and took a sip and wrinkled her nose. The sweet without the salty was much too syrupy. Her gaze traveled down the bar to land on Paul who, for once, wasn't interacting with his usual buddies. Now, his gaze was focused out the big picture window that overlooked the bay beyond.

Through it, one could see Falcon Island. Paul's expression was enigmatic.

Kathy and Anissa followed their friend's gaze.

"What? Do you think Paul might know something about the dead guy?" Anissa asked.

Tori shrugged. They were about the same age. "What if Charlie Marks—or Mark Charles—*had* been his friend?"

"And what if he wasn't?" Anissa asked.

"Paul's practically attached to this bar from sun-up to way past sunset," Kathy pointed out.

Tori lowered her voice. "Yeah, but when you think about it— we don't know anything about him except he owns this place, Noreen is his second wife, and he seems to be a nice guy."

"Well," Kathy began, but then didn't seem to have much to add to the conversation.

Anissa leaned in. "He used to ride a motorcycle."

"We *think*," Tori pointed out. "I mean, Noreen said *she* used to ride, but she never mentioned if Paul rode—only that she met him here while on a charity run."

"Didn't he once say he was a local?"

"If he did, I don't remember," Anissa said.

"How could we find out?" Kathy asked.

"There are websites where you can look up where people went to high school. I could start there," Tori volunteered. "What if Paul and the dead guy were in the same class?"

"That might be telling—then again, maybe not," Anissa said.

"Isn't that a pretty big leap in logic?" Kathy asked.

"Great discoveries are often made by people who have hunches."

"If you say so," Anissa said, rolled her eyes, and took a sip of her beer.

"There are ways to find out," Tori said.

"Like what?" Anissa asked.

"Aren't some high school yearbooks available online?" Kathy asked.

"Yeah," Tori agreed, already planning her Internet search.

"Okay, but so what if they were in the same class? The dead guy apparently had a double identity," Anissa pointed out. "And he was declared dead almost twenty years ago—and yet he turns up dead again just last week."

"Yeah. We definitely need to do more research," Tori said.

"Or none at all," Kathy pointed out. "That's what the members of the Sheriff's Department get paid for."

"Can I help it if I'm curious?" Tori asked.

"Anybody with a molecule of curiosity would be," Anissa said.

Kathy pouted. Of course, she had other real—monetary—concerns. She couldn't be distracted from what she needed to do to get her fledgling business up and running. But Tori and Anissa had no such constraints. Except ... jobs.

Anissa took a deep drag on her beer. "What are the odds we'll get some food out of the kitchen tonight?"

Tori looked in that direction. "I'm thinking they're poor."

"I have to agree," Kathy said.

"Should we just leave some money on the bar and head back to McDonald's?" Tori asked.

"I wanted to treat you girls to something a little better than that," Anissa said.

Tori shook her head. At lunchtime, Anissa had been worried about treating them to lunch might cut into her profits. "I'm good with Mickey D's—how about you, Kathy?"

"As long as I don't have to cook it—I'm good, too. We'll eat something healthy tomorrow night."

Anissa stood, reached into the pocket of her bib overalls, and extracted a couple of tens, placing them on the bar. "Let's go. There's a burger with my name on it and I'm ready to meet it."

ori's Internet search for Charlie Marks was a bust. She couldn't even find a story about his disappearance, which wasn't really surprising. He'd been just a nobody and the story was probably not important enough for someone to upload a newspaper clipping to the World Wide Web. She didn't find anything on Paul, either, save for a few Yelp reviews on the bar.

With that search behind her, Tori did some digging and found a couple of Etsy shops that featured broken china jewelry. Clearly, there were various degrees of difficulty in the process. YouTube videos were a great way to learn a new craft—and Tori was determined to master this one. Of course, first, she needed the tools. Amazon was only too glad to sell them to her. While on the site, she thought about the upcoming dry run at Swans Nest.

Tori's mother had always been a stickler for the rules of propriety and would never have arrived at a dinner party or other social occasion without bringing a hostess gift. Kathy certainly wouldn't expect one—but she would definitely be pleased if Tori brought one. Wine was too pedestrian—they bought bottles for the house all the time. She typed 'hostess gifts for women' in the search box and was almost immediately given a list with accompanying photos of suggestions.

Should she bring six pairs of pastel cat socks? A spa gift set? A set of silicone spatulas (in three fun colors!) with funny sayings on them? Then her gaze settled on a realistic faux orchid. She clicked on the picture to enlarge it and had to admit that if the photo gave a true representation of the product, it looked pretty darn real. She winced at the price but hit the buy button anyway.

With that taken care of, Tori shut down her computer and hit the sack.

The phone rang before her alarm went off the next morning, and Tori was happy for another day of gainful employment. Once June rolled around, there'd be no substitute teaching until the fall. Oh, how she hoped she wouldn't have to take another full-time teaching job.

She was showered, dressed, and out the door before Kathy even got up. She left a note on the kitchen table and headed for Warton-Erie High School. Today she'd be monitoring students in a math class. Math wasn't really her thing, but she did what she could, and assigned homework for the four classes she taught that day. But there was somewhere she needed to go before the end of classes and was happy she was free that last period of the day.

The school library was filled with hushed voices and giggling students at tables, ostensibly doing homework. Tori stopped at the main desk. Librarian Leona Root looked up. "Oh, hi, Tori. Need some help?"

"Yes. Uh, I was wondering if the school has back issues of its yearbook?"

"Yeah." Leona jerked a thumb behind her. "They're in my workroom in the Media Center."

"Any chance I could have a look?"

Leona frowned, but then shrugged. "I can bring them out to you. What year do you need?"

"That's just it, I'm not sure." Tori gave her a range of years.

"Be right back." Leona disappeared for a minute or more, and then came back with three large tomes. "Here you go."

"Thanks." Tori took possession of the copies of *For The Record* and carried them back to an empty worktable and sat down.

The first was the oldest. Tori flipped pages, looking at the young faces—none of them familiar—taking in their earnest, and often bored, expressions. Would she even recognize a younger Lucinda Bloomfield? She was still an attractive woman, but what if she'd worn her hair in a crazy do all those years ago? And who said she even attended public school? Her parents had been the richest in the county. There were plenty of private schools in Rochester—or would she have gone to boarding school in some other city or even state?

Skipping to the senior pictures, Tori looked through the pages. No Bloomfield. She closed the book and chose the next year's edition. Ten minutes later, she abandoned that tome, too. This could be a colossal waste of time. Was it even worth it to look through the remaining volume?

As she flipped through the pages she came to the senior section, with pictures of those predicted to be the "most likely to succeed" as well as the "class clown." She paused to look at one listed as "The Three Musketeers" and was surprised to recognize the first of the names: Paul Darcy. What a baby he'd been with a full head of hair and the impish grin he had never abandoned. With him were Charlie Marks and Ronnie Collins. She'd found Charlie Marks dead in the water. And Ronnie Collins.... Tori squinted. Could that fresh-faced teen actually be Lucinda Bloomfield's dour butler?

Tori flipped through the pages until she reached the senior pictures. Sure enough, there was Lucina Bloomfield. She'd obviously employed a different photographer than the rest of her classmates. Her portrait was much more sophisticated than the other girls pictured on the same and facing pages. Turning a leaf, she found Ronald Collins's picture. The twinkle in his youthful eye hadn't been evident on the day Tori had met him at the Bloomfield estate. Did he feel beaten down by his former classmate, or had life just dealt him an unhappy hand? Or had he just adopted a rather stoic countenance which would be appropriate for the title of "gentleman's gentleman" even if he worked exclusively for a woman?

Tori turned the page to find Paul Darcy's senior portrait. He looked happy. Like he didn't have a care in the world. He hadn't looked that way the evening before, which wasn't like him. He'd always been nice to her—friendly and jovial. But not last night. She flipped through the pages until she came to Charles Marks's picture and frowned. There was something about the man—teen, she reminded herself—that she didn't like. Was it the set to his eyes, or the odd quirk to his mouth?

She closed the book, then reopened it and searched again for the picture of the Three Musketeers, studying the trio's faces. The smiles they'd shared with the camera had been genuine. Hands held up for a high five, their expressions were carefree. After all, at that point in time, they had their whole lives ahead of them.

Frowning, Tori remembered the yellowed Valentine Kathy had found in Mark Charles's shabby, littered cabin. *"Luv you always"* Lucinda had written. She'd known the dead man—had been infatuated with him—and she now employed another of the Three Musketeers as a trusted employee. And what about Paul Darcy? In the almost-year that Tori had known him, Paul hadn't let on that he and Lucinda had ever been acquainted. Of course, people move on. Tori was no longer in contact with the people who'd attended her high school, either. Not one of them. She'd spent those years in Columbus, Ohio, pining for Lotus Bay.

She closed the yearbook, unsure what to make of the pictures she'd seen. Her reactions were purely subjective. Judgments made on people solely by black-and-white photos from the past.

Tori stacked the books and stood, returning to the main desk. "Hey, Leona, can I take this old copy of *For The Record* home for a few days?"

Leona shook her head. "No can do."

Tori frowned. "Can I make copies of the pages?"

Again, Leona shook her head. "The copier's down—we ran out of toner. But if you only need a couple of pages, I can let you scan them."

"The perfect solution," Tori agreed and followed the librarian to her office. Within minutes she'd scanned the pertinent pages and sent the files to her e-mail address. She'd print them out when she got home and share what she'd learned with Kathy.

But what did it all mean? Okay, Paul, Lucinda, Collins, and Charlie Marks had all known each other. Charlie had disappeared a year or so after graduation only to reappear some twenty-five years later.

Why had he disappeared?

Why had he been presumed dead?

Did his friends look for him, and if they didn't, why not?

Something about the whole situation didn't feel right. What did Paul Darcy and Ronnie Collins know about the missing piece of their triad? And what part—if any—had Lucinda Bloomfield played in the scenario?

Tori had those and many more questions on her mind. Was there any chance they'd ever be answered?

Kathy stood over the newly patched guestroom floor, studying it in great detail. "How on earth did you match the stain so perfectly?"

Anissa grinned. "It's that old Jackson magic. My daddy taught me everything I know about stains and poly, and compared to him, I still know nothing—but I know enough."

Kathy looked at the patched wall, which had been sanded to perfection. "Can I put primer on this?"

Anissa nodded. "And tomorrow you can start painting the whole room."

"I've been ready for days."

"It'll take you a day to do that, and few hours to put up the border, but then this room will be ready for habitation."

"I can't wait to start decorating. I've been itching to do it since the day I first saw this place."

"You *have* been decorating. The downstairs is gorgeous."

"Yes, but the heart of the guest experience is the boudoir."

"Fancy-schmancy name for a bedroom," Anissa scoffed, "but I know what you mean."

"If you're not busy this Saturday night, maybe we could do our dry run."

"Busy? You mean like with a date or something? Honey, I haven't had a date in I don't know how long."

"You're not the only one," Kathy groused. From what she could tell, the local talent was nothing to get excited about. But then, the only places she ever seemed to go were the grocery store, Reynolds Hardware, and The Bay Bar.

"Anybody home?" came Tori's voice from the first floor.

"Upstairs," Kathy hollered.

Seconds later, Tori appeared.

"Well, don't you look like teacher Barbie," Anissa said.

"Yes, this is my favorite school outfit." Which consisted of black slacks, white blouse, a tailored black jacket, and black flats. "If only I wore glasses, the look would be complete," Tori agreed.

"You've even got a matching pocket folder," Kathy commented.

"Yes, and it's what's in the folder that will be of interest to you ladies—or at least Kathy."

"Why wouldn't I be interested?" Anissa asked, irked.

"You tell me." Tori opened the folder and withdrew five sheets of paper, handing several to each of her friends.

"Whoa!" Kathy said.

"Holy crap! Is that old lady Bloomfield?" Anissa asked.

"You got it."

"The Three Musketeers," Kathy murmured, studying the image.

"Okay, you found their yearbook pictures. Now what?" Anissa asked.

"By his reaction last night, Paul has obviously been thinking a lot about the past."

"Yeah, and he didn't seem interested in sharing those thoughts with anyone," Kathy said.

"He must have shared them with Noreen."

"Yeah, and she was the Ice Queen. If you think you're going to get anything out of her—and I'm sure Paul told her something—you're crazy," Anissa asserted.

"There are other sources of information—ones we haven't tapped."

"Like whom?" Kathy asked.

"My Gramps, for one. I haven't spoken to him since Charlie

or Mark was identified. He's the only other person I know who lived here at the time Charlie disappeared. He might know something."

"Maybe you should give him a call," Anissa suggested.

"I will." She looked around the room. "Hey, the wall and the floor are fixed. It looks great."

"Yeah, I'm going to put a coat of primer on those patches, and tomorrow I'm going to start painting."

"I wish I could help, but I've got those windows to put in that cottage up at the Point," Anissa said.

Kathy looked at Tori. "Do you think you'll be substitute teaching tomorrow?"

Tori shrugged. "I won't know until or unless the phone rings in the morning."

"Even if I have to do it all on my own, it *will* get done," Kathy said, and neither of her friends looked like they doubted her. She glanced around the room. "This is no longer my prettiest room, but it will be again."

Anissa smiled. "You got that right."

TORI RETURNED to the Cannon Compound and changed clothes before returning to the kitchen where she usually called her grandfather. Sometimes Herb and Irene went out for an early-bird special, so she wondered if she should wait until later in the evening to call.

Oh, what the heck. If Herb wasn't home, she'd try again later. She punched in the number on the old touch-tone phone and listened as it rang three times before it was picked up.

"Hello."

"Hi, Irene, it's Tori. Is Gramps around?"

"It's not Sunday," she said, sounding rather surprised.

"What?"

"You always call on Sundays," Irene clarified.

"I know, but I need to talk to Gramps about something."

"I'll go see if he's available," she said in that saccharine-sweet voice that made Tori's molars hurt. Did Irene talk to Herb in that tone? It drove Tori nuts.

"Tori?" Herb asked.

"Hi, Gramps."

"It's not Sunday."

"I know," she said and sighed. "I need some information on something that happened on the bay years ago."

"No how are you? How's it going?"

"Hi, Gramps," Tori started again. "How are you? How's it going?"

"Fine and fine," he said, and she could picture him smiling. "It was your grandma who liked a good piece of gossip. Not that she spread it—but she listened."

"Did she tell you what she heard?"

"Sometimes, but I didn't always listen. Now, what is it you want to ask?"

"First, do you remember a young man going missing about twenty-five years ago? His name was Charles Marks—Charlie for short."

"That was no secret. Everybody in the area talked about it for months."

"Well, he's the guy Kath and I found washed up at the south end of the bay last Friday, only now he was called Mark Charles. Apparently, he came back to the area a few years ago and was living on Falcon Island. I guess he pretty much kept to himself, but Tammy at the hardware store said she knew of him and that he came to the grocery store now and then."

"So?"

"Well, did you ever know him?"

"Now why would I? I worked full-time when he disappeared, and unless he bought bait from me, I probably never laid eyes on him."

Tori let out a breath. Well, she hadn't really expected her Gramps would know everyone on the bay.

"Is there anything else you want to tell me?" Herb asked. Something about his tone seemed off.

"Uh, not that I can think of. Why?"

"Just wondering. You gonna call me on Sunday at the usual time?"

"Of course. I always look forward to talking to you, Gramps."

"Yeah, and I like to hear from you, too," he said, his tone softening.

"Okay. Sunday it is. Talk to you then."

"Good-bye."

Tori hung up the receiver and chewed at her lip. Who else could she talk to? She thought about it for a moment. Maybe some of her older, regular customers. And maybe chief competition, Don Newton at Bayside Live Bait & Marina across the bridge might have some ideas. They weren't exactly friends, but they weren't enemies, either. He'd sent some business her way, and she'd done the same. That's what neighbors did.

It was getting a little late in the day for friendly visits. Then again, Don was open year-round, twelve to fourteen hours a day. No wonder he was still a bachelor.

The phone rang, disturbing Tori's revelry. "Cannon Bait and Tackle. This is Tori."

"Tori dear," came Irene's simpering voice once more.

"Irene?" Why the heck was she calling?

"Your grandpa was telling me you're interested in hearing about Charlie Marks."

Of course! Irene was known as one of the biggest gossips around. Her church's Ladies Circle was probably bored without her reporting the latest scandals from near and far. Tori should have just bypassed her grandfather and gone to the real source of information.

"Did Gramps tell you that Kathy and I found the poor man?"

"Oh, yes, but then...I already knew that."

Of course she would. Despite moving to the Sunshine State, she probably still kept her entire espionage system back in Ward County working at full tilt.

"What do you remember about him?" Tori asked.

"Oh, there were terrible rumors ... just before he disappeared."

"Rumors?"

"Oh, yes. That he was a young man you didn't want near your daughters."

"Oh?"

"Apparently, he didn't know the meaning of the word 'no.'"

"Did he force himself on women?"

Irene lowered her voice. "The word r-a-p-e had been bandied about, but as far as I know, no one pressed charges."

Charlie Marks had disappeared two and a half decades before the #Metoo Movement, when sexually aggressive men often had their way with members of the opposite sex and considered it their right.

Had Lucinda Bloomfield been one of Charlie Marks's casualties? Her father had been the richest, most influential man in the county. Could he have been responsible for Charlie's disappearance? But that didn't make sense. Charlie had been declared dead. And who had done that? Tori really had a lot more questions that needed answering.

"What else do you know?" she asked Irene.

"Well, it seems there was a fight at a bar up at Lotus Point over a young woman. Rumor was a couple of Charlie's friends were upset that he had ... had his way with a young woman, and had beaten her up. So ... they beat him up. Pretty badly, too. Charlie was taken to Lakeside Hospital—they closed it about ten years ago. Such a shame. Now we have to drive all the way to Rochester—and can you imagine how much an ambulance ride costs?"

"A lot," Tori said, frustrated for the interruption in the narrative.

"Better that than a Mercy Flight," Irene went on. "I don't trust those helicopters one bit!"

Tori was losing her patience. "What happened after that?"

"Charlie was discharged a day later, but then the Sheriff's Department was called to his house. He had disappeared. His bedroom had been ransacked and there was blood on the floor and bedclothes. It was assumed he was murdered, but there was no fingerprint evidence of anyone having been in his room— except for him and his mother. Eventually, Mary Lou, his mom, had him declared dead because she had a small insurance policy on him and that was the only way she could collect. Poor thing, she died just a few months later."

No wonder Noreen hadn't wanted to talk about Charlie Marks. It would have brought up the subject of the fight at the bar—and it was probably something Paul hadn't wanted to dredge up. But knowing that Charlie Marks had been alive decades later would have exonerated Paul. Or did he think that Mark Charles's death might be pinned on him or Ron Collins? Had Paul even known Mark Charles was in the area? And what about Collins?

Why would Charlie make it seem like there'd been more violence done to him and then up and disappear? And he had obviously taken Lucinda's Valentine along with him as—what? As a sick souvenir?

But why, why, why?

"It's getting on to dinnertime. I'm making a nice meatloaf

and we're having mashed potatoes and peas with it. It's your grandfather's favorite dish. I made an applesauce spice cake this morning. To cut down on calories, I didn't make frosting but just to make it look pretty, I put a paper doily over the top and dusted it with confectioners' sugar."

Oh, dear. If Tori didn't get off the phone, Irene would soon be telling her about her latest shopping trip to the nearest Publix grocery store and what all their weekly specials were.

"I'd better let you get to it. It was so nice to chat with you, Irene. We need to do this more often."

"Yes, we should. Maybe we can have a little chat when you call your grandfather on Sunday."

Oh no!

"Um, that would be nice," Tori lied.

"I'll look forward to it."

"Irene!"

Gramps to the rescue!

"Gotta go. Talk to you on Sunday," Irene said and hung up.

Tori let out an exasperated breath and hung up the phone once more. Though grateful for the gossip Irene felt no qualms about passing along, Tori was *not* looking forward to Sunday.

15

*K*athy locked Swans Nest's front door and headed toward the Cannon Compound. The big willow in the property's south side was beginning to yellow—a sure sign of spring. Within a month, most of the trees would be fully leafed, the spring flowers would be winding down, and once Memorial Day hit, bookings at Swans Nest should bring her to near capacity—she hoped. Kathy entered the house and found Tori standing at the counter, just staring into space. "What's up?"

Tori shook her head. "I just got off the phone with Irene."

"But I thought you were going to talk to your Gramps."

"I did. Irene called back. She's not known as the biggest gossip in Ward County for nothing."

"She spilled all?"

"All that she knew—which was more than I expected. It seems that a couple of Charlie Marks's friends beat him up because he sexually assaulted a woman."

"And do we think we have a clue who that woman was?"

"Who else could it be but Lucinda Bloomfield? They confronted him at a bar on Lotus Point—beat him up enough to send him to the hospital. And then he disappeared a couple of days later, apparently making it look like he might have been a murder victim."

"So Paul and Ronnie were suspects?"

"They couldn't prove they'd made Charlie disappear because there was no evidence to support it."

"Wow. So where does this leave us?"

Tori shrugged. "Nowhere, really. I mean, that only gives us information on why Charlie Marks left twenty-five years ago. Not why he came back and, at this time, no way of knowing if his death was an accident or a murder."

Kathy shook her head. "It's too bad we didn't hang around The Bay Bar last night to listen to all the gossip. I'm sure there had to be some juicy stories being passed around."

"Maybe. But from the look of Mark Charles's cabin, he liked to drink beer. Okay, he drank alone—but what if he sometimes went to bars. There's only The Bay Bar and Cunningham's Cove at this end of the bay, but there are at least three bars up at Lotus Point. Maybe we should hang around there for an evening on a kind of listening tour."

Kathy grimaced. "There's a reason we stopped hanging out in bars."

"Getting hit on by lowlifes?"

Kathy nodded.

"Noreen met Paul in a bar and said it was love at first sight," Tori reminded her.

"Yeah," Kathy agreed.

"It's too early to go now. What do we do in the meantime?"

"I think there's a box of mac and cheese in the cupboard."

Tori grimaced.

"It's not the stuff in the blue box—it's the good kind," Kathy assured her.

"Oh, okay."

"I'll make supper and you can work on Anissa's website. By the way, how's it coming?"

"I'd say it's about fifty percent done. I need those pictures you talked about. And we need to order those business cards. When do you want to present her with the site, anyway?"

"Not until the cards come. The gift needs to be a complete package."

Tori nodded. "It will take longer for the cards to get here than for me to finish the site."

"Why don't you go online and find a printer. I'm sure it won't take long to set it up."

"Okay, but it needs to go on your credit card. Mine's about maxed out."

"Really?"

"Yeah, I had a couple of ... unexpected purchases this month. Between that and setting up Anissa's site—I don't want to get in too deep."

Kathy studied her friend's face. Did Tori look just a little guilty? She was free to spend her money any way she pleased, and she certainly hadn't splurged on anything in almost a year —since she lost her regular teaching job. Kathy gave a mental shrug. Tori would talk about it when she was ready.

"Let's get going," Kathy said and turned for the cupboard to get a saucepan to cook the macaroni, while Tori headed for the office. A piece of cheddar sat in the fridge's butter compartment. She'd grate that onto the hot pasta to enhance the taste. And she was pretty sure there was still a bag of mixed vegetables in the freezer. She could cook some bacon and toss that with the pasta, for extra protein. If they were going to have a couple of drinks while at the Point, they'd need to fill their stomachs to keep the booze from hitting them too hard.

Kathy filled the pan with water and set it on the stove to boil.

It occurred to her that they were probably wasting their time. Who really cared that Charlie Marks/Mark Charles was dead?

Then again ... maybe somebody should.

EVEN THOUGH THE summer season wouldn't officially begin for another five weeks, Tori and Kathy were surprised to find very little street parking on Lotus Point. They left Tori's truck in the municipal lot across from the convenience store and had to walk to the most boisterous bar.

They'd dressed casually in slacks, blouses, and sweaters which wouldn't have looked amiss in any of the establishments on Bay Street.

The Pour House was certainly the liveliest place on the main drag. Loud classic rock blared from speakers mounted in the overhang above the sidewalk. "This looks like the most popular place," Tori shouted above the racket, "but will we be able to hear ourselves think—let alone what anyone else has to say?"

"We'd better move on to the next one," Kathy advised, and they kept going east down Bay Street.

They paused before The Lakeside Grill, taking in the large two-story building with a huge outdoor deck which was not yet in use.

"What do you think?" Kathy asked.

"It looks more like a restaurant and bar—and a lot more expensive. But it's going to be an older crowd that remembers Charlie Marks, although its clientele aren't likely to be the gossipy type."

"You've got a point," Kathy agreed. "But maybe the bartender doesn't mind telling tales. If it's a bust, we can head back to that first bar near the highway—Schooners—and as a last resort, The Pour House."

"Okay, but that's it. I can't afford to pay for more than three drinks—and especially can't handle a DUI arrest."

The place wasn't what you'd call elegant, but it was tastefully decorated and the chairs—what Tori thought of as the ballroom type, the kind you sat on at wedding receptions in hotels—had been embellished with fabric covers, looking more upscale, but not delivering much in the way of comfort.

As Kathy suggested, the place seemed to cater to an older crowd, but there were younger people sitting at tables near the bar and that was the direction the women gravitated toward. They sat at the end and looked around.

"What are the odds anyone here is going to talk about a scandal that happened two decades before?" Kathy asked.

"Zero," Tori guessed. "But we're here and we should at least try to engage the bartender."

They glanced toward the man behind the big oak-topped bar. He didn't look much older than them. What were the chances he'd know about Charlie Marks/Mark Charles? That would be yet another zero.

"We're wasting our time—and our money," Kathy observed.

"Maybe," Tori said, looking around.

The bartender approached. "What can I get you ladies?"

"I'll have a gin and tonic," Kathy said.

"A Margarita," Tori replied.

The man nodded and retreated.

"Think we can get him to give us some chips or popcorn?" Kathy asked.

Tori shook her head. "Not a chance."

"Is that you Tori Cannon?" came a male voice from behind them.

Tori turned around to see the owner of Bayside Live Bait & Marina.

"Don Newton?"

"That's my name," said the man who slid onto the stool beside Tori.

"What are you doing here?" Tori asked.

"I could ask the same of you."

"Hi, I'm Kathy Grant," Kathy said, reaching around Tori and offering her hand.

"Don Newton."

"Yes, I know." They shook on it. "I'm the owner of Swans Nest Inn—across the street from Cannon's and Tori and I came out to celebrate."

"A little premature, isn't it? I thought you weren't opening until the first week in May."

"You're well informed," Kathy said.

"I've visited your website," Don said. He signaled the bartender, who wandered over.

"Heineken?"

Don nodded.

"Coming right up." The bartender turned away.

Newton looked different than he did when behind the counter of his bait and tackle shop. When Tori had seen him there, he'd either been dressed in a grungy T-shirt or a plaid flannel shirt. He'd spiffed up for a night on the town—or rather, the Point—looking rather dapper in a nicely ironed blue dress shirt and sports coat, sans tie. He looked younger, too. Tori guessed him to be in his early forties instead of ... older. Clothes really did make the man.

"I've never seen you ladies here before," Newton said.

"We haven't been here. We usually hang out at The Bay Bar."

Newton frowned. "I wouldn't have thought that was your kind of place."

"You're right, but we're friends with Noreen—the cook and co-owner."

Newton nodded.

The bartender returned with an opened bottle of beer and a glass, setting the latter on a cocktail napkin. "Can I get you anything else?"

"Chips?" Tori asked hopefully.

"Coming right up."

Of course. Now that they'd been joined by a *man* they were getting a little more attention.

Newton poured his beer. "So, you ladies found Mark Charles's body?"

Tori blinked. "Yeah."

Newton nodded. "I read about it online."

"Did you know him?" Tori asked.

"Not really. I recognized his face from the news report. He came into my place a couple of times to buy ice—nothing else— and that was a couple of years ago."

Tori took a sip of her Margarita. They'd learn nothing new about the dead man from him.

"But my dad remembered the whole scandal," Newton said and picked up his glass.

Both Tori's and Kathy's heads whipped around to look at him.

Then again....

"Oh, yeah?" Kathy said.

Newton sipped his beer and the bartender returned to place a paper napkin-lined bowl filled with potato chips in front of them.

"Let me know if you need anything else," he said and left them.

Newton set his glass back down on the bar.

"Scandal?" Tori asked innocently. "What did your dad say?"

"It seems there was a bar fight at what's now The Pour House."

"We also heard Charlie Marks was beaten up pretty good

and then disappeared," Kathy said, toying with the napkin under her drink.

"We heard it was a couple of his friends that attacked him—and it was over a woman," Tori said, selecting one of the smaller chips.

Newton nodded. "Lucinda Bloomfield," he said with disdain. Tori already knew that Newton had a poor opinion of the woman thanks to a conversation they'd had the summer before. He considered Lucinda to be a slumlord—even if they were located in rural New York.

"Why would Charlie Marks's friends beat him up?" Kathy asked wide-eyed.

"Because word was he'd taken liberties with Lucinda."

Liberties was a lot nicer word than rape, Tori thought. "I heard they were called the Three Musketeers."

"That was in high school. The incident I'm talking about happened a couple of years later."

Tori frowned. "How much later?"

Newton shrugged. "I'm not sure. A couple of years, I think. All three guys worked for old man Bloomfield at his canning factory."

"I didn't know they made their money that way," Kathy commented.

"Oh, sure. They canned fruit and vegetables for all the local and lots of name-brand companies under license. They still do, but the old man sold out about a decade ago. Still, Ms. Bloomfield will never have to work a day in her life," he said, bitterness tinging his voice. What was his beef with Lucinda? That she was rich and he wasn't? He made a very nice living from his marina and especially his boat launch. There must be another reason, but Tori wasn't sure that this was the time to push for that explanation.

"What else do you know about it?"

Newton shrugged. "I guess Lucinda used to visit the factory and got to know Charlie. There was that whole rich girl/poor boy dynamic. Her father was not pleased. And then—something must have happened."

"But what?" Kathy asked.

Newton shrugged. "That's all I know."

"Who would know the rest of the story?" Tori asked.

Don looked at her without blinking. "Who else? Lucinda."

ewton turned the conversation from decades before to the present and he and Tori started talking shop. It didn't take long until shop talk became flirt talk and Kathy felt like a third wheel.

But it was Tori who put a halt to it by glancing at the digital clock behind the bar that gave the date and time and said that anyone born after the current day would not be sold liquor.

"I really need to get home. The phone could ring just after five and I might have to go to work substitute teaching."

"You must be counting the days until the season starts," Newton said, and Kathy was afraid he'd bend Tori's ear for another twenty minutes, so she stood. "I've got that bedroom to paint in the morning, too. It was sure nice talking with you, Don."

"Yes," Tori agreed. "Maybe we can do it again sometime." She smiled at the man. Kathy knew that look.

Newton stood. "I'd sure like that," he said, his gaze riveted on Tori's face.

Kathy paid their tab and grabbed her best friend's arm. "See you soon," she called cheerfully, dragging Tori along with her toward the exit.

"Hey, don't be so pushy," Tori admonished her. "Don shared a lot of good information with us."

"Yes," Kathy agreed as they ventured into the cold evening air. The noise level at The Pour House had not dropped one decibel and they had to wait until they were nearly to the municipal lot before they could hear each other speak.

"So what do you think about what Don said?" Tori asked.

A young jeans-clad couple stood under the glow of a lamp-post, passing a joint back and forth, the heady aroma wafting their way. "Let's talk about this in the truck," Kathy advised.

Once inside the cab, Tori started the engine and pulled out of the lot. "Did you want to try that bar up the street?"

"I think it would be a waste of time. If we hadn't run into Don, going to The Lakeside Grill would have been a waste."

"Yeah, what were we thinking?" Tori asked, but in the wan light Kathy could see a smile quirking the corners of Tori's mouth.

"You like him," Kathy accused.

Tori shrugged, but kept her eyes on the dark road, "What's not to like?"

"He's *old*," Kathy accused. "At least ten years older than you. And he's a workaholic."

"And we're not?" Tori accused.

"We have goals."

"Who's to say Don doesn't have goals? And he was out on a weeknight, just like us."

"We don't make it a habit," Kathy said. "That bartender knew what he drank. He must go there on a regular basis—which means he's probably looking to get laid."

"Ya think?" Tori asked. "That place wasn't exactly hopping.

Wouldn't his chances of finding a willing partner have been better at The Pour House?"

"How do I know? I don't know anything about the local nightlife."

"And maybe you ought to. Your guests might want to visit some of these places."

Kathy frowned and turned her gaze to the road, which she could only see in the truck's high beams. "I guess," she admitted. "So what do we do next? Visit a new bar every weekend?"

"That's not my plan," Tori said. "I was thinking more about Lucinda Bloomfield and her heroic saviors."

"I don't know that they were saviors. More like revenge seekers. But it begs the question: What happened among those Three Musketeers? The yearbook made it seem like they'd been and were destined to stay friends forever."

"Yeah. That's been niggling at my brain ever since Don told us about the incident. How would we find out?"

"By asking them?"

"Them who?" Tori asked, sounding wary.

"First of all, Lucinda. You've got a great in with her."

"How?"

"That contract you got from Rick Shepherd. You did promise her you'd speak with her again before you made a decision."

"I've already made my decision. I'd rather The Lotus Lodge stay shuttered rather than give away control of it."

"Lucinda doesn't have to know that. You could say you're looking for advice."

"Uh-uh," Tori said and shook her head. "There's no way I'm going to go to her house under false pretenses to ask about the man who apparently raped her. We're not friends. She wouldn't confide in me just because I also have a uterus."

Kathy sighed.

"Don't try to guilt trip me," Tori said. "If our places were reversed, would you want to walk in that house and ask her about what was probably the most emotional and physically painful incident of her life?"

"Well, when you put it that way—no."

"And neither do I, so don't suggest it again."

Kathy wasn't about to promise anything when it came to that particular subject.

"You should ask Paul," Tori said.

"Me?"

"You're the one who wants to get to the bottom of all this. You ask him."

"I'm not going to ask him about it," Kathy declared.

"He would probably be more willing to talk about it than Lucinda."

"You did see how he ignored us the other night, right? He wouldn't even look us in the eyes."

"And why was that? Was he embarrassed that he'd come to a woman's rescue? I would think he'd be proud of that."

"It was a fight in a public place. We don't even know if he and Collins were arrested. If they were, it could be a reason Collins has had a job with the Bloomfield family for what appears to be years."

"Maybe," Kathy said.

Tori turned onto Ridge Road, heading east toward the Cannon Compound. "Noreen knows. She's the one we should talk to."

"She's not about to discuss it at the bar."

"Then maybe we should ask her to lunch."

"And go where? Cunningham's Cove?"

"Why not at Swans Nest? You can say you're testing recipes for your brides. It would also show her you don't hold a grudge for her sending you the people who trashed your bedroom."

"But I *do* hold a grudge," Kathy said. "I'm pissed as hell."

"At Noreen?" Tori pressed.

Kathy let out a sigh. "No. If she could have accommodated them, she would have."

"Yeah, and then it would've been her room that was trashed."

"It wouldn't have taken almost a grand to fix it," Kathy muttered.

Tori didn't seem to have a retort for that remark. "Of course you know, we don't have to do anything. We can just go on with our normal lives—"

"There's nothing normal about our lives," Kathy pointed out.

"We could just forget all about this. You're the one who wanted to do so just days ago," Tori reminded Kathy.

"I know ... but now I feel like we have a stake in this."

"Why?"

"Because ... I don't know. I kind of admire Lucinda Bloomfield. She's gracious, and she's had a traumatic past."

"She's also rich and beautiful."

"And alone."

"Like us?" Tori asked.

"The way you were looking at Don tonight, who says you'll be alone much longer."

"Oh, stop it," Tori protested.

"Okay, okay."

"And think about what I proposed with Noreen. You know she hasn't got a lot of friends—just acquaintances at the bar."

"Like us?"

"We've shared Christmas dinner. We're more than just acquaintances," Tori stressed.

"I guess you're right. But I can't do it tomorrow. I need to get that bedroom painted."

"If I don't get called in for school, you know I'll help."

"Yeah, but—I don't have anything to feed the poor woman. We haven't gone grocery shopping in almost two weeks. My cupboards have nothing but baking supplies, and yours are just about empty."

"Yeah, and it would look really last-minute to say 'Come over and try these appetizers.'"

"Why appetizers?"

"Because I like them, and you make the best," Tori said, sounding hopeful. "Besides, if there are any leftovers, you can feed them to Anissa and me when we do our dry run, which you mentioned might be Friday."

"If I have to make a load of appetizers, it might be Saturday —or next week."

"So why don't you give Noreen a call tomorrow before the bar opens and invite her to lunch or tea or whatever you want to call it. If I can, I'll be there for moral support."

"Big of you," Kathy said with sarcasm.

"Oh, come on Kath. Do you want to see this thing settled or not?"

"Yes." Even though it really wasn't any of their damn business. For some reason, Kathy *did* want to know the truth about what happened to Charlie Marks. She did want to extend the hand of friendship to both Noreen and Lucinda. But would reaching out to them—asking terribly personal questions about Noreen's husband and Lucinda's traumatic past—also make them enemies for life?

17

*T*he phone rang at just after five thirty, waking Kathy who groaned. The sound meant that Tori would be gainfully employed that day and unable to help her paint the guest room at Swans Nest.

She listened as water ran for a shower, and then got up, tying her bathrobe cord around her middle, and headed for the kitchen to make coffee. Tori usually didn't bother with tea on days she had to work—"a waste of teabags" she often lamented —and Kathy pulled a couple of muffins from the freezer, waiting until the coffee was brewed before nuking her own. She sat down at the table to wait for her friend.

Tori breezed into the kitchen, once again Teacher Barbie, with her hair tied in a ponytail. "Hey, you didn't have to get up."

"A ringing phone makes a great alarm."

"I'm sorry, but—"

"Don't be sorry. This household needs the income," she said with just a tinge of bitterness.

"Once Swans Nest is up and running, you'll be up to your chin in money."

"From your mouth to God's ears," Kathy said. "You've got time for a muffin and a cup of coffee before you go."

"Yeah." Tori peeled the paper from the apple strudel muffin, set it on a plate and in the microwave and set the timer for thirty seconds. "I've been thinking...."

"About what?" Kathy asked.

"Well, there was nothing online about Charlie Marks's disappearance, but what if the *Times of Ward County* ran a piece?"

"How would you look it up?"

"Their office isn't that far from the high school. I could stop by and see if they have old files they'd let me look at," she suggested as she poured herself a cup of joe.

"It's an idea," Kathy agreed.

The microwave went *ding*, and Tori withdrew her muffin. She didn't bother to sit to eat her breakfast, standing over the sink so the crumbs would fall in it and not on her. She gulped her coffee. "I need to get going."

"What are you going to do for your lunch?"

Tori headed for the fridge, opened the freezer door, and grabbed another muffin. "This will do."

Kathy shook her head. They really needed to eat some healthy food. At least the muffin had fruit in it.

"Don't forget to give Noreen a call this morning," Tori encouraged her.

"Oh, yeah—I'm *real* eager to do that."

"Kath!" Tori said sternly.

"Yes, dear."

"Gotta go," Tori said.

"Okay. See you later," Kathy said as Tori grabbed her purse, lunch, and jacket and rushed out the door. Kathy sat down again with her unfinished breakfast and listened as she heard Tori's truck take off. It was just after six in the morning—a little too early to start painting. But *not* too early to start decorating the other rooms at the inn, or at least taking a look at what she'd collected *to* decorate them.

But first, more coffee!

§.

KATHY HAD STOWED several large totes full of treasures in Swans Nest's east bedroom. It wasn't the largest room in the inn, but it did have the biggest closet. She set the top tote on the unmade queen-size bed and was about to start sorting through the linens and knick-knacks when she heard the front door slam. "Kath!" Anissa yelled.

"Upstairs."

Kathy pulled out a white cotton dresser scarf embroidered with bluebirds and flowers and was admiring the workmanship when Anissa joined her.

"Hey, that's pretty. My great grandma used to make those kinds of things. I've got a few of them. I ought to take them out and enjoy them."

"I love vintage linens. Think of the time and effort it took to embellish a plain piece of cloth and make it pretty."

Anissa nodded. "My mother hates this kind of stuff, which is why I've got it all." She sighed. "She likes everything modern and stark. She'd probably break out in hives if she stayed here." Which was pretty much what the vandals had said.

"Well don't jinx my next guests—which will be you and Tori," she reminded her friend. "But the thing is, *you* appreciate your great grandma's work and think how happy that would have made her."

"I was only five when she died but I still remember her," Anissa said fondly.

"And there's part of her left behind in you and her linens. But that's not what you came over to tell me."

"Besides, where's Tori?"

"Working—thank goodness. And your story is?"

"My window job has been postponed because they came in the wrong size—not *my* mistake. The owner ordered them himself because he thought I might jack up the price. The short of it is, I'm yours for the day."

"The list of things for you to do should only take you about an hour to finish."

"I came to help you paint."

Kathy shook her head. "I can't afford to pay you for stuff I can do myself."

"And who said you have to pay me?"

"I do."

Anissa shook her head. "I want to stay in that room during the dry run, which is supposed to happen tomorrow night."

"Or Saturday," Kathy interjected.

"Or Saturday. Let's get it all prettied up. If we start now, we can get a second coat in after lunch, put the furniture back in place, and have it looking spectacular again before Tori gets home from work."

"It would be fun to surprise her."

Anissa smiled. "Then let's get to it."

TORI WAS happy that her last class of the day was just after one, but the back-to-back classes with recalcitrant teens had been brutal. The sunny day gave the kids spring fever, and they barely paid attention to her as their gazes kept being drawn to the windows. But spring in Western New York is fickle. While the temps were warm that day, it could just as easily snow tomorrow.

It didn't take long for Tori to drive to the offices of the *Times of Ward County*, which was housed in a shabby brick building in the county seat. She parked on the street and entered the newspaper's front office, which wasn't much more than a reception desk with a fifty-something woman seated in front of a computer.

Tori walked up to the counter. "Hi. I was wondering if you have back issues of the newspaper available to look at."

The woman tossed her head in the direction of the counter. "There's last week's issue. That'll be a buck."

"Um, I was thinking of some much older issues."

The woman looked up from her keyboard. "How old are we talking?"

"Twenty-five years or so?"

The woman looked at her skeptically.

"I'm a teacher at the Warton-Erie High School," Tori said, which was technically true for that day—and lots of others, too. "I wanted to look up some information on a former student."

The woman's gaze didn't falter.

"I found some material in old issues of the school's yearbook, but I wondered if you might have more information on him."

The woman sighed. "We have bound issues by year. What were you looking for?"

Tori gave her a range.

"This isn't something we ordinarily do."

Tori dipped her head and did her best to look desolate.

"But...I guess I could let you have a look at them."

Tori brightened. "I'd be so grateful if you could."

The woman got up from her chair and went through a doorway into the back room.

Tori stood in the reception area, waiting and waiting for a good four or five minutes before the woman reappeared.

"I had to dig through the file cabinets to find the years you wanted."

"I really appreciate it," Tori said.

"Do you have a subscription to the paper?"

"Uh, no. But I sometimes buy it at Tom's Grocery Store in Warton," Tori fibbed.

"A subscription will save you forty percent off the list price." She gave Tori the bad news and, feeling guilty, Tori found herself surrendering her credit card. If nothing, else, she could at least leave copies of the rag hanging around the bait shop. Maybe her customers would like to read them while waiting in line to be helped. That is ... should there actually *be* lines of customers come summer.

After the transaction was completed, the receptionist—Ellie, by her nametag—left Tori to leaf through the fifty-two issues bound in one thin volume. It didn't take long to find the five-paragraph story she was looking for.

The Ward County Sheriff's Department reported the arrest on Saturday (4/21) at 11:18 p.m. of two Ward County men for committing assault against a third.

Paul M. Darcy, age 21, of Frederick Street, and Ronald T. Collins, age 20, of Lucky Avenue, were arrested following a fight at The Jolly Roger in Lotus Point.

It is alleged that Darcy and Collins confronted Charles Marks, age 22, accusing him of sexually assaulting a mutual friend. A fight broke out in the bar's parking lot and deputies were called. Marks was taken to Lakeside Hospital for treatment.

Paul Darcy and Ronald Collins were taken into custody and transported to the Ward County Sheriff's Department for processing. The men were arraigned in the Town of Lotus Court and remanded to the Ward County Jail in lieu of $1,000.

Darcy and Collins will appear in the Lotus Town Court at a later date and time to answer the charges.

The story pretty much corroborated what Don had told her the night before. She flipped through more pages until she came to a related story.

On Wednesday, State Police questioned Paul M. Darcy, age 21, of Frederick Street, and Ronald T. Collins, age 20, of Lucky Avenue, in the disappearance of Charles Marks, age 22.

Darcy and Collins allegedly assaulted Marks on 4/21 at a Lotus Point bar. Marks was treated at Lakeside Hospital and released. He disappeared three days later after his bedroom was apparently ransacked.

Darcy and Collins were the chief subjects in the disappearance, but were released when it was determined there was no physical evidence to indicate that they had been present in the Marks home.

It wasn't an exoneration but came pretty close to one. Tori leafed through the rest of the tome but there didn't appear to be any follow up stories. Taking out her cell phone, Tori took a few photos of both articles to show Kathy later. She closed the book.

"I don't suppose you have a story in the current issue about the murder of Charles Marks, who was also known as Mark Charles?"

Ellie merely smiled. "You'll have to read our next issue, which should arrive in your mailbox on Friday."

18

*E*llie's remark about the mailbox reminded Tori that she was expecting her Amazon package to arrive that day and wanted to intercept it before Kathy did, just in case Kath wanted to see what she'd bought. But Kathy wasn't there—probably over at Swans Nest—and so Tori unpacked her tools and examined them. She couldn't wait to start work on her first piece of broken-china jewelry, but first she thought she ought to cross the road to see if Kathy needed help with painting her guestroom.

After squirreling away the tools and the faux orchid, which had also been delivered, Tori changed her clothes and headed over to Swans Nest, not at all surprised to see Anissa's truck parked out front. Taking out her key, she opened the door. "Anybody home?"

"Upstairs," Anissa hollered.

Tori climbed the stairs and headed straight for The Floral Room, pausing at the door, taking in the glowing lamps, the bed piled high with lacy pillows, the furniture all back in place, with floral pictures on the walls. "Oh my God, it's finished—and it's gorgeous! How did you manage to pull it off since just this morning?"

Kathy giggled. "Teamwork. What do you think?"

"It's just as pretty as before the trouble. Even the border looks good."

"Yeah, I might not be in a hurry to change it," Kathy said with pride. "You're late getting in. Did you go to the newspaper?"

"Yeah, and forty bucks later, I got to read the old stories about the fight at the Jolly Roger Bar."

"Say what?" Anissa asked.

Tori explained.

"I'm not sure about the hint that there might be something potentially explosive in Friday's issue. I mean, the receptionist could have just been giving me a line of bull," Tori said.

"Or she could be telling the truth," Anissa said.

"We haven't heard anything else from the Rochester news," Tori said.

"We're not exactly tuned into what happens back there," Kathy pointed out. "We don't watch much TV, and we don't read the Rochester paper. And anyway, Mark Charles's death won't mean a thing to anybody in the city."

"You're probably right," Tori admitted.

"What could be potentially explosive?" Anissa asked.

"The cause of death?" Tori suggested.

"Maybe," Kathy agreed. "But even if they announce it, the body was so decomposed, are they ever likely to determine the circumstances of his death?"

Tori shrugged. "I guess we'll just have to wait and see."

§&

DINNER WAS DECIDEDLY MAKESHIFT—AGAIN. "When are we ever

going to go grocery shopping?" Kathy asked, rinsing what had been her dinner plate. Ha! She'd prepared boiled corn, toasted bread heels (fresh from the freezer) and oven-browned French fries. Talk about a carb-heavy dinner. And except for yet more breakfast muffins, the freezer was devoid of any other meal potential. The fridge contained milk for coffee and tea, some limp celery, and half a carton of eggs. No doubt about it, the women were on the verge of potential starvation.

"We'll go to the store tomorrow," Tori said.

"If we don't have other things to do."

"Which reminds me," Tori said. "Did you call Noreen today."

"Noreen?" Kathy asked, as though she'd never heard the name before.

"Yeah, our friend across the road. The one you're supposed to be inviting to lunch tomorrow."

"Lunch. With no food."

"That's why we need to go grocery shopping," Tori reminded her friend.

"Yeah," Kathy admitted, and finished loading the dishwasher, "but I will."

"In the meantime, wanna hear about my latest money-making idea?"

"Tell all," Kathy encouraged.

"First, what happened to those dishes we found at Mark Charles's cabin?"

"They're in unit three of The Lotus Lodge, why?"

"Hang on," Tori said, grabbed her keys from the hook by the door, and disappeared. A couple of minutes later, she returned with the saggy box full of chipped china. Truth be told, most of it was pottery, but the floral motifs were pretty—and from the nineteen thirties, forties, and fifties.

"What are you going to do with them?" Kathy asked.

"Remember that necklace Tammy at the hardware store wore that I admired?"

"Yeah." Then Kathy made a face. "You're going to make pendants from broken pottery?"

"Yeah, and sell them in the shop—maybe on Etsy. Who knows? I could be the next broken jewelry queen of Ward County."

"Talk about delusions of grandeur," Kathy muttered.

"Oh, shut up. If nothing else, it'll be something to do while I sit in the bait shop over the summer. I can offer them for sale on site, and if I make too many to sell here, then maybe I'll try online. I only invested about fifty bucks so far—that's not a lot to lose if it doesn't pan out."

"You're right." Kathy picked up one of the plates. "And some of these designs are pretty darn cute." She traced her finger around the pattern of little blue flowers on the rim of the plate. "I wouldn't mind having a pendant made from these little guys."

"Maybe you could offer them at Swans Nest, too."

Kathy opened her mouth—but didn't speak.

"But *only* if you liked them. We're only dealing with theory right now."

"Okay," Kathy said cautiously.

Tori picked up the crimpers she needed to cut the plates into pedant-sized pieces. "Hmm. I wonder if I should wear eye protection when I play with these things."

"Definitely," Kathy agreed.

"In the meantime, make that call," Tori advised.

"Oh, all right," Kathy groused. She pulled her cell phone from her pocket and hesitated. She could just send Noreen a text message. She'd done that many times during the past year, but an invitation to a somewhat formal lunch deserved a call—if not a face-to-face request for her presence. She wasn't up to walking across the road and asking. Kathy wasn't sure she could bear an in-person rejection.

Opening her phone's contact list, Kathy glanced at it and then tapped Noreen's name. It rang twice. "Hey, Kath, what's up?" Noreen asked, but her voice was flat—not the funny, sassy tone Kathy was used to hearing.

"Hey, Noreen. What are you doing for lunch tomorrow?"

"Lunch?" Noreen sounded wary.

"Yeah, I'm experimenting with some recipes that I want to serve to my brides either at showers or weddings and I thought you might enjoy trying them out. If Tori doesn't have to work, she and I thought you might like to join us."

"Well, I ...." There was a long pause before Noreen spoke again. "It sounds very nice."

"Great. Come over to Swans Nest tomorrow around noon and we'll chow down. There might even be a mimosa or two—or more—served."

"Then how can I say no?" Noreen asked.

"Wonderful."

"Kath," Noreen started, but then there was another long pause. Kathy listened—sure another apology was on the way, but then Noreen simply said, "I'll see you tomorrow."

"Great. Looking forward to it. Bye."

"Bye."

The connection was broken.

Kathy put her phone away.

"So?" Tori asked.

"She said she'd come."

"And?"

Kathy shrugged. "I have a feeling it'll either be a time of catharsis—or the end of our friendship."

Tori scowled. "Don't be so melodramatic."

"I'm worried. I value Noreen's friendship. I sure as hell hope that crap from the past—a situation that has nothing to do with either of us—won't threaten it."

"Yeah," Tori agreed. "Me, too."

The two friends looked at each other for long moments. It was Tori who spoke first, her eyes widened with anticipation. "So, what are you going to make for lunch?"

19

*D*espite the financial loss, Tori was actually glad when the phone didn't wake her at way-too-early o'clock the next morning. The day offered much more interesting opportunities. She got up and wandered into the kitchen to find three happy cats eating their breakfast, a fresh pot of tea under its knitted cozy, and Kathy perusing a folder of recipes she'd clipped or had copied out of books.

"You're just in time. What kind of muffin do you want this morning?"

Tori sighed. "No offense, Kath, but I'm getting really tired of muffins."

"Yeah, me, too, but someone's got to eat my test results, and I've narrowed it down to ten recipes, so they're coming off my experimentation repertoire."

"And what's taking their place?" Tori asked, grabbing a Lotus Inn mug from the cupboard.

"Egg recipes. I suppose I'll have to offer Eggs Benedict—I mean, doesn't every B and B present that?"

"I wouldn't know. I've only been to one B and B. Our dry run tomorrow will make that two. You are offering Anissa and me breakfast, right?" Tori asked and poured the tea.

Kathy picked up her coffee cup and took a sip. "Of course. It wouldn't be a dry run without it."

Kathy pulled out a piece of notebook paper from her folder. "I've made a list of stuff to get at the grocery store. Half is for here, and half is for Swans Nest. Of course, I'll cough up for those."

"Of course," Tori repeated.

"But I'm buying the stuff for lunch with Noreen, too. And you're welcome to join us."

"I'm pretty sure I heard my name mentioned when you talked to Noreen," Tori said.

Kathy nodded and offered a smile. "It didn't hurt to say it out loud."

Tori poured milk into her tea, took out a spoon from the drawer, and stirred it. "Tom's Grocery opens in less than an hour."

"Yeah. I'd better get showered and dressed. I want to be early so that I have time to pull something together for lunch."

"Are you going to make tea sandwiches and scones?"

Kathy shook her head. "Not enough time. I thought I'd make a quiche, have a nice side salad, and defrost a bunch of cookies. I've got a punch recipe I want to try, too."

"I thought you said something about mimosas. It might take liquor to get Noreen to talk about Paul's past."

"I thought of that. We should make a quick stop at the liquor store before we head home."

"Can do."

"Great, now that that's settled, I'm going to get ready. Eat up and then you can hop in the shower."

After Kathy had left the room, Tori caught sight of the contract Rick Shepherd had sent. She picked it up and leafed through the pages. The more she studied it, the more she was determined *not* to enter into a business deal with the local mogul. She set it down and looked out the back door's window. The sun was shining and the big plastic thermometer that hung from the Siberian elm in the yard said it was already near fifty. It would be a warm day in April—they hadn't had nearly enough of them yet. Maybe she'd open the shop and take her jewelry-making equipment out there. That's where she intended to do most of the pendant creation, anyway. It would be a dry run for her to see if the shop could double as her studio. She smiled. *Studio.* She liked the sound of that. Now to hope she'd have talent when it came to actually making the necklaces.

THE SHOPPING TRIP went well and they made their stops at the grocery and liquor stores and still managed to be on the road for home just after nine. Tori stopped at Swans Nest and helped Kathy take in the groceries before she headed for the compound. But when she pulled up by the house, there were two familiar cars in the lot.

Damn! Amber and Rick Shepherd had returned—and why had they arrived so early and apparently at the same time?

Not seeing the pair, Tori still had to contend with a frozen pizza, veggies, and milk. She slammed them into the fridge and freezer and hurried outside. There was no sign of the intruders by The Lotus Lodge, so that meant they had to be either by the bait shop or the boathouse.

The shop was still locked, but the door to the boathouse was open, and Tori heard voices as she approached.

"Excuse me," she called in the open doorway.

"Tori," Amber said, in the same simpering tone Irene

employed. "I was just having a nice little chat with your new business partner."

"What are you doing here, Amber?"

"Just another friendly visit. How lovely that I was able to meet Rick. We're becoming fast friends."

"Yes, we are," Shepherd agreed. "I was just telling your cousin my plans for this boathouse."

"Were you?" Tori asked, unable to keep an edge from entering her tone.

"A combination great room and kitchen with stainless steel appliances and granite countertops that opens to a big deck overlooking the bay. Some built-ins for storage and a covered bar will have guests swooning. Then in the loft, we'll add an outstanding bedroom suite with a big picture window so guests can watch the sun set and gaze at the stars at night."

Tori had had thoughts along those lines, too, but she wasn't about to voice them then. "What can I do for you, Mr. Shepherd?"

"I came to see why I hadn't heard from you."

"You could have called."

"I was on my way to check on another of my properties—" Talk about presumptuous! "—and thought I'd just stop by."

Tori bit her tongue to keep from commenting.

"And I'm learning *so* much about partnerships," Amber said.

"Shouldn't you be at work?" Tori countered bluntly.

"I called in sick. I needed a mental health day." Amber gave a feeble laugh.

Tori wasn't amused.

"So what do you think of my proposal?" Shepherd asked.

"I've read it over a couple of times," Tori said, hedging.

Shepherd's smile was oily. "Great." He reached into his inner suit coat pocket and withdrew a pen. "Then let's seal the deal."

"I haven't made a decision. I need to talk to my business consultant about it."

"And who would that be?" Amber asked sourly.

"You wouldn't know her. Like Mr. Shepherd, she also owns a number of properties and businesses here in Ward County. I'm sure you've heard the Bloomfield name before, Mr. Shepherd."

Shepherd's smile evaporated. "Yes," he said tersely, and he definitely wasn't pleased.

"Lucinda Bloomfield has volunteered to act as my mentor," Tori continued.

"Which means Tori's too wishy-washy—or just plain stupid —to make her own decisions," Amber volunteered.

"I wouldn't put much stock in what the local slumlord has to say," Shepherd grated.

Shepherd was the second man to intimate that Lucinda was a hard-hearted bitch when it came to collecting her rents. But Tori wasn't sure about that. It was easy to denigrate someone; much harder to probe for better answers about their actions and motivations.

"Did you have a deadline in mind for my decision, Mr. Shepherd?"

"Call me Rick," Shepherd said for at least the tenth time. "Yes. If we're to get this property up and running by the Fourth of July, you need to sign that agreement by Monday."

"What happens then?" she asked, wondering if the compound would suddenly burst into flames or sink into the bay forever. "And if I don't?" she added.

Shepherd's eyes narrowed. "I'm a very busy man, Ms. Cannon. I've made you an extremely generous offer. You'd be wise to accept it."

Or what? Tori was tempted to push. If Shepherd thought he could intimidate her, he had another thing coming.

"Or it's null and void, and you'd be making a very big mistake."

Tori frowned. "That almost sounds like a threat, *Mr.* Shepherd."

Shepherd's eyes narrowed. "Take it any way you want, Ms. Cannon."

*T*ori watched as Shepherd's Mercedes pulled out of the compound's lot and onto Resort Road to head west on the highway. That was one pain in the neck gone, but there was still Amber to contend with. Tori turned to face her cousin.

"What are you doing here?"

"You changed the locks on the house," Amber said, not sounding at all pleased.

"Of course I did—to keep *you* out."

"That wasn't very friendly."

"You're not my friend."

"I'm your *family*—and you haven't got much."

"More than I need right now."

"If you want to know the truth, I'm scouting out a property here on Lotus Bay."

"What for?" The last thing Tori needed was for Amber to become a neighbor.

"None of your business."

"Fair enough. And my business isn't *your* business, either. Please leave. And don't come back."

"Oh, I'll be back. Guaranteed," Amber said and stalked off

toward her car. She got in, started the engine, and hit the gas, sending gravel flying as she took off.

Tori watched until the little white car had disappeared before she reentered the house. The first thing she needed to do was call her grandfather and tell him about her visitor before Amber had a chance—putting the wrong spin on the impromptu meeting. But when she punched in the number on the landline, it rang and rang. That was odd. Her grandfather had an old-fashioned answering machine because he couldn't figure out voice mail. Usually, the machine picked up calls after the fourth ring.

Tori replaced the receiver and looked at the clock on the wall. It was getting close to nine-thirty. Herb and Irene had probably gone out to breakfast. The old man hadn't had two nickels to rub together for most of his life, but since winning the lottery the previous summer, he'd been living high on the hog. Of course, his version of that meant eating at diners and maybe getting a beer, not five-star restaurants with tablecloths and a maître d'. She'd try to call again in an hour or so.

In the meantime, she collected her jewelry-making equipment and took it out to the bait shop, along with her laptop. She'd play with the silver tape and soldering gun to see if she could make a decent join. She might have to do it several times before she got the hang of it. So be it. Maybe she'd have her first necklace finished to show Kathy and Noreen come lunchtime. At least, that was her plan.

Before she sat down on the stool behind the counter, Tori switched on the shop's glowing OPEN sign. She was officially ready for business. Now all she needed were customers.

It didn't take long.

The sound of a motor broke the quiet and Tori looked up to see Dickie Sanderson's fishing boat tie up to his slip at the dock. The engine hadn't sounded quite right and Dickie pulled up the ten-horse-power Mercury motor and began to tinker with it. Tori went back to her soldering iron and prettied up the seam, pleased with her work. By the time she looked up again, she saw Dickie headed toward the shop.

"Hey, Dickie—what's up?"

"Aw," and then he let loose with a string of profanity, the gist of which pertained to the prop from his motor and the big chunk of metal that was missing from it.

"How'd that happen? Did you hit a rock?"

"No—something a lot bigger. I think there's a car sunk in the bay not far from Falcon Island."

"A car?" Tori asked.

"Something pretty big. I poked at it with an oar."

"Did you report it to the Sheriff's Department?"

"Yeah. Someone came out and took a look, but I didn't hang around to find out more. I need to get this prop replaced. My brother's coming down tomorrow and expects to get in some bass fishing."

"Well good luck with that," Tori said and watched as Dickie headed toward the compound's parking lot.

She took out her crimpers and started to cut another section of flowers from one of her broken plates. A sunken car.

Nobody had mentioned whatever happened to Mark Charles's truck. Could that be what was sitting in the mud at the bottom of the bay? Did someone run it off the Falcon Island bluff? Could Mark Charles have been in it at the time? If someone had wanted to make him disappear, at least for a few months, they might have rolled down the windows so the truck would sink faster and then eventually the body inside could have floated out.

The very idea gave her the willies. The fact it was plausible, even more so.

❧

KATHY FUSSED at the dining room table, rearranging forks, and adjusting the napkins folded in a Bishop's Miter on top of each plate. It was too bad she hadn't thought to stop at the florist to get a small arrangement for the table. Still, the large silver bowl filled with apples looked adorable, and everything else looked as pretty as she could make it, from the vintage table linens she had lovingly ironed to the polished silver, and pretty china settings. The house smelled like baking, thanks to the quiche in one oven and homemade Parker House rolls in the other.

Kathy glanced at her watch. Noreen was late—only by five minutes—but Kathy wondered if she might have changed her mind about attending the somewhat spur-of-the-moment luncheon. If nothing else, Kathy and Tori could feast on something better than peanut butter and jelly sandwiches or more mac and cheese.

The doorbell rang and Kathy glanced in the mirror over the sideboard to check her hair—perfect—then hurried to answer the door.

"Hey, Noreen, come on in. I'm glad you could make it."

Noreen's usual attire was one of The Bay Bar T-shirts and jeans, but that afternoon she'd donned dark slacks, a black blouse, and matching sweater, and wore silver jewelry—rings, necklace, and bracelets. Good grief! She looked like she'd just come from a funeral.

"Can I take your sweater?"

"No, I'm fine," Noreen said, looking around the foyer. She'd seen it before—from the wreck it had been on the day Kathy had taken possession of the property, through months of refurbishment and restoration, but she hadn't been inside the house in almost two months. "Would you like the grand tour now that it's finished?"

"I don't want to put you to any trouble."

"Are you kidding? I've been waiting seven months to show it off."

Noreen had already seen the first floor, so Kathy started the tour in the basement, which was totally unlike the rest of the home's early twentieth century charm. Instead, it was like a modern-day family room, with a large sectional with cream-colored slipcovers. It was a risk going with lighter shades on the Berber carpet and furniture, but since all of it was washable, it helped to brighten what could have been a dark and depressing place. A large-screen television took up the west wall, and a polished oak bar with six stools lined the south wall. Behind the couch was a table, and bookshelves stood nearby filled with board games, bestsellers, and folk art pieces she and Tori had found the previous summer when scouting yard sales and auctions.

"Wow—you really nailed this room."

Kathy practically beamed. "I'm glad you like it. I hope my guests will, too."

Noreen bit her lip but said nothing.

"The mechanical room is over here," Kathy said, throwing open a door. "Anissa did a heck of a job pulling everything together, from the tankless water heater to coordinating with the HVAC guys. She did all the plumbing. The inspector was very impressed."

"She's a chip off the old block," Noreen agreed. "Her father was so talented."

"I couldn't have accomplished all this without her. Come on, I want to show you the second floor."

Again, Noreen seemed to stiffen. That was where the vandalism had taken place. For a moment Kathy thought she'd beg off that portion of the tour, but then Noreen waved a hand in the direction of the stairs. "Lead the way."

At the top of the stairs, Kathy held out a hand to direct her guest toward the first of the three guest rooms. "This is the Lilac Room, so named because of the lilac bushes that separate our properties. I can't wait to see them in bloom in a couple of weeks."

"You'll be grateful for the foliage to help deaden the sound of our jukebox," Noreen said.

"To be honest, Anissa and I took that into consideration when we repaired the walls. We added in soundproofing. I just hope it's enough."

"We usually turn the jukebox down around eleven—if that helps."

Kathy sure hoped it would.

Staying with the floral theme, the Lilac Room sported pastel purple walls, and one wall was covered in a lilac wallpaper in tones of gray and white. Coordinating fabric covered the bed and shams, and antique furnishings looked quaint, but not precious. A digital clock sat atop the nightstand on the left side of the bed, and a vase of faux lilacs graced the other.

The bathroom was a little tight, but Anissa had managed to squeeze in a slipper tub. As a good innkeeper, Kathy had tried it out and could attest that it was pure bliss to soak in.

Next up was the Daisy Room.

"Isn't that the name of Tori's cat?" Noreen asked.

"Yes, but it's the wallpaper that inspired the moniker." Again, said wallcovering had been used as an accent, and the rest of the room was an antique white with vintage oak furnishings. Its bathroom was larger, and a little more luxurious, which meant that Kathy could charge that much more for it.

"Wow," Noreen said. "I wish my bathroom was this nice."

Kathy felt the same way. The bathroom at Tori's house was cramped and shabby, straight out of 1952 with plastic pink tiles with a black border. Tori had no money to upgrade it and until

Kathy could build onto the back of Swans Nest to create her own home, she would have to be content squatting at the little bungalow on the Cannon Compound. Still, she was grateful that Tori had never asked her for a cent for her keep during the past ten months. She wasn't sure she would ever be able to repay her friend for the kindnesses she'd been shown.

Kathy pointed Noreen toward the last of the finished bedrooms. She hoped to turn the attic into a gorgeous master suite, but that wouldn't happen until she had a successful season or two under her belt. Still, the infrastructure was there for a sumptuous bathroom and bedroom with dormers that over-looked Lotus Bay to the north. *One day* Kathy thought and sighed.

Noreen looked around the newly reconstructed room. Her lower lip trembled before she spoke. "Is this where...?" But she couldn't seem to form the words to complete the sentence.

Kathy nodded. "We don't need to talk about it."

"Well, I think we do." Noreen swallowed, and her eyes filled with tears. "I contacted my customer who vouched for your first guests."

When Noreen didn't say more, Kathy asked, "And?"

Noreen's lip again trembled. "He said he didn't know what I was talking about."

Taking in her friend's anguished gaze, Kathy felt an over-whelming sense of compassion.

"I promise you, Kath, I trusted that man. He was our customer for *years*. He lied to me. He misrepresented those people he recommended and now that could destroy *our* friendship."

Kathy shook her head and stepped forward to grab Noreen in a hug. "No. You were acting in good faith. You wanted to do well by your customer. It isn't your fault."

"Maybe not," Noreen said, almost a sob, "but you've had to suffer a financial loss because of it."

That was true, and Kathy would never again accept a referral from Noreen—but she also knew that the Darcy's would never again *ask* her to take their guest overflow.

"Our friendship is worth more to me than anything that happened last weekend," Kathy said.

Noreen pulled back, her expression the epitome of anguish. "I'm so sorry. I can't tell you how sorry I am—"

"You have and as far as I'm concerned we never have to discuss this again."

"You're way too kind," Noreen said.

"No, *you've* been kind to me. When I got the house, you took days away from your own business to help me clean out the rubbish that was here. You fed me, Tori, and Anissa burgers, bought us drinks, and you've been a true friend. I couldn't ask for anything more."

Noreen wiped at the tears leaking from her eyes. "Liar."

Kathy smiled. "Not at all."

"Hello!" came a voice from downstairs: Tori.

"Coming," Kathy called. "Holy cow, I had better check my rolls in the oven and hope they aren't burnt. Come on. I've planned a lovely lunch. Let's go downstairs and enjoy it."

Noreen smiled. "I'd love to."

ori's gaze traveled around Swans Nest's dining room. Kathy had outdone herself when serving her first meal in the completed dining room, even if it was a simple one. Everything looked so darn pretty. She set down her fork and reached for another one of those light-as-a-feather rolls. "These are too good, Kath."

Kathy laughed. "Then be grateful they didn't burn. Another minute in that oven and they would have."

The conversation had been pretty innocuous, with no mention of Charlie Marks/Mark Charles. Tori hadn't brought up her run-in with Shepherd and Amber, saving that bit of news for later when she and Kathy were alone. When she'd helped Kathy in the kitchen, she'd been told that Kathy hadn't had time to broach the subject with Noreen before Tori's arrival. And yet, tension still seemed to fill the dining room.

It was Noreen who finally approached the subject. "I need to apologize—"

"We've already discussed that," Kathy began.

"Let me finish," Noreen insisted and drank the last of her second mimosa. "The other night when you guys and Anissa came to the bar, I acted rather coldly toward you because ... because I was afraid you were going to bring up the subject of Charlie Marks."

Tori and Kathy exchanged looks, but said nothing.

"I mean," she started again. "You *did* find his body on your property, and that was just a little too close for comfort for Paul and me." She seemed to think about it. "Mostly Paul. You see, he and Charlie Marks had been friends. But that changed just before Charlie disappeared for the first time."

Nothing we didn't already know, Tori thought and reached for the teapot, pouring herself another cup. She was about to pour one for Noreen, who shook her head. Kathy did likewise.

"There was a fight at a bar up at Lotus Point and ... Charlie ended up going to the hospital."

"Yeah, we kind of heard about that," Kathy admitted.

Noreen managed a weak laugh. "I'm not surprised. Memories around here are long. Of course, all this happened long before I even knew Paul. I'm not proud of him for fighting—God knows the last thing we ever want in our bar is a fight—and it's come close to that a few times, but Paul's become a pretty good bouncer. To stay in business—he had to."

And, Tori had to stop herself from urging.

"If you heard about that, you probably heard what they were fighting about."

"Yeah," Tori said.

"For a while, the deputies thought that Paul and Ronnie might have killed Charlie. They were arrested after the fight, but there was no real evidence of them ever being in the Marks's house—even if Charlie's room was made to look that way."

"We heard there was no fingerprint or other evidence to implicate them," Tori said.

"That's right—and of course, Paul and Ronnie were sweating bullets for a while there, but they always did figure that Charlie just up and left before something worse happened. I mean, you don't rape Horace Bloomfield's daughter without ramifications."

"Had Charlie been threatened by old man Bloomfield?" Tori asked.

"The old man wanted to kill him—and a lot of people around here thought he did just that."

"Kill Charlie himself?" Kathy asked aghast.

"Or *had* him killed," Noreen said.

"But how come nobody mentions that part of the story?" Kathy wondered aloud.

"Because money talks. He didn't want the whole county to know what had happened to Lucinda. But, of course, plenty of people *did* know."

Like Irene Timmons, who had been only too happy to report the story decades later.

"Mr. Bloomfield invited Paul and Ronnie up to the house after Charlie's disappearance."

Tori's eyes widened. This was a new dimension to the story.

"And?" Kathy urged.

"And he thanked them for beating the crap out of Charlie and told them they'd have jobs for life."

"And that's how Ronnie got to be a butler?"

Noreen shook her head. "Not exactly. They both went back to their jobs at the canning factory, and when it was sold a few years later—the new company fired everybody and closed down the plant."

"But I thought it was still running," Tori said.

"It was bought by a conglomerate a few years ago and reopened. It's now bigger and better than it ever was," Noreen said.

"So what happened to Paul and Ronnie?"

"Mr. Bloomfield asked them what they'd like to do. When things were slack at the canning factory, Paul worked as a fill-in bartender for the former owner of The Bay Bar. The old man knew it was up for sale, and he bought it—drove a pretty hard bargain for it. Then he sold it to Paul for a song. Still, it took him eight years to pay off the loan, but you won't ever hear Paul say a bad word about any of the Bloomfields."

"And Ronnie became their butler?" Tori asked.

Again Noreen shook her head. "He wanted an education. So the old man paid for him to go to Cornell and their school of hotel management."

"Wow, I wish *I* could have gone there," Kathy said. She'd gotten a good education in the same discipline, only for a much lower price at a state school.

"And then he became a butler?" Tori asked again.

"Not quite. Ronnie did the same as Kathy—started by assistant managing a motel in Syracuse. He bopped around the state for a while. I guess he loved the work."

"I wish I could say the same," Kathy muttered, but then it was what she learned on the job that encouraged her to go into business in the hospitality business for herself.

"So how did he become a butler?" Tori insisted.

"Well, he ... kind of ... got shot."

"What?" Kathy practically yelled.

"Yeah. Seems someone tried to rob one of the places he was managing. Ronnie would have given him whatever money was on the premises—but the guy had an itchy trigger finger and shot first. He fled the place with no cash—and they caught him hours later. He didn't realize there were cameras in the parking lot and lobby."

"What an idiot."

Noreen nodded. "He got fifteen years in jail, and Ronnie lost his taste for managing hotels. So he took a course and became a butler," she said, giving Tori a nod. "When Lucinda heard, she hired him on the spot. He's been working for her ever since."

"Are they friends?"

"You'd have to ask Lucinda that," Noreen said. "I've never spoken to the woman."

"What do Paul and Ronnie think about Charlie reappearing? Did they know he was in the area?"

Noreen shook her head. "No. I think Ronnie would have gone berserk if he'd known."

Tori couldn't imagine Collins, as Lucinda called him, going off the wall. The time she'd seen him he'd been so reserved, kind of like an automaton.

"Are Paul and Ronnie still friends?" Kathy asked.

"Not really. He comes into the bar now on a regular basis on what Paul calls spy missions for Lucinda."

"What do you mean?"

"He sits in a corner with a redneck hat on, listens to the gossip, and then reports what he hears to his boss."

And that was probably how Lucinda knew about the deal Shepherd had proposed to Tori. It all made sense now.

"Did you know Anissa was hired to clean out Mark Charles's rental cabin?" Kathy asked.

Noreen shook her head.

"Yeah, Kath and I helped her. And Kathy found a card that Lucinda had written to Charlie saying 'luv you always.'"

Noreen frowned. "I doubt it."

"I can show it to you—later. It's over at Tori's house in our office. I was going to turn it over to Detective Osborn ... but I haven't gotten around to it yet."

"From what Paul told me, they barely knew Lucinda. But—it seems Charlie was obsessed with her. In fact, he kind of stalked her."

"What do you mean, kind of?"

"He took pictures of her in high school, hung them in his locker. Everybody knew he had a crush on her, but she wouldn't give him the time of day. He tried to date her, but he wasn't in her league, if you know what I mean."

"Where did he get the Valentine's Day card?"

"It must have been a phony," Noreen said.

Tori wasn't so sure. She took a sip of her tea and found it had gone cold. She set the cup down. "What do you—and more importantly Paul—think happened to Charlie?"

Noreen shrugged. "We don't know what to make of his actual death. But Paul did say that Charlie changed after high school. He hated working in the canning factory. Thought it was beneath him. He stopped hanging around with Paul and Ronnie. Well, by that time Paul and Ronnie had stopped hanging around with each other much, too. They both had girl-friends and they didn't like each other. Paul later married his girl."

The first wife, Tori knew. Noreen was his second. They'd only been together about six years.

"What were the circumstances of Lucinda's ... attack?" Kathy asked.

"That's something just weird. Paul and Ronnie ran into each other up at the Point, and they were both leaving the bar when they heard a woman scream. That's when they found Charlie raping Lucinda behind a Dumpster at the restaurant next door."

The same one Kathy and Tori had gone to just the other night.

"She'd been to dinner with friends and left the restaurant to walk to her car. Apparently, Charlie had seen her enter the place and waited for her to leave. She rebuffed his advances one time too many, I guess and...." Noreen didn't finish her sentence.

Rebuffed him one time too many? That almost made it sound like it was Lucinda's fault she was raped. For too many men, the answer "no" was simply not enough.

"Anyway," Noreen continued. "Paul and Ronnie beat the tar

out of Charlie. Someone called the cops, and there was a deputy in the village on another call and he got there soon after, but by then, Lucinda's friends had whisked her away. Paul and Ronnie told the deputy about the rape, but they didn't report who the victim was. Charlie wouldn't admit to anything."

"But people did know," Tori insisted.

"Sure, but nobody, least of all Lucinda, wanted to go on record to report it."

"And that's why old man Bloomfield was so grateful to Paul and Ronnie," Tori guessed. "They'd stopped Charlie, and then kept the whole thing quiet."

"They did lie, saying they didn't know the woman's identity," Noreen said, "and Paul has no qualms about keeping quiet."

"And since there was no 'victim' to press charges, he was never going to be prosecuted, either," Kathy said.

"You got that right. But the whole thing was moot anyway when Charlie disappeared less than a week later."

"Hmmm," Tori muttered.

Noreen picked up the napkin from her lap and folded it, placing it beside her now-empty plate. She glanced at her watch. "Wow, look at the time. I need to get back to the bar and get the French fry grease up to speed for tonight's dinner crowd." She stood. "Thanks for the tour of the inn. You've done a terrific job with it. And thanks for the lunch. I wish I could do more than burgers, wraps, and soups. Your brides and guests will be very lucky indeed to be entertained at Swans Nest."

Kathy's grin was so wide Tori worried her face might crack.

"I'm sorry to run out on you when you've got dishes and everything."

"Don't worry about it. I'm here to help," Tori said. "And this has been the best meal I've had in a while. I'm hoping there're leftovers, and if there are—I've got dibs on them."

They walked Noreen to the door, exchanged hugs, and

promised to see each other soon. Then Kathy closed the front door and looked at Tori. "Well?"

Tori shrugged. "We know more than we did this morning."

"Yes, but what does it all mean?"

"I don't know. But there's one thing that wasn't mentioned."

"And what's what?"

"Charlie Marks's cause of death. Once we know that, it could just give us a lot more questions."

22

*K*athy and Tori collected the plates, cutlery, glasses, and serving dishes from the dining room and brought them into the kitchen, then while Kathy rinsed, Tori stacked them in the dishwasher. While they worked, Tori told her about the vehicle that sank in the bay.

"Wow."

"Yeah. I sure hope they put a buoy up if they can't pull it out pretty quick." Tori changed the subject. "What are we going to do about that Valentine's card?"

"I suppose I really should give it and that other piece of paper I found to Detective Osborn, and then we can ask if the medical examiner has determined Charlie Marks's cause of death."

"Do you actually think he'd tell us?"

"If he doesn't, it'll be made public at some point anyway."

"Holy smoke," Tori said. "The *Times of Ward County* might be reporting it in the current issue. That could be what the receptionist was hinting at the other day. The issue was supposed to be delivered to our mailbox today."

Kathy looked at the clock on the wall, the hands on its face pointing to the roman numerals of two and six; in other words, two-thirty. The mail usually arrived late in the afternoon. "We'll just have to wait a bit longer."

"And in the meantime?" Kathy asked.

"You should call Detective Osborn."

"Why me?"

"You were the one who found that card and the paper," Tori reasoned.

"You're right," she conceded. "And in the meantime, you should call Lucinda Bloomfield."

"What for?"

"To talk."

"About her being raped?"

"Well, maybe not that, but you can talk *around* the subject."

"How?"

"You're a teacher—you know how to get people to think outside the box."

Tori ignored the statement. "I don't know her number."

"But you know the name of her property management company," Kathy pointed out.

Yeah, Bloomfield Properties. Tori pulled out her phone and looked up the number online.

"And what do I say to whoever answers the call?"

"That you want to speak to Lucinda, of course."

"They're not going to give me the number," Tori said.

"Then ask them to pass on a message for her to call you."

"Why would they do that?"

"Just call," Kathy ordered.

Tori picked up the phone and punched in the number. It rang three times before it was answered.

"Bloomfield Properties: Avery Simons at your service."

"Mr. Simons? This is Tori Cannon. We last spoke last Saturday when Ms. Bloomfield invited me to tea at her home."

"Of course."

"Uh, Ms. Bloomfield asked me to contact her about a business proposal."

"Ah, yes. She's been waiting to hear from you."

"I don't have her number. Can you please give it to me?"

"Why don't I have her call you?" he said instead.

Naturally. "That would work," Tori said, resigned.

"Fine. She'll be in touch."

But before Tori could say "thank you," Simons had ended the call.

"Well?" Kathy asked as Tori punched the phone's end-call icon.

"Mr. Simons is going to have her call me."

"And what do you want to bet the number will be blocked?"

"No bet because you'd win."

Kathy nodded. "Then how long do you think it will be before she calls back?"

"An hour or more. She probably won't want to look too eager."

"Uh-huh," Kathy said.

"And I'll bet she'll expect me to jump at the chance to talk to her."

"Then maybe you should stall her."

"Why?"

"If nothing else, it would show that you're not desperate to seal a deal."

"I'm not," Tori protested.

"And you shouldn't be willing to mortgage your future for the pittance Shepherd wants to give you."

"Lucinda already told me she wants almost as much."

"We both know you'd never take either offer so that discussion is moot."

"Yeah," Tori said, feeling defeated—not by refusing the

offers, but knowing that she probably would never be able to afford to resurrect The Lotus Lodge.

"If nothing else," Kathy went on, "you can ask if Lucinda needs a friend."

"Why would I do that?"

"Because she's got to be in terrible turmoil with everybody talking about Charlie Marks's death. And what if, unbeknownst to Paul and Ronnie, she actually *was* Charlie's girlfriend."

"You think she'd be slumming with a guy like that?"

"Who knows? Maybe she was a rebellious teenager."

"But me bringing up the past could make Lucinda an enemy for life."

"What have you got to lose?"

"She's a powerful woman in this county," Tori reminded her friend. "What if she blackballs me with the bank I deal with, or the Chamber of Commerce, or who knows what other influences she has—from getting me barred from running ads in the *Pennysaver* to souring my relationships with any or all of my vendors?"

Kathy frowned. "When you spoke to her last week, did you really get the idea she was so ruthless?"

Tori scowled. "She's very polite—almost guarded. But she *did* reach out to me."

"Then you should try to reach out to her."

"And what about the card? I can't show it to her if you give it to Detective Osborn. And what if I showed it to Lucinda and she decided to destroy it. Then that could potentially be evidence tampering, and I don't want to go to jail."

"We could make a copy of it."

"I guess. But here's another question for you. What are you going to tell Osborn?"

"About what?"

"The card. You found it on Tuesday. This is Friday. He's going to want to know why you didn't contact him before this."

Kathy looked thoughtful. "It slipped my mind?"

Tori glared at her. "You made me make a call, now it's your turn."

Kathy frowned. "Oh, all right." She turned and opened a drawer, withdrew a business card and stalked over to the phone that hung on her kitchen wall, then punched in the number. "Yes, I'd like to speak with Detective Osborn." She paused. "That's too bad. I'll call again later. Thank you."

"He's unavailable?" Tori guessed.

"Yes. I'll try again later."

"What do we do in the meantime?" Tori asked.

"Finish cleaning the kitchen. Then I guess we go back to your place and wait."

"What about the dry run?"

Kathy shook her head. "I don't think I'm up to it today. Do you mind if we postpone it until tomorrow night?"

"I'm good with that, but you need to tell Anissa."

"I'll text her," Kathy agreed. "Come on, let's get this kitchen back in shape. But first," she said, indicating the plate that still contained half a dozen cookies, "have one or two of these."

"What for?"

"Strength and fortitude."

Tori looked at the sunflower seed and chocolate chip oatmeal cookies. She would need more than a couple of cookies to get through her upcoming conversation with Lucinda Bloomfield. But then she figured what the heck—and grabbed a cookie, then went back to loading the dishwasher.

TORI AND KATHY returned to the Cannon Compound and

changed into more comfortable attire. Kathy put the Valentine's Day card on the printer/scanner and made a two-sided copy on heavy-duty paper.

Then they sat in the tiny living room to wait.

"Oh," Tori said suddenly, sitting up straighter. "I forgot to tell you who was waiting for me when I got back from the store this morning."

"Don Newton?" Kathy guessed.

"No. Rick Shepherd and my cousin Amber."

"What were they doing here?"

"Snooping around. Amber said something about she's looking for property in the area."

"I thought you said she never liked Lotus Bay."

"That's what she always *used* to say."

"And where is she coming up with the money to buy this property?"

"She was being coy."

"Maybe she just wanted to rankle you."

"I *am* rankled," Tori admitted. "And just as bad, Shepherd practically threatened me if I don't sign his contract."

"Which you aren't going to do," Kathy said vehemently. "What did he threaten you with?"

"He wasn't specific. But he made it sound like I'd be very sorry if I didn't deal with him."

"Then maybe Noreen and Lucinda are right about him. And maybe when we talk to Detective Osborn, we ought to mention that Shepherd tried to intimidate you."

Tori shrugged. Then she remembered something else. She dipped into the pocket of her jeans and came up with the pendant she'd made. "Take a look. What do you think?" She handed it to Kathy.

"Wow—it's cute."

"And it was fun to make. I can see myself doing this a lot over the summer when things get slow. And if they don't sell in the bait shop, maybe I can sell them online."

"Would you do craft shows?"

Tori shook her head. "That would take me away from the shop. Jewelry making would be a hobby sideline. My summer income is dependent on the bait shop and the marina. In the meantime, I need to find a source for inexpensive, but fairly good quality chains. Women are going to want to wear the pendants right away."

"I would," Kathy said.

They heard the sound of an engine outside. Tori got up and headed into the kitchen to look out the window. "It's the mail truck."

"Oh, good—go see if the *Times of Ward County* has arrived. While you do that, I'll text Anissa."

Tori hiked out to the mailbox and retrieved its contents. Among the items were the utility bill for both the shop and the house, circulars, a bait catalog, and hot off the press, the most recent issue of the *Times of Ward County*. Sure enough, the top story was about Charlie Marks.

Tori hurried back to the house and dumped the mail on the counter. "Kath—come here," she called and began to skim the story. Charlie Marks, aka Mark Charles, had not died of natural causes. Kathy began reading over her shoulder.

"Gunshot?" she muttered in disbelief.

"Yeah," Tori read aloud. "'Despite the body's state of decomposition, a small caliber bullet was recovered from the victim's chest cavity.' That sounds revolting."

"Okay, now the question becomes ... who killed him, and why?"

"I wonder if Osborn has any ideas," Tori said.

Tori's ringtone sounded, startling them. She withdrew her

phone from her pocket and glanced at the screen—it was the same Bloomfield Properties number she'd called earlier.

"Is it her?" Kathy whispered.

Tori shook her head and answered the call, putting it on speaker so that Kathy could listen in. "Hello?"

"Ms. Cannon. Avery Simons returning your call."

"I had hoped to speak with Ms. Bloomfield."

"She prefers to communicate in person. She'd like to invite you to meet with her again. Would tomorrow at one be convenient for you?"

Tori hesitated before answering. She didn't want to look too eager, either. "Well, I did have plans, but I suppose I can make other arrangements."

"Very good. I'll let Ms. Bloomfield know. Thank you." And with that, he ended the call. Tori set her phone on the counter.

Kathy shrugged. "At least you'll get a good meal."

"If she doesn't throw me out before I get to eat it," Tori griped. "And what am I going to wear? I can't wear the same outfit I had on last Saturday."

"You can borrow one of my dresses. You'll look adorable."

"I don't think that's going to matter to Lucinda."

"If you look wide-eyed and innocent, it might make all the difference in the world."

Tori wasn't convinced.

The ringtone on her phone sounded once again. She looked down at the instrument and groaned. "Oh no! It's Gramps. Amber must have gotten to him before I could."

"Then don't answer it."

"I *have* to answer it," Tori said and stabbed the call button. "Hi, Gramps," she called cheerfully, but this time didn't hit the speaker icon and turned away from her friend. "I'm surprised to get a call from you on this phone."

"Oh yeah?" Herb's voice was filled with challenge.

"Yeah, I tried to call you this morning, but it rang and rang—the answering machine didn't even kick in."

"We had a power outage last night. It screwed up everything that had a clock—including the answering machine," he explained, but his voice hadn't grown any warmer. "Irene and I went to the grocery store this morning, and when we came back I got another call from Amber. She had a lot to tell me—stuff you apparently weren't *prepared* to tell me."

Tori wasn't sure how to react to that statement, so she said nothing.

"What's this about a possible buy-out of The Lotus Lodge?"

"Amber told you that?"

"Yes. Now answer me, are you going to sell?" Herb demanded.

"No!" Tori answered

"Then, will you take on a partner?" he accused, sounding just as angry.

"I don't know. I've seen a proposal, but I don't like the terms. The second offer was almost as bad."

"You've had *two* offers?" Herb practically shouted. When the property had been for sale for three months the year before, he hadn't had even a nibble.

"Yes," Tori said. "I've had seven months to think about the situation and it's obvious that without a big infusion of cash, there's no way The Lotus Lodge can ever reopen."

"Why would you even want to reopen that money pit? Your grandma could never make it pay. It nearly killed her doing all that work alone."

That was the key. Josie Cannon *had* done all that work alone. As far as Tori knew, they'd never hired anyone to help her. Tori's father had told what he found to be amusing stories about how he and his sister had shirked jobs at the Lodge that they thought were too boring to do or beneath them. Chores like laundry, cleaning, and vacuuming the little motel's guest rooms. In their teens, both had found employment away from The Lotus Lodge because those businesses paid better than what their parents could afford to give them.

Both children had left home as soon as they could. And when they'd had kids of their own, they'd dumped them on their parents during the summers instead of paying for expensive camps or other daycare. Even as a child, Amber had been a nasty little piece of work, but Josie had always seemed to bring out the best in her, although it had been obvious to everyone—including Amber—that Tori was her favorite. Maybe because she loved the place so much. Because she was never bored by the rural landscape. Because she *had* loved to help Josie with the laundry and making every room at The Lotus Lodge pretty again after every guest went home. She'd learned to make beds with hospital corners while Amber refused to help but was jealous of the dollar a day Josie paid Tori.

Years before, there'd been a little convenience store just across the way that sold bread, milk, beer, candy, and chips. Tori would indulge in the latter, and Josie encouraged her to share—even though Amber would usually grab and gobble whatever treat Tori had bought. That was when Tori learned to save her cash, letting Josie hold onto it until it was time for her to leave at the end of the summer. Of course, then her mother made her use that money to buy school supplies. Something, in retrospect, Tori thought her parents should have shelled out for.

There was a reason Tori wasn't especially fond of her parents and had always thought of Lotus Bay as her real home. And when Tori's nuclear family had moved to Ohio—ripping her away from her beloved second home—she had become a different child. Less outgoing. Less willing to trust. And profoundly unhappy.

"Tori? Are you still there?" Herb asked.

"Yes, Gramps." She thought about his question. "Gramps, you might not understand this, but...I really think that reopening the Lodge can be successful."

"How?" he demanded, his voice hard.

"Because the bay is becoming more of a tourist attraction. Kathy's inn is going to bring in more business at the south end."

"From people with money," Herb said sourly. "The Lodge ain't gonna attract that kind of clientele."

"No, but thanks to the Internet, I can market it better than Grandma ever could."

"She did the best she could," Herb said sternly.

"Yes, she did. But I have many more tools, and Internet marketing is the way to go. It doesn't have to be expensive. I've already got a website up—"

"Yeah, Irene showed me that on her computer," Herb grudgingly admitted.

"And I've got a Facebook page and a Twitter account for the bait shop. I'll do the same should The Lotus Lodge reopen."

"Doesn't that cost a lot of money?"

"These accounts are free, Gramps. Of course, Facebook will do everything it can to suppress my posts if I don't take out ads... but I know ways around it."

"Hmmm."

"Anyway, you shouldn't worry about any of this. The Lotus Lodge is *my* problem now—not yours."

"Old habits die hard," Herb said.

Yeah. They did.

"You gave me the property. I hope that meant that you trusted me to make the right decisions on how to go forward with it."

"You're right. I was never gonna make the damn place pay. If anyone can make a success of it, it's gonna be you, girl."

Tori smiled. "Thanks, Gramps. I'll make you proud. I swear."

Herb laughed. "Your grandma wouldn't like to hear you cuss."

Tori laughed, too. "I know. We'll talk again soon, Gramps."

"And I'll look forward to your call. I always do."

"I love you, Gramps."

"And I love you, too, Tori. Bye."

The call ended. Tori turned around to see Kathy watching her.

"Sounds like it went better than it could have," she said optimistically.

"Maybe."

"I'm sorry, Tor."

"For what?"

"Well, I know you've never said anything, but it didn't escape me that it was you who bought that winning lottery ticket for your gramps. I know he gave you the whole compound, but ... well, he's got millions. He could do even more for you. He could—"

"Don't go there, Kath. I gave my Gramps that ticket. It only cost me a dollar—and the computer picked the numbers, not me. He didn't owe me a damn thing. I'm grateful he gave me what I wanted most: a chance to stay here on the bay. I'm not going to fault him for what he did or didn't do beyond that."

Kathy pursed her lips and said nothing for long seconds. "You're right. We're both very lucky to get what we wanted most in life at so early an age."

"That's right."

"And we'll figure out some way to get The Lotus Lodge back on its feet. Thanks to what you and Anissa have already done, it's in better shape than when we first looked at it last summer. If you do nothing but maintain what you've got, when you do get an influx of cash, it will be easier to resurrect it."

Tori nodded. That was her hope. And maybe with her fledgling broken jewelry business, maybe that day would come sooner than she anticipated. That was if she could entice customers to buy her creations. She thrust her hand into her jeans pocket and fingered the silver and china pendant—her first creation.

She could choose to feel despondent or hopeful.

She chose hope.

23

*I*t was later that evening when Kathy realized that although she'd promised to call Detective Osborn with her discovery of the Valentine's Day card and the list of phone numbers, she hadn't done so. However, that lack of action hadn't gone unnoticed by Tori.

"I thought you were going to call the detective," she casually mentioned as they were cleaning up the supper dishes.

"I was. He'll be off duty by now. I may as well wait until tomorrow."

"And what makes you think he'll be working on a Saturday?" Tori asked.

"Um...." Kathy had no real answer to that question. "I was thinking, maybe it would be better to learn what Lucinda's reaction to the Valentine's Day card would be, first."

"If it's genuine, that's immaterial," Tori declared.

"We don't actually *know* it's legitimate," Kathy countered. "The way Charlie carried on in high school, he might have bought it himself and had someone sign it just so he could show off. And what if Lucinda says it isn't legit, and she's not telling the truth? Maybe they didn't hang around in school, but it sounds like they *could* have had a secret relationship afterward."

"I suppose she *could* say it isn't her signature, but would we believe her? We don't have any reason to think she'd lie," Tori said.

"Maybe, but now that we know Charlie Marks was murdered...."

Tori shook her head. "I *want* to believe her."

"Why?" Kathy asked.

"I dunno. She has a reputation around these parts, but I don't think it's warranted. She seems like a genuinely nice person to me. Okay, she *is* a businesswoman and her terms weren't especially generous, but they are better than what Rick Shepherd offered."

"You have nothing in writing from her," Kathy commented as she wiped down the counter. "And people like Don Newton have said disparaging things about her."

"Who else besides Don?" Tori asked.

Kathy opened her mouth to answer, but then realized she didn't have an explanation.

"We know Rick Shepherd has a similar reputation. I don't consider him a reliable character witness. Maybe we should try to get more information on her. I don't know who else to ask?"

"You're sure to get some customers at the bait shop tomorrow. Saturday is your best day no matter what the month. And there's always Irene," Kathy offered.

Tori scowled. "I'll call her only as a last resort."

Kathy shrugged. "So be it. In the meantime, will you be working on Anissa's website tonight?"

"I could. Why?"

"Because the business cards I ordered online and paid extra to get sooner, should be arriving tomorrow. I'd like to give them to her and show her the site tomorrow evening."

"I could go work on it now if you finish cleaning the kitchen."

"Why not?" The truth was Kathy kind of enjoyed cleaning, which was good because until the inn was in the black, she wouldn't have the money to hire help.

Ten minutes later, she joined Tori in the little office they shared.

"Take a look," Tori said and pushed her chair away from the computer.

"You changed the home page."

"Uh-huh, I played with Photoshop and decided to add Anissa to some of the pictures. I think this one standing in front of your new porch looks good."

"Should I prepare a testimonial?"

"Definitely. Click through the pages, and then write it and I'll add it to the contact page. While you do that, I'll go get a cup of tea. Do you want one?"

Kathy shook her head. "Not right now." Tori left the room and Kathy sat in her friend's chair and flipped through the new web pages. Considering Tori wasn't a trained web designer, she'd done a credible job. The site was quite professional looking.

Moving to her own workstation, Kathy opened a document and composed her statement. It wasn't hard to write a gushing endorsement and she'd finished by the time Tori returned. "Read this and tell me what you think?"

Tori set her mug on the desk and scanned the document. "It's a little long," she said, ever the English teacher. "I'll edit it and then get your approval. Email it to me, will you?"

Kathy did and swung her chair back and forth as Tori worked, her thoughts returning to Charlie Marks.

How had the man survived since his return to the area? He had to have had a job. His next-door neighbor had only mentioned lawn-cutting jobs. When Detective Osborn came to collect the card, and she was pretty sure that he would, she'd ask him about that.

"See what you think," Tori said, and Kathy stood to look over her shoulder. She read the text. Pared down, it read as a concise summary of Anissa's strengths—of both skill and character. "Wow. Did I actually say that?"

"You did. Just a little less wordy."

Kathy smiled. "Have you ever thought about freelance editing?"

"What—you mean like books or something?"

Kathy shrugged. "It might be something you could do during off hours—or during the winter when you don't have substitute teaching days and when the bait shop is closed."

"I never gave it a thought. Hmm."

Kathy studied her friend's face, glad she had given her something to think about.

She returned to her chair. "I've been thinking about Charlie Marks."

"And?" Tori queried.

"Well, there's still a lot we don't know about him—his life. I could kick myself for not asking more questions when I had the chance while talking to his neighbor."

"Like what?"

"Nobody can live without money, and as far as we know, his income was seasonal. How did this loser guy pay his rent during the winter? How could he buy all those beer cans Anissa took to the recycling center? How did he feed himself—let alone his dog?"

"He wouldn't want to draw attention to himself by applying for welfare or SNAP benefits," Tori said.

"Right, so he had to have some way to pay his way, and I'm

betting whatever it was, was under the table. Otherwise, he would have to file a ten-forty with the IRS like the rest of us."

"Good point," Tori conceded. "So how do we find the answers to these questions?"

"By asking more questions," Kathy said.

"But of whom?"

Kathy sighed. "I wish I knew the answer."

AVERY SIMONS'S invitation to meet with Lucina Bloomfield had not mentioned the word "tea," so Tori figured she had better eat lunch before she drove up Resort Road to meet with the county's number one millionaire.

She'd borrowed one of Kathy's summer dresses, but it was much too cold to go sleeveless this early in spring, so she'd donned a white sweater so that she wouldn't catch a chill.

After parking her truck in the drive near the front of the house, Tori once again stood before the big door and rang the bell. It took long moments before it swung open, once again attended by Collins.

"Hello," Tori said. "I believe Ms. Bloomfield is expecting me."

"Yes. Come in, Ms. Cannon."

Tori swallowed. It was like being addressed by one of her students, but Tori didn't feel any kind of love, or even welcome, from the never-smiling Collins. He led her to the luxurious living room where Lucinda stood gazing at an oil painting of an older woman above the fireplace. She turned at Tori's entrance.

"Hello, Tori. Thank you for contacting me."

"Hi. Thanks for seeing me."

Now why had she said that? It was Lucinda who wanted to see *her!*

Lucinda nodded toward the folder Tori held in her hand. "Did you bring the Shepherd Enterprises proposal?"

"Yes."

Lucinda waved a hand toward the seating arrangement in front of the big fireplace. "Please sit. Collins, would you bring us some tea."

"Very good, Madam." And he nodded and left the room.

Tori took a gold brocade wing chair and Lucinda settled on the long white couch. She held out a hand and Tori handed over the paperwork.

Lucinda withdrew a pair of reading glasses from a blue-and-white porcelain box on the coffee table, and settled back to inspect the pages.

Tori found her mind wandering as her gaze settled on the various objects that decorated the room. Kathy would probably sell her soul to get inside the mansion to study what professional decorators had done to transform the place. But Kathy was no slouch when it came to décor, either. Swans Nest might have had a beer budget, but the champagne results were a credit to Kathy's thrifting ways and frugal living.

At last, Lucinda sighed and set the proposal on the coffee table just in time for Collins to bring in a brightly polished silver tray with a bone china tea set. A small plate held cookies that were commercially made—something with a chocolate coating. He poured before retreating.

"So," Tori said, picking up the creamer and pouring a small stream into her cup before stirring. "What do you think of Mr. Shepherd's offer?"

"Not much. I assume you've read it through."

"A number of times," Tori agreed.

"And your reaction?"

"I'm not prepared to sell my soul to reopen The Lotus Lodge. I'd have to do so to sign that contract."

"Then am I to assume that you wouldn't consider my offer to be worth deliberating, either?"

Tori shook her head. "My grandfather sold me the compound with the belief that I alone would be its steward. He was not happy to hear that I might take on a partner."

"I see," Lucinda said coolly. "Are you considering alternate possibilities?"

"You mean like going to a bank and asking for a loan?"

Lucinda nodded.

Tori shook her head. "I doubt I could get one. If I'm going to turn the business around, I'm going to have to do it on my own initiative. It might take me a decade or more—if ever—but that's going to have to be the way it is."

"That's too bad," Lucinda said. "But it seems to me that you're a determined young woman. If it's something you really want, you'll find a way."

"Yes," Tori said with authority, "I will."

"I admit I'm disappointed, but I'm also not surprised," Lucinda continued and picked up her own cup, taking a sip of tea. She reached for one of the cookies—or was it a biscuit? "I sense the contract wasn't the only thing you wanted to talk to me about."

"You're right, but...it's a delicate subject, and I wonder if showing you what Kathy found might be upsetting."

Lucinda's eyes narrowed. "Found?"

"As you know, your neighbor, Anissa Jackson, is a contractor and woman of all trades. She was hired to clear out the cabin Charlie Marks was living in."

Lucinda's expression didn't change at the sound of the man's name, but her gaze seemed to harden. "I don't think I understand what you're getting at."

Tori opened the folder once again, taking out the facsimile of the old Valentine's Day card. She handed it to Lucinda. There was no flicker of recognition as the older woman gazed at the front of the folded paper and Tori wished she'd cut it down to actual size. However, Lucinda's eyes widened and her breath caught in her throat when she opened the paper and took in the signature.

"Where...where did you say you found this?" she asked rather breathlessly.

"In Charlie Marks's cabin. He was living there under the name Mark Charles. It was his body Kathy and I found down by the water next to Swans Nest last Friday."

All color had drained from Lucinda's face. She swallowed. "This isn't the original."

"No, it's being given to Detective Osborn of the Ward County Sheriff's Department."

Lucinda's gaze seemed riveted on the signature. "I see. I don't suppose—" she began, but then didn't finish the sentence. "This ... card ... represents an awfully uncertain time in my life."

"Did you love Charlie Marks?" Tori asked.

"Of course not. I was an infatuated girl. I had no concept of what love was, as I'm sure you didn't at the same age."

When it came to that, after her disastrous relationship with Billy Fortner that had ended the year before, Tori wasn't sure she had a clue what real love was.

"I thought you should know of its existence. The detective is sure to come and ask you about it."

Lucinda nodded. "I appreciate the warning, thank you."

There didn't seem to be much else to say.

Tori collected the papers from the coffee table, but didn't pick up the copy of the Valentine's Day card.

"I ought to get going. Kathy's doing a dry run at Swans Nest tonight. She's got real guests next week and wants to make sure she's ready."

"And you'll be staying there tonight?"

"Yes. If there's a problem, she wants to know before its opening day."

"A prudent decision," Lucinda agreed. She stood. "Thank you for coming today, Tori. I hope we'll have more opportunities to chat in the future."

"Me, too," Tori said.

Lucinda walked her to the door and they exchanged cordial goodbyes.

The door behind Tori closed softly, but she couldn't help but feel as though she was being watched as she walked toward her truck, got in, and then backed out of the driveway. For some reason she couldn't pinpoint, she felt uneasy. But when she turned to look, there was no sign of Lucinda Bloomfield.

24

*K*athy couldn't seem to sit down during the time Tori was gone to visit the lady at the top of the hill. She'd start to clean something, get distracted, and then do something else—like check email, or pick up a magazine, only to abandon it and go look out the window in the front door that overlooked the Cannon Compound's parking lot. And yet, it wasn't all that long—maybe half an hour—before Tori returned, the tires of her truck crunching on the gravel parking lot.

Kathy leaned against the worn Formica counter, trying not to look like she was lying in wait for her long-time roommate to reenter the house, and yet it seemed like every muscle in her body was tense and she had to rein in her propensity to pounce as soon as Tori entered the house.

"So? How did it go?"

Tori sighed and peeled off her sweater. "It went."

"That's not a satisfactory answer."

"Okay, she took the fact that I don't want to take on a partner well. I mean, she seemed a little disappointed, but not floored to hear my decision."

"And the card?"

"That threw her for a loop," Tori admitted. "Not so much the card itself, but when she saw her signature, she kind of freaked —but in a totally passive kind of way."

"What the heck does that mean?" Kathy asked.

"She didn't seem to remember the card itself, but she sure seemed to recognize the signature."

"So, there was more than just a crush going on with Charlie Marks. She had feelings for him, too?"

"I don't know. It seemed more like she was ashamed than anything else."

"Ashamed?"

"She admitted she didn't think she was in love with Charlie. I wonder if you might have been right. Maybe she was just a mean girl who led him on."

"But you can't be sure," Kathy said.

"No. I can't."

"And you didn't ask?"

"Kathy, when the woman saw the card, she was gobsmacked."

Kathy frowned. "You and your Anglophile descriptions."

"Hey, you're the one who's determined to serve afternoon tea."

Kathy nodded. She sure was.

"After showing her the card, I kind of got dismissed."

"But what about the Shepherd proposal? Did she offer better rates?"

"Not really. And she actually seemed encouraging when I told her I was determined to revive The Lotus Lodge on my own."

"Good for her. I think you can do it. It just might take a couple of years."

"Or never," Tori groused.

Kathy didn't like to encourage negativity.

"Did you call Detective Osborn?" Tori asked.

Kathy ducked her head. "Uh, no. I mean—it's the weekend! Why would he give up a couple of days off? Charlie Marks will still be dead on Monday. I'll call him then. I promise."

"See that you do," Tori warned. "Meanwhile, what are we going to do about supper?"

"I thought we might wait for Anissa and then go across to The Bay Bar. I want Noreen to know that she can count on us remaining her friends. I can afford a greasy supper for the three of us, and then we'll go over to Swans Nest together. I've got snacks ready, and a bunch of chick-flick DVDs to choose from. Add to that a couple of bottles of wine to celebrate Anissa's new website, and afterward the three of us can retire for the night in the three guest rooms. Then in the morning, I'll cook you guys a sumptuous breakfast and you can let me know what you think about your stay—good *and* bad."

"I hardly think we'll find anything worth complaining about."

"But you need to. If there's something a guest could possibly gripe about, I *need* to know about it before the paying public arrives."

"Okay—okay. I'll be so critical you'll want to ban me from ever darkening your door again."

"Well, I didn't exactly say *that*," Kathy cried.

But then Tori's lips curled into a smile. "I don't think you have to worry. You've been obsessing over this for seven months. I have a feeling I'll never again have such a wonderful guest experience."

Tori's faith in her gave Kathy a shot of much-needed confidence. By tomorrow morning, she'd have her answer.

Kathy crossed her fingers and hoped for good results. And she was determined that no matter what happened during the dry run, that she would be able to fix the flaws.

She had to.

֍

ANISSA SHOWED up at Tori's front door, duffel in hand, just after six that evening. "When does the party start?" she asked, grinning.

"Not until after supper," Kathy called from her station at the sink, where she was polishing the copper bottoms of the old Revere Ware pans Tori's grandmother had used for more than three decades. They had held up nicely despite the years.

"Kathy's buying us dinner over at The Bay Bar," Tori said.

Anissa's answering smile looked forced. "Burgers. Again?"

"Nah, they've got wraps on the menu, too," Tori said, but Anissa didn't look encouraged.

"They've also got a salad bar—and that's what I'm going to have," Kathy said, rinsing the bottom of the pan and putting it in the sink-side rack to dry. "Let me grab my purse and I'll be ready to go." She stopped. "Oh, shoot. The cats!"

"I'll feed them," Tori volunteered and picked up the morning dishes. Hearing the bowls clink was like a siren song to the felines, who showed up for their dinners hours early with no qualms.

"Are you packed?" Anissa asked Tori.

Tori pulled the tab on the cat-food can and Daisy wrapped herself around her ankles, meowing quietly in encouragement. "Pretty much. All I'm bringing with me is a sleep shirt and a toothbrush."

"Are you going to try out the soaker tub?"

"I hadn't given it any thought."

"Well, I have." Anissa indicated her duffle. "I've got a change of clothes as well as my nightie. Plus a book, a flashlight, and my cell phone. I like to be prepared for any circumstance. Besides, I never know if I'll have to fix somebody's toilet at the crack of dawn. I need to be able to get up and get out if the need arises."

Facing high schoolers didn't sound all that bad when faced with that alternative, Tori decided. She placed the bowls down in their usual spots and the cats wasted no time in attacking their meals.

Kathy returned with her purse and a small suitcase. Tori got her things and then followed her friends out, calling, "Goodnight, guys. Henry, you're in charge." She switched on the outside light before locking the door behind them.

They hiked across the road and into The Bay Bar. Since it was early, the place wasn't crowded. Kathy and Anissa took their usual seats at the bar, setting their bags down on the floor, and Tori ambled over to check out the salad bar. It didn't contain as many offerings as the one at Cunningham's Cove, but it would do. And she at least knew the potato salad was made by Noreen —not something from one of their suppliers.

Seated at one of the tables near the big window was a guy hunched over a glass of beer. There was something familiar about him, but Tori had other things to think about as she joined her friends at the bar.

"Are we going to have a drink?"

"I am," Anissa said.

"I've got wine chilling over at Swans Nest," Kathy cautioned.

"Oh, all right, then," Anissa said.

"What'll it be ladies?" Paul asked as he approached them after pouring a beer for another of his patrons.

"We're just here for the grub," Anissa answered.

"What's it going to be?" Paul asked.

"Salad bar," Kathy said.

"Salad bar," Anissa echoed.

"Make that three," Tori told the barkeep.

"If you want soup, it's Noreen's famous New England clam

chowder. Help yourself when you're ready," he said and headed back down the bar.

"I'm ready now," Anissa said and led the way.

After they'd piled their plates with lettuce, other veggies, plus pasta and potato salads, with dressings of their choices on the side, they headed back to the bar and chowed down.

"Are you nervous about the dry run?" Anissa asked Kathy.

"Of course not. I think—or at least hope—I've anticipated your every need."

"I'm sure you have," Tori said, but if there was anything lacking in Kathy's welcome, she had already decided she'd honor Kathy's request to be brutally honest. There was no way she wanted Kathy to be embarrassed when her first real and *paying* guests arrived in the not-too-distant future.

Anissa dipped a fork into her dressing and stabbed a piece of pepper. "We need to talk about the addition to your house," she told Kathy. "We need to figure out where it's going to go and how big it will be before we build that gazebo you want in the backyard. I mean, if we set the gazebo in the wrong location, and then your new home comes later, it could screw up the whole aesthetic, and it would be expensive to relocate."

Kathy sighed. "I've thought about it. But I don't have the money to consult an architect."

"No, but you have me. If you want, I'll draw up a plan that I think might work, and then give you an estimate on the cost."

"Of the addition, or the gazebo?" Kathy asked.

"Both. But let's face it, you aren't going to be in a position to build the addition until you've got a year or two behind you."

"True enough," Kathy acknowledged.

"But you need that gazebo if you want your brides to get married on site."

"Yes."

Anissa nodded. "I can give you an estimate in a couple of

days. Will that do?"

"Yes, thank you."

Somebody plugged a few quarters into the jukebox and a sad song about love gone wrong boomed from the speakers above them, the bass line vibrating through them.

"I'm so glad we added that soundproofing to the east side of Swans Nest," Kathy muttered.

"We went way beyond code, but I'm still not sure it'll be enough," Anissa said.

"Well, that's the room I've given myself," Kathy said sounding worried.

"What room have you given me?" Tori asked.

"The Daisy Room. I hope you don't mind, but since Anissa has done so much to bring that poor sorry house back to life, I thought she should get The Floral Room. Besides, your room was partially named after your cat. It seemed appropriate."

Tori smiled. "Yeah, it does."

"Aw, you didn't have to do that," Anissa said, but she sounded grateful none-the-less.

"Are you kidding, you told me yesterday, in no uncertain terms, that you wanted it," Kathy said and laughed.

"Yeah," Anissa admitted. "But Kath, you've got to change the name of that room. It really sucks."

"Yeah," Kathy agreed, "it does."

Since their mission at The Bay Bar had been only to consume food, the women plowed through their salads in no time flat. Tori did go back to the salad bar for another helping of Noreen's potato salad, which tasted almost as good as what her grandmother, Josie, used to make, but Kathy and Anissa passed on seconds.

Kathy paid the tab and they called goodbyes to Paul and to Noreen, who came out to wish them well on the dry run.

Ready or not—Swans Nest was about to be tested.

25

No sooner had the women retreated to Swans Nest's game and media room, than Kathy fired up the popcorn machine that sat on the bar on the south wall. It made smallish batches of popcorn that tasted like the kind you get at the movies, and neither Tori nor Anissa complained—especially when she broke out the wine.

"Let me propose a toast," Anissa said, raising her glass. "To Swans Nest Inn."

"To Swans Nest," Tori agreed and the three of them clinked glasses and drank.

It was Kathy who spoke next. "But the inn is not the only thing we have to celebrate tonight."

"Oh, yeah?" Anissa asked. "Is it somebody's birthday?"

"Not mine," Tori said.

"Nor mine," Kathy agreed, "but it is a gift-giving occasion."

Anissa looked puzzled. Kathy got up from her seat on the sectional and went behind the bar, bringing back an oblong box wrapped in cheerful paper of colorful balloons; it was actually birthday wrap, but Anissa didn't have to know that. On top was a big pink bow, which wasn't exactly Anissa's favorite color, but the only one Kathy had on hand.

She marched over to the sectional and handed the box to Anissa, who seemed taken aback.

"What's this?"

"You won't know until you open it," Tori said and giggled.

Anissa gave them both a hard look before she began to rip the paper from the box. She lifted the lid and for a few seconds didn't seem to know what to make of the contents. Then she ran a finger over the top and plucked a card. Her eyes widened, and then she burst into a toothy grin. "Get out—what is this?"

"Read the last line," Tori directed.

"Anissa Jackson contractor dot com?" she asked in wonder.

"Uh-huh—that's the second part of the surprise."

Kathy returned to the bar and bought out her laptop, which was already connected to the Internet. She set it on the coffee table before them. "Take a look."

"Holy crap!" Anissa hooted. "This is fantastic!"

"Tori made the site," Kathy said. "I just supplied the pictures."

Tears filled Anissa's eyes as she clicked through the web pages. "This is ... this is fantastic," she managed, her voice cracking. She turned her gaze on her friends. "You did this for me?"

"Well, we wanted the world to know what a great contractor you are. We're so proud of your work—we thought you should have an Internet presence so that others could find you, too."

A single tear rolled down Anissa's cheek and she wiped it away. "I don't know how to thank you."

"I think you just did," Tori said and laughed.

They toasted once more, stuffed their faces with popcorn, and watched a favorite chick flick that made them laugh and cry. And suddenly it was almost eleven o'clock. After a long day, they were ready to head to the second floor and their respective guest rooms, with Anissa taking her box of business cards with her. Finally they said good night.

As Kathy undressed she noted she could vaguely hear the pounding beat of the jukebox next door, but as Noreen had promised, once the clock downstairs struck eleven, the vibrations ceased entirely. Kathy crossed her fingers that her neighbors would keep that promise when the inn opened the next weekend.

The bed was comfortable, the sheets were sinfully soft, and Kathy had no trouble falling asleep in the Lilac Room. In fact, upon awakening Sunday morning, she wished she could stay in that room instead of returning to the lumpy mattress in the room she slept in over at the Cannon Compound. Some things just weren't meant to be...at least for the foreseeable future.

Still, she was up well before six and showered and dressed before stripping the bed and heading downstairs to prepare breakfast. She wanted her dry-run guests to be as pampered as those she hoped to host in the not-too-distant future.

And what a breakfast it would be. Omelets made to order, two different kinds of muffins, sweet rolls, coffee, and tea. She would offer more when the guest roll amounted to more than two, but she knew what Tori and Anissa were used to and didn't want to overdo her menu.

Tori was the first to come down the stairs, but Kathy heard the water running for quite a long while, which meant that one of the baths was being filled.

"Yup—Anissa," Tori affirmed. "She told me she was determined to try out that soaker tub."

Kathy smiled. "Do you want to eat now or wait for her?"

"I'll wait," Tori said, "but I sure could use a nice cup of tea."

"Already made," Kathy said and pulled a mug from the cupboard. "Of course, when it's time to serve breakfast in the dining room, you'll have a bone-china cup. You can choose any pattern you want from the cabinet."

"No, that's okay. Whatever you select will charm me no end."

"Flattery will get you—" She was about to say everywhere, but that wasn't what Kathy needed to hear. "Do you want to talk about your experience now or wait until Anissa gets down here?"

"Now is fine with me," Tori said and accepted the mug that Kathy gave her.

"And?" Kathy asked with trepidation.

Tori shrugged. "I'm happy. I would be a very happy person staying here in this beautifully restored historic home."

"And?" Kathy asked again.

"I love the antiques, but I also am in love with that game and media room. It was so neat to kick back with you guys. It felt like a real family room, except better because of the popcorn machine and wine."

"And the bedroom?"

"The bed and sheets were great. I had no trouble falling asleep. I like the bathroom, but I'm not a tub person, so a walk-in shower would be better for me personally, but I understand the appeal to the B and B crowd."

"And the bedroom decorations?"

"Pretty, but not overly so. I've seen pictures online of some of your competition and they're either a little too quaint, or like something from the seventies example of country décor. I think what you've done hits the nail on the head, if I may use a cliché as a descriptor."

"Fine with me," Kathy said, feeling inwardly relieved and yet proud. But then, what was her best friend supposed to say?

Tori frowned. "I know that look, Kathryn Grant. You're wondering if you can trust me on this."

Kathy shrugged.

"If I thought there was something wrong, I would tell you. I want this to be the best B and B in the area. I think once you get that gazebo built and get more of the landscape under control, you'll have a hit on your hands. But that's going to take time—and you need money coming in to pay for those improvements."

"In other words, I have to start somewhere?"

"Another cliché, but also a truism," Tori said neutrally. She sipped her tea.

"In the meantime, I've still got few things to do before breakfast can be served." And with that, Kathy headed to the fridge and took out an onion, a red pepper, and a block of cheddar cheese.

"Which reminds me, I should take this opportunity to go home and feed the cats. They've been alone for more than twelve hours. We're no doubt going to suffer their wrath by being completely ignored for most of the day."

"Crap you're right."

Tori left the kitchen and Kathy heard the front door close. She would be ready and waiting for make those omelets the minute Tori returned. But first—coffee!

❧

TRAFFIC WAS non-existent that quiet Sunday morning as Tori crossed Ridge Road and headed toward the Cannon Compound's mailbox, gravel crunching under her shoes. She opened the box and found it empty. Duh! Kathy had said Anissa's business cards were to arrive the day before and she'd obviously retrieved the mail in order to collect them. Tori closed the lid and started toward the house when sunlight glinted off something at the side of the home.

Glass. Broken glass.

Tori's heart picked up speed and she broke into a jog, but then practically skidded to a halt.

"Oh, no!" she cried, taking in the living room's broken window. Most of the glass was on the inside.

Feeling torn, Tori wasn't sure what to do. Should she risk entering the house and find a burglar inside—or run back to Swans Nest and call the Sheriff's Department from there?

She remembered what Anissa had told her: someone who was determined to get in the house would get in. Had Amber paid her a visit the evening before?

Fear turned to anger as Tori pictured Amber rummaging through her things looking for—what? She didn't have much of value. Just the computers and—

"Oh my god! The cats!"

Throwing caution to the wind, she rushed to the front door but it wasn't locked. She darted inside, only stopping to grab her grandmother's rolling pin—the only weapon she could think of. "Daisy! Henry! Larry!"

The kitchen hadn't been touched, but the two bedrooms and the office had been trashed. Oddly enough, the computers were still there, but Tori wasn't sure if anything else had been taken. The closets had been rifled and every drawer had been dumped.

Tears of frustration welled in her eyes, but she had more important things to think about.

"Daisy?" she called again. It was later than the cats usually ate and they should have come running when they heard her call. Pulling the tab off a can of cat food might be easier than plowing through the clothes, books, papers, and clutter that littered the three rooms to search for the felines, praying they hadn't already escaped.

Tori made her way back to the kitchen, her hands shaking. Obviously, whoever had entered her home was long gone. Was it just some teenaged kid having fun? Then why not trash the kitchen, living room, and bathroom?

But what in the world would she do if Daisy was gone? How could she tell Kathy that Henry and Larry might be missing, too?

Setting the rolling pin down, she grabbed a can of cat food from the lower cabinet and called, "Breakfast!" Daisy knew what that word meant: food!

No sign of the cats.

Grabbing the bag of treats, Tori walked into the living room and shook the bag. "Treats!"

Black cat Larry emerged from Kathy's bedroom and headed for his bowl. "Henry! Daisy! Treats!" she called.

Henry, also known as "The Big Orange," because he was a fourteen-pound orange tabby, also emerged from Kathy's room.

But where was Daisy?

The boys were obviously glad to see a familiar face and twined around Tori's ankles, asking for the promised treats—or at least their morning meals. "Good boys. I'll get you something to eat," she promised, her stomach feeling shaky. Where was Daisy?

The phone rang. Tori wasn't sure if she should pick it up. She'd already contaminated a crime scene, but her cell phone was back in the room she'd occupied at Swans Nest. She grabbed it on the third ring.

"Tori?" Kathy sounded annoyed. "What's taking so long?"

"Oh," Tori said, close to tears. "Someone broke into the house overnight."

She heard Kathy's quick intake of breath. "The cats?"

"The boys are with me here in the kitchen. I haven't found Daisy."

"Oh, no. I'll be right over."

"No. The Sheriff's Department is going to be pissed at me for messing up their investigation—if it comes to that. I have to secure the window so that the boys don't get out.

"Forget that. If you can get them into their carriers, bring them here."

"Are you sure?"

"Definitely. I'll be right over to help." The line went dead, and Tori replaced the wall phone's receiver.

The boys were getting impatient. Tori picked up their dinner bowls and got three bowls down from the cupboard, still hopeful that Daisy would appear.

Kathy arrived just as the boys tucked in. "Did you find her yet?"

"I haven't had time to look. Did you tell Anissa where you were going?"

"She hadn't come down yet," Kathy said and crouched down to pet her cats. They were more interested in breakfast, but she didn't seem to care. "Go look for Daisy."

"Shouldn't I call nine one one first?" Tori asked.

"We're in no danger, but you've got to find Daisy. If she's not here, we've got to start scouting the neighborhood ASAP."

Tori nodded. "You call."

"Go!" Kathy commanded.

Tori tore off for her bedroom. If there was one place Daisy would feel safe, it would be there. But she felt heartsick as she entered her room. Some of her keepsakes—glass from picture frames, and a princess figurine her grandmother had given her for her eighth birthday—were smashed. It didn't make sense—unless it had been Amber who'd done the damage. Why not try to destroy the pictures of Tori and her beloved grandparents—ruin a gift that had meant so much to her? But then Kathy's room hadn't escaped the same treatment, and Amber didn't even *know* Kathy. Did she even know Tori had a roommate? Herb might have mentioned it, but what if he hadn't? Would Amber have just assumed that Tori had taken over two rooms in the little bungalow?

"Daisy?" she called, stepping over the mess on the floor, and in some cases, kicking the debris aside. "Baby, come out for your mama."

Still no sign of the little orange tabby.

Tori crouched down, and then pushed the mound of clothes aside and got down on all fours, pulling up the dust ruffle and looking under the bed. Two shining eyes stared back at her. "Oh, sweetie, please come out," she coaxed, but Daisy—who had never been particularly brave—stayed put.

Well, at least she was safe. But that broken window in the living room had to be covered so that the cats couldn't get out. Then again, Kathy had been right. It would be better to pack up a litter box and get the three cats over to Swans Nest until the Sheriff's Department had gone over the home.

"I'll get your breakfast. You can eat it under the bed," Tori told her girl, hoping that she might use food to coax the cat out. "Be right back," she told Daisy and climbed back to her feet.

Kathy was hanging up the phone when she arrived back in the kitchen, and the boys were licking their chops, perfectly content.

"They'll send a deputy out as soon as they can. They asked us to vacate the premises."

"Just as soon as I get Daisy out from under the bed."

"Oh, good. You found her."

"Yeah, but she seems pretty terrified. Whoever did this must have scared her silly."

"Do you have any theories on who it might have been?" Kathy asked.

"Oh, yeah. And she is not about to get away with it," Tori swore.

26

*N*o sooner had Tori disappeared to take food to her cat, than the phone rang. Kathy grabbed it, thinking it might be the nine one one dispatcher once again.

"Where is everybody?" Anissa demanded.

"Here, obviously," Kathy answered. "Someone broke into Tori's house overnight!"

"What? I'll be right over," Anissa said and broke the connection.

First things first, Kathy thought and headed for the utility room, where they stored the cat carriers and litter boxes. They kept three of the latter, but they'd only take one over to Swans Nest. And where was she going to put the cats? She couldn't put them in one of the living areas. Cat hair and dander were not conducive to people who might have allergies. The best—the only viable place—she could keep them was in the butler's pantry. The cats usually got along pretty well, but being cooped up in such a small space wasn't going to be easy on them—especially poor Daisy who was outnumbered by the bigger and more aggressive boys. The situation was not a good one, but it was temporary, Kathy told herself.

She'd brought her two carriers into the kitchen and had easily captured Henry, who went into his box rather docilely, but Larry saw his carrier and bolted for the living room. He knew that being confined in the carrier meant a trip to the vet. She was still scrambling to corner the cat when Anissa arrived.

"What happened?" she demanded, sounding almost as upset as Kathy felt.

"I haven't had a chance to check things out. Tori's in her room trying to grab Daisy. Why don't you go and help her?"

Anissa nodded and disappeared, but only for seconds. "There's a gale blowing through that broken living room window."

"We need to secure it so that when we can get back in here, the cats will be safe."

"I'll get right on it," Anissa said and headed out the door. She might not be a cat person, but Kathy knew that Anissa understood what Tori's and her cats meant to them.

Once Larry had been confined, Kathy began gathering up bowls and other paraphernalia that the cats would need once they'd been transferred to Swans Nest. She was about to grab the first carrier and take it across the street when Tori emerged from the living room carrying Daisy.

"Is she okay?"

"Purring like a happy kitten," Tori said, sounding relieved. "She ate a little bit, and I managed to grab her. I'd like to take her over to your place before the deputies get here."

"Agreed. Anissa is out looking for something to cover that window."

"I think there's some wood paneling in the boathouse. She probably knows what's out there better than I do."

Kathy nodded. "I guess one of us should be here in case the deputies show up."

"You stay and I'll ferry the cats across the road. I won't feel better until I know they're settled."

"Absolutely," Kathy agreed.

As it happened, all three cats were carried across the road and made comfortable in the pantry when Tori returned to the Cannon Compound, and still no one from the Sheriff's Department had shown up. Apparently, breaking and entering wasn't considered that uncommon an event in rural Ward County.

Anissa had covered the broken window, if only to keep the heat in, and had headed off to the hardware store to buy a new piece of glass, saying she'd have it fixed before lunch.

All that waiting had given Tori more than enough time for her anger to grow to the boiling point, Kathy watched as her roommate paced the kitchen grumbling to herself.

She sighed and thought about the items she'd assembled that were sitting in the fridge at Swans Nest. They weren't likely to have breakfast any time soon.

After way too long, it wasn't a deputy who finally arrived, but Detective Osborn himself.

"Since when does a break-in warrant Osborn's attention?" Tori asked as they watched the detective get out of his unmarked car.

"Since I may have directly asked for him to come," Kathy admitted. "After all, we still need to give him that Valentine's Day card we found in Mark Charles's cabin."

They invited the detective inside.

"You shouldn't even be in here," the man chided. "It's a crime scene."

"What were we supposed to do? Stand outside and freeze?" Tori demanded.

"If you've been in every room, then you've contaminated any evidence that may have been there."

"We had our cats to think about—which we've relocated to my house across the street until we can secure this one," Kathy asserted.

"Cats, schmats," Osborn groused. Nevertheless, he left the kitchen to poke around the rest of the house. When he returned a few minutes later, he took out a notebook. "Tell me about it."

Tori related how her cousin had violated her privacy a week before and then had shown up the previous day. Osborn wasn't impressed.

"Means nothing. Unless you've got an eyewitness, it's just hearsay."

"Well, *somebody* broke into my house!" Tori almost shouted.

"What could your cousin be looking for?"

"I don't know. But she's jealous that my grandfather let me have this property. He won the lottery last year and hasn't given any of my other relatives a nickel. They're a jealous lot."

Kathy studied her friend's face. She knew it had taken a lot for Tori to admit that fact.

"The items that are broken were things I've treasured most of my life, and now they're ruined."

"But what's the monetary loss?" Osborn persisted.

"Not much," Tori admitted, her cheeks growing pink.

"It looks like malicious mischief to me," Osborn said. "It may surprise you to know that most homes are burgled during daylight hours. Still, your burglar is probably just a teenaged boy. That's what usually happens. You might want to make some security upgrades. Like motion-activated lights around the outside of the house. Get a sign that says BEWARE OF DOG." He put the notebook away without writing down a thing. "Now where's this evidence regarding Charles Marks?"

"If I can go back in the office, I'll get it," Kathy said.

Osborn didn't object, so she trundled off to the very messy office.

Kathy had left the card in a manila file folder on the side of her desk, under a pile of magazines, but when she searched through the contents on the littered floor, she didn't come up with it. Her anxiety began to mount as she started stacking items on the desks and chairs, but could not find the folder.

Finally, she shuffled back to the kitchen, where Tori was still ranting about Amber.

When she got the opportunity to interrupt, Kathy said, "It's gone."

"What?" Tori asked.

"The folder the card was in is gone, along with that list of telephone numbers Mark Charles had hidden."

Osborn looked annoyed. "You said you had the evidence since last Tuesday. Why didn't you call me sooner?"

"We were busy," Kathy offered lamely.

"I don't suppose you thought to make a copy of the card."

"As a matter of fact, we did," Kathy said.

"And where is it?"

Tori looked sheepish. "I gave it to Lucinda Bloomfield."

"Why in hell would you do that?" Osborn bellowed.

"Because she offered to help me financially. I thought it was the least I could do in light of her generosity." Tori explained about the Shepherd Enterprises proposal and that Lucinda had asked to counter it.

"When did you give her the copy?"

"Yesterday."

"I assume you know what her relationship was with Charles Marks."

"We know he was accused of raping her."

"Did you know that one of the men who beat up Charlie Marks before his disappearance was Lucinda Bloomfield's butler, Ronnie Collins?"

By the look on his face, Osborn hadn't been aware of that

fact. Still, he ignored the information. "That card could have proved to be a motive for revenge—for murder," he said sternly.

"I left the copy with her because I like her," Tori said. "Just go up the road and ask her for it."

"You like her—but do you trust her?" Osborn asked.

Kathy saw the look of indecision on her friend's face.

"I think so. I have no reason to doubt her sincerity."

The word "yet" seemed to hover in the ether. The three of them looked at each other for long seconds. Osborn spoke first.

"I'll go speak with Ms. Bloomfield, and then I'll get back to you."

"Should we clean up? I mean, maybe the card is still in the office buried under something," Kathy said, hoping she might be right.

"Go ahead," Osborn agreed. "There's nothing else the Sheriff's Department can do here." He sounded distinctly annoyed.

Without another word, the detective turned and exited the kitchen, the door slamming behind him.

"He seems a tad upset," Kathy offered.

"Pissed off, more like it. Was it a bad decision to show that card to Lucinda?" Tori asked.

"I know you want to trust her, but ... maybe that wasn't the most prudent decision."

Tori's frown bordered on profound. "Is it wrong to want to think the best of people?"

"Absolutely not," Kathy affirmed. And yet.... According to Don Newton, Lucinda Bloomfield was a slumlord. She detested "trade." Tori's bait shop could definitely be considered trade located at the bottom of Resort Road, which Lucinda's family had long wanted to be gentrified, probably to increase the neighborhood's property values. Did she own more on Resort Road than just the mansion on the hill? Had she intimidated other owners on the road to sell to her like she'd tried to do with Anissa's farther? Mr. Jackson had told his daughter in no uncertain terms that he felt bullied by the Bloomfields to sell. Stubborn old cuss that he was, he had refused. At first, Anissa had wondered if Lucinda had been behind her father's death, but in the end, it had been something—and someone—much more sinister.

The sound of tires on the compound's gravel drive caused the women to look up and through the window on the home's front door. Anissa had arrived, presumably with the replacement glass for the broken window. They left the house.

Anissa got out of her truck. "I've got everything I need to fix that window."

"Thank you," Tori said, sounding grateful.

"It'll take me all of twenty minutes—maybe half an hour. Do you think by then I can finally have something to eat?"

Kathy forced a smile. "You better believe it. But I don't have anything that's lunch worthy. Are you still willing to eat breakfast?"

"I'm about ready to eat my foot," Anissa declared.

Kathy laughed. "I promise, you won't have to do that."

"Then let me get working on this window."

"Um, we've got some other stuff to tell you," Tori admitted.

"Do it while I work. And Kath, go on back to Swans Nest and start getting my breakfast—or lunch—ready."

"Will do," Kathy said. "Tor, if Anissa is done before the detective gets back, leave him a note to tell him where we are."

"Will do," Tori promised, and accompanied Anissa to the side of the house.

Kathy headed back toward Swans Nest, figuring she might have four to cook for—depending on if Detective Osborn returned before Anissa fixed the window. Feeding the man might actually make him a little more friendly.

And if not ... well, she'd deal with whatever situation presented itself.

She really had no other choice.

*a*nissa had just smoothed out the last of the putty and replaced the storm window when Osborn's vehicle pulled into the Cannon Compound's lot once again. As he got out of his car, Tori could see that the deputy was not pleased.

"And?" she prompted.

Osborn walked slowly toward her. "Ms. Bloomfield looked at me with innocent blue eyes and said she didn't have a clue what I was talking about."

"Excuse me?" Tori challenged.

"You heard me. She said she didn't have any knowledge about a Valentine's Day card and suggested I go back to the source and ask for a better explanation. So, I'm asking."

Tori's anger blossomed once again. "Kathy found the card in Mark Charles's cabin when we were cleaning it out—after the Sheriff's Department had already gone through the place. Knowing Charlie Marks had disappeared after a parking lot brawl behind a bar, after allegedly raping Ms. Bloomfield, we thought it might be evidence."

"You couldn't have thought hard enough about it to wait five days to let me know of its existence."

"That was a mistake," Tori acknowledged. "But that doesn't negate the fact that we found it and always intended to turn it over to you. The card said, 'Charlie, luv you always, Lucinda.' Ms. Bloomfield studied the copy I gave her and her expression told me that she recognized the writing as her own."

"Well, she didn't admit it to me," Osborn said. "As far as I— and the Ward County Sheriff's Department—am concerned, it's your word against hers."

Tori glared at the detective.

He glared back.

"What about my house? Someone trashed it. Aren't you going to at least make a report?"

"I'll send a deputy to do that."

"Thank you," Tori managed, unable to keep the sarcasm out of her voice.

Osborn turned and returned to his car.

Anissa joined Tori and they watched as the law officer started the engine, backed out of the lot, and drove off.

"That man is *cold*," Anissa commented.

Tori said nothing, afraid of what she *might* say.

"What are you going to do?"

Tori looked toward Resort Road. "I'm going to go to that woman's house and confront her."

"Do you think that's a good idea?"

Tori turned to face her friend. "Have you got a better one?"

Anissa shook her head. "Do you want some backup?"

Tori let out a breath. "I think I can handle this by myself."

Digging into her jeans pocket, Tori removed her keys, walked over to her truck, and got in. Then she drove to the Bloomfield mansion.

Once again, Tori parked in front of the big house at the top of Resort Road. She marched up to the big front door and pounded on it.

She waited for at least thirty seconds—which she counted off in her head—before she pounded once again. It took another twenty seconds (one Mississippi, two Mississippi) before the door opened and Collins once again stood before her.

"Yes?"

"I'm here to see Ms. Bloomfield."

"I'm sorry, she isn't available."

"Excuse me, Detective Osborn of the Ward County Sheriff's Department was here not ten minutes ago and she sure as hell was available to see him."

"I'm sorry," Collins said again and went to close the door, but Tori stuck her foot over the threshold and he wasn't able to shut it.

"She *will* see me, and if she doesn't, I guarantee she will be very, *very* sorry she didn't."

Collins seemed to size her up. "I will inquire if Madam is available."

"Yeah. You do just that, *Ronnie*," Tori said contemptuously.

Collins's eyes widened and he did not seem pleased, but his training and years of service didn't allow him to show much more. He opened the door and allowed her to enter, leaving her standing there as he left her and ventured deeper into the house.

Tori shifted her weight from one foot to another, fuming, not sure what she was going to say to the lady of the house. Lady? She wasn't at all sure Lucinda deserved that title after blatantly lying to Detective Osborn. A lady should be a person of honor. Perhaps the locals had been right. Perhaps she was nothing more than a slumlord who took advantage of people with no other options, who forced them from their crappy rental properties when they were down on their luck and unable to pay.

Perhaps Lucinda was the bitch everyone thought her to be.

The bitch in question appeared from a door at the end of the hall and seemed to glide to the foyer. "Ms. Cannon," she said in greeting.

"Oh, so we're no longer on friendly terms, Ms. Bloomfield?"

"Why would you ask that?"

"Let's not fence," Tori practically spat. "Why did you tell Detective Osborn you knew nothing about the Valentine's Day card?"

Lucinda's features remained immobile, but she at least had the grace to blush. For a moment Tori wasn't sure Lucinda would answer, but then she seemed to remember her manners.

"Won't you come inside?"

"I think we can say what we need to right here," Tori said.

Lucinda frowned. "Very well." She paused, as though to compose her thoughts.

"That card brought back a lot of unpleasant memories of a very unhappy time in my life."

"I understand that, but lying to the detective doesn't erase what happened."

"That card has nothing to do with the current investigation into that man's death."

She couldn't even utter Charlie Marks's name. Then again, since the man had attacked—raped—Lucinda, was that even surprising?

"I know nothing about why or where he disappeared to all those years ago, and I'm not interested in knowing anything more about the man."

Tori wasn't about to be so cavalierly dismissed. "I gave you the courtesy of seeing that card before we gave the original to the Sheriff's Department. Only now my home was burgled and trashed, and the only thing we know for sure that is missing is the original card. Apart from Kathy and Anissa, nobody knew about it—except you."

"Are you accusing me of breaking and entering your home?"

"Not at all. But I wouldn't be surprised if one of your employees did the deed for you."

Lucinda said nothing.

"It's too bad, Ms. Bloomfield. If we weren't to become business partners, I thought at least we might become friends. I won't make that mistake in the future."

And with that, Tori turned, wrenched open the front door, and stalked out of the mansion.

AFTER TAKING copious amounts of photographic evidence, Tori and Anissa returned to Swans Nest for a brunch break. The food was excellent, but the celebratory mood they'd all experienced the night before was now a distant memory. After tidying the kitchen, the women returned to the Cannon Compound to set to work tidying the house. It took several hours to get it back in shape—and for a deputy to show up to take their statements. Despite Osborn's assurance they could clean up the mess, the deputy was annoyed that they had done just that. Since Tori, Kathy, and Anissa had assumed the deputies weren't going to bother to do more than make a report, they weren't the least bit apologetic.

"What gets me," Anissa said, as the three of them flopped down on the living room chairs, "is who else could have known about that card?"

"Like I told the detective," Tori said, "the three of us—and Lucinda."

"We did talk about it at the bar last night," Kathy pointed out

"As I suggested to Lucinda when I confronted her, our burglar could have been one of her employees."

"Who do you suspect? Avery Simons or Collins the butler?"

Tori thought about it. "I've had some time to think about it, and I think it was Collins. It's been bugging me since last night. One of the guys sitting alone at a table at The Bay Bar, nursing a beer, looked familiar, but I couldn't place him, probably because of his clothes. I've seen him there before, too. I think it was Ronnie Collins slumming."

"Noreen did say he was Lucinda's spy," Kathy pointed out. "We need to cross the road to get the cats back home; why don't we stop in The Bay Bar and ask before we do."

"Would Paul tell you?" Anissa asked.

"I don't know. But Noreen told us the other day that he and Ronnie weren't exactly friends anymore, but she didn't mention they were enemies, either."

"Maybe he'd tell us where Ronnie lives," Tori suggested.

"You could Google him. There are lots of sites that have public records," Anissa suggested.

"Let's try that first, but then we need to get going," Kathy said. "Those poor cats have been cooped up in my pantry for hours."

The computers were back online, so Tori sat down in front of hers and typed the name into the browser. The search turned up eighty-five Ronald Collins. She looked at the *Times of Ward County* news account she'd read days before and got Collins's middle initial. That narrowed the possibilities to three, and one of them was in Ward County. The report gave his address as Lake Bluff Road.

Coincidentally, Lake Bluff Road was the way one arrived at the bridge to Falcon Island.

"Yeah, but it's also about five miles long and strewn with farms, tract houses, and single trailers, not to mention the big campground where RVers filled with weekenders and snowbirds resided," Kathy said.

"What's the number?" Anissa asked. "We can do a drive-by on Google Street View."

Tori pulled up the appropriate page and moved the mouse until she found the property in question: a shabby, run-down single-wide trailer, surrounded with knee-high grass and looking derelict.

"What's the date on the drive by?" Kathy asked.

Tori frowned. "Three years ago." She stared at the screen. "Somehow, I can't imagine Collins the butler living in a dump like that. I mean, his clothes were impeccable. And if he's the cook, too, he's almost as good as you, Kath."

"I wonder if we could find out when he bought the trailer."

"Some counties in the state have a GIS system that lists who owns what properties," Anissa said. "Unfortunately, Ward County isn't one of them."

"Paul might know that, too."

"We can but ask," Tori agreed.

"Do you need me for anything else?" Anissa asked.

Tori shook her head. "We've already infringed on your only day off."

"Yeah," Kathy agreed, "and I'm sorry the circumstances ruined your breakfast. I still feel I owe both of you a stress-free gourmet meal."

"I'll take a raincheck," Anissa said, grabbed her jacket, and headed for the front door.

Tori and Kathy followed.

They gave Anissa a wave as she drove her pickup out of the compound's lot and Tori and Kathy crossed the road for The Bay Bar.

The bar had been open for a couple of hours, but they didn't see much in the way of traffic this early in the day. Paul stood at the end of the bar talking to one of the three bikers nursing beers and gave the women a wave as they entered. They took their usual seats near the kitchen and waited until Paul excused himself and headed their way.

"Kinda early for you girls to visit," he commented

"Yeah," Tori admitted.

"We saw the Sheriff's cruiser over at your place. Everything okay?"

"Somebody broke into my house overnight and trashed the place."

"Whoa. Not nice," Paul said. "How bad was it?"

"Mostly messy," Kathy said. "Whoever it was broke a window and dumped the dresser drawers and went through the closets in our bedrooms and office, but the rest of the house was untouched. We think they were looking for something specific."

"And they found it," Tori said.

"And we think the person who broke in knew we wouldn't be home last night because he heard us talking about the dry run and watched us leave the bar."

Paul's expression darkened. "Who?"

"First answer this question; was Ronnie Collins in here last night?"

Paul's gaze dipped. "Yeah. You think it was him?"

Tori and Kathy nodded.

"Why?"

"Because earlier this week, Anissa was hired to clean out the cabin rented by Mark Charles—aka Charlie Marks. We helped her and Kathy found a Valentine's Day card that was signed by Lucinda Bloomfield."

Paul's eyes widened. "That doesn't make sense. Charlie never had a shot with Lucinda."

"Apparently he had more than a shot," Kathy offered. "The card was signed 'Luv you always, Lucinda.'"

Paul's expression could only be called skeptical. "It had to be a phony."

Tori shook her head. "I showed Lucinda a copy—and hours

later the original was stolen. It was the *only* thing missing from the house after the break-in."

"Well, not exactly," Kathy said, but didn't go into details. "Tori gave a copy of the card to Lucinda yesterday afternoon. We don't know if she showed it to Collins, but he could have been listening in on their conversation and then decided to liberate the original. Without it, there's no proof that Lucinda ever had a relationship with Charlie."

Paul frowned. "It still doesn't make sense to me."

"Collins has been protecting Lucinda for years. Maybe he figured he still needed to protect her from being barraged with media attention and memories of the past," Tori explained.

"Okay, I get that," Paul said. "But I can't wrap my head around Lucinda Bloomfield having any kind of a relationship with Charlie Marks."

Tori sighed. "Not surprising. You're a *man*."

"And by your tone, I feel like I've just been insulted."

"Not at all," Kathy assured him. "But I'm betting you know nothing about alpha males."

"Excuse me?" Paul asked, sounding confused.

"In romance novels, lots of women are attracted to alpha males."

"Also known as bad boys," Tori added. "You know, tough, macho guys, with big hairy chests and arms."

"Yeah?"

"Well, maybe not all *that* hairy, but they're often misogynists."

"Sounds like those kinds of guys are just jerks."

"Yes, but it's the love of a good woman who redeems them—at least in fiction. In real life? Not so much."

"Is it out of the realm of belief that Lucinda, poor little rich girl, would have wanted to rebel and chose someone her parents would never have approved of to ... fool around with?"

Paul still didn't look convinced.

"Think of it this way," Tori continued. "You guys didn't believe Charlie when he boasted about knowing Lucinda back in high school. So if he actually *was* seeing her later, after you all had graduated, once again, you probably wouldn't have believed him."

"She wouldn't be the first woman to be branded a cock tease," Kathy said.

"Try this on for size: What if Lucinda wanted something her parents didn't want to give her—like more freedom, she could have used Charlie as leverage. 'Let me do X, or I will be involved with Y.'"

"Sounds pretty devious."

"Young people often are when they want something," Tori said. After teaching high school students for more than seven years, and having been one herself, she pretty much had them pegged.

Paul didn't seem convinced. "I'm telling you, I pulled that piece of shit off of her. She was terrified, she was brutalized. There's no way she was faking that."

"No, but if Charlie Marks felt like she'd been stringing him along, he might have felt she deserved what she got."

"That's a terrible thing to say," Paul hissed.

"I don't believe it—I'm saying *he* might have believed it. We'll never know because we can't ask him."

"What I don't get is why did Charlie—or Mark or whoever he was—come back to Lotus Bay in the first place? What did he hope to gain? Why did he change his name? Why did he dare to come back to a place where he was hated?"

Paul shrugged. "I've been trying to figure that out ever since I heard he was back—and dead."

"And more importantly, why would someone kill him?" Kathy suggested.

"Well, it wasn't me. I had no clue the guy was here. And whatever beef I had with him was long since over. Ronnie and I don't talk much anymore, but I'd say the same was true for him, too."

"Yes, but you don't work for the wronged person," Kathy said. "How many people in Ward County are butlers?"

"It's a job," Paul said flatly. "From what he's said, he cooks, he cleans, and he manages the estate—but under Lucinda's eagle eye."

"We looked him up on the Internet," Tori said. "Saw that he lives on Lake Bluff Road in a trailer."

"He doesn't live there," Paul said.

"Then he's moved?" Kathy asked.

"No. That's a rental property he owns. He has a room up at the Bloomfield mansion."

Tori and Kathy glanced at one another and shared a knowing look. Ronnie Collins was the estate's butler, but was he also Lucinda's live-in lover? It really wasn't any of their business, and they weren't about to voice the idea to Paul, who obviously had never considered the possibility. But it explained a lot. Lucinda might *not* have asked Collins to trash Tori's house, but if he was in love with her he might decide to intervene on her behalf if only to spare her from more embarrassment from the past. That said, was he as clueless as Paul that Lucinda had actually *had* a relationship with Charlie Marks? If he had been—he no longer was.

"Is there a chance Ronnie Collins knew Charlie Marks was back in the area?" Kathy asked, echoing Tori's thoughts.

Paul shrugged. "I have no idea. I sure as hell didn't. I'm betting Charlie shied away from his old haunts."

"His neighbor did say he kept to himself. She said he did odd jobs. Doing work under the table might be a way to stay out of the IRS's sights, too."

"Hey, Paul!" one of the guys at the end of the bar called. "Another round."

"Sure thing," Paul said and moved to the taps to pour three more beers. He didn't return to speak with the women.

"We ought to go rescue our cats," Kathy suggested, her voice edged with defeat.

"Yeah," Tori agreed.

The women got up from their stools and headed for the door. Paul didn't bid them a cheerful goodbye.

They hadn't learned anything of real value by talking to Paul, but they did have a better understanding of what might have gone on decades before.

Still, they had no clue as to who killed Charlie Marks, which was a real bummer.

28

While the cats weren't eager to return to their carriers, they were happy to come back to their real home and let Kathy know that they deserved treats for their hours-long ordeal. Soft touch that she was, she obeyed their commands.

By then, it was time to think about food—and what they'd have for dinner. Tori had forgotten to freeze the chicken breasts they'd bought two days before, so Kathy took out three and put the rest in plastic bags to freeze. Now all she had to do was decide what to do with them. She assumed Anissa would be coming to dinner—she usually did—and so Kathy wasn't surprised when the blue pick-up rumbled into the compound's lot.

"Anissa's here," she called to Tori as she sat down at the kitchen table with one of her cookbooks.

Tori emerged from the newly tidied office just as Anissa knocked on the door and then entered the kitchen. "I'm back."

"We noticed. It's almost suppertime. We're having chicken. You staying?"

"I never say no to chicken. Or burgers. Or hot dogs, or even leftovers," Anissa said and grinned.

"Sit down and I'll pour us some wine," Tori said. "Then we can trade stories about the horrors of the rest of the day."

"My day wasn't that horrible," Anissa said, peeling off her jacket and hanging it on one of the pegs by the door. She took her usual seat at the table. "When I got home, there was a strange message on my answering machine from none other than Rick Shepherd Enterprises."

"On a Sunday?" Tori asked.

Anissa nodded. "Yeah. Apparently, he's looking for someone to take care of his lawn-cutting operation in the Lotus Point area."

"But you're a contractor, not a landscaper," Kathy said.

"Don't I know it," Anissa said. "The message said that they'd had someone with a single mower take care of the small yards at the Point, and they wanted to contract that out."

"And the significance of that is?" Tori asked.

"Think about it. Mark Charles was a guy who cut lawns around the Point with his lawnmower. If he wanted anonymity, might he have worked for someone like Rick Shepherd? The people whose grass he cut wouldn't know him by name, only that he showed up once a week during the summer and made their lawns look tidy."

"That sounds plausible," Kathy said, "but how do we prove he worked for Rick Shepherd, and what's the significance if he did?"

"Well, the person on the phone—and it wasn't Rick Shepherd himself because I would have recognized his voice—dropped the name of one of my customers who suggested I might be able to help them out. I called my customer to say thanks and left a message asking about mower guy. He might have seen Mark Charles's picture in the paper. If so, that would be a good ID."

"Is he likely to call you back?" Kathy asked, flipping pages and studying the pictures of various chicken entrees.

Anissa nodded. "He's waiting for a quote on rebuilding his front steps, so I *will* be talking to him by tomorrow at the latest."

"Great," Tori said.

"Wait—how does your customer know Rick Shepherd?" Tori asked, measuring to see that everyone's glass had the same amount of Zinfandel.

"He didn't say. I'm guessing he might have once rented one of Shepherd's properties because he definitely owns the house he's fixing up piecemeal. He's interested in hiring me for the jobs he doesn't want to tackle."

"Which sounds like you aren't desperate enough to cut anyone's grass," Kathy guessed.

"I don't even like cutting my own. Whatever happened to all the teen and tween boys who wanted to make a little dough and would bum their dad's mower and some gas to cut lawns and make a few bucks?"

Tori passed the wineglasses around. "Probably making videos on YouTube and raking in much bigger bucks and without all the sweating."

"Did you call Shepherd back?" Kathy asked.

Anissa shook her head. "I figured I'd wait until business hours tomorrow."

"Maybe you could ask a few more questions about the job—get a better idea of what properties you might be working on."

"What for?"

"Well, if we hadn't lost the list of names and telephone numbers, we could have compared them."

"Well, you *did* lose it—so what's the point?"

"I guess you're right." Kathy sighed. "What do you think about oven-baked chicken barbeque?"

"Hot or sweet sauce—or both?" Tori asked.

"I was thinking sweet."

"Honey, as long as I don't have to cook it, I'm happy with anything," Anissa said and took her first sip of wine.

Kathy got up from the table, taking the cookbook with her. "It's going to take at least forty-five minutes to cook, so I'd better get started." She set the book aside, set the oven temperature, and took the chicken out of the fridge. Next, she pulled the aluminum foil out of the pantry and lined a baking sheet.

"I have to admit," she said as she put the chicken in the oven. "I've been thinking an awful lot about Ronnie Collins."

"I can't think of him as *Ronnie*," Tori said, frowning. "Just Collins. Ronnie sounds like it might be a fun name for a fun person. Collins is just plain dull."

"And he probably burgled your house," Anissa pointed out.

"Don't think I haven't forgotten that," Tori muttered.

"So, if he's so protective of Lucinda," Kathy went on, "why shouldn't he be the one to kill Charlie Marks? You think he's dull, but maybe he just keeps himself under tight control."

"So controlled he could shoot a man in cold blood?" Anissa asked.

"Why not?"

"And the motive?" Tori asked.

"Like I said. He might have felt he was protecting Lucinda."

"What kind of a threat was Charlie Marks to her all these years later?" Anissa asked.

"Bringing up the whole rape thing. Nobody wants to relive that kind of a nightmare," Tori said.

"I don't know. We have no proof that Collins even knew Marks was living in the area."

"Okay, we know that Mark Charles cut lawns in the summer.

What if he left a flyer on the door of the property Collins owned? He doesn't live there, but I'm betting he wasn't going to cut the grass at the place—not and get his fancy butler outfit covered in grass stains."

"So you think he could have called Mark Charles and recognized the voice after more than twenty years?"

"Maybe."

"Except that Mark Charles disappeared in December. He'd hardly be cutting lawns at that time of the year," Anissa pointed out. "And I didn't see a snow blower on the property when we cleared it out."

"A snow blower is a lot heavier to haul around than a lawnmower," Tori agreed.

"So where could Charlie aka Mark have run into Collins?" Kathy asked.

The three of them sipped their wine, the only noise in the kitchen being the aging fridge, which seemed to be humming awfully loud.

"Remember what Tammy at the hardware store told us," Tori said. "Mark Charles used to come to Warton for groceries and to go to the pharmacy. Collins could have run into him there. He wouldn't have confronted him in town, but what if he found out where the guy lived and paid him a visit, shot him, and pushed his truck over the bluff into the bay."

"How would we know if Collins even owns a gun?" Kathy asked.

"Everybody in these parts seems to own at least one gun," Anissa said. "I'm a minority in more than one way around here."

"I don't own a gun," Kathy said firmly.

"No, but Tori does."

"I've never used it," she said defensively. "But I have thought about getting rid of it. In fact, I didn't think to look to see if it was still in the closet after the break-in."

She got up from the table and left the room. She was gone for an awfully long time before returning to the kitchen. "It's gone."

"What? Your Gramps's gun?"

She nodded. "I think I'd better call Detective Osborn. He might think the theft of a shotgun was at least worth noting." She went into the other room to make the call.

Kathy got up to make the barbeque sauce for the chicken. "Well, I won't sleep better knowing that some creep has Mr. Cannon's gun," Kathy said.

"And if that creep is Ronnie Collins?"

"Especially if it is. Tori practically accused the guy of ransacking the place. What if the stoic butler comes back gunning for Tori?"

"You better not say that out loud to Tori," Anissa warned.

"Scare *her*? *I'm* scared," Kathy admitted. She took out the ketchup, brown sugar, cider vinegar, Worcestershire sauce, and yellow mustard and started mixing.

"Is that all you're putting into the barbeque sauce?" Anissa asked.

"When it comes to my sauce, less is more," Kathy asserted.

Tori returned to the kitchen. "Big surprise—Osborn's off duty. I had to leave a message."

"The guy deserves a couple of hours off a week," Anissa said reasonably.

"He seems to take off those hours only when we need to talk to him," Tori grumbled.

Kathy removed the chicken from the oven and began brushing on the sauce. "We should eat in about half an hour. More than enough time for another glass of wine."

"I'm game," Tori said and played bartender once more, while Kathy selected peas as their vegetable, and took out some frozen rolls as the meal's accompaniment.

Tori and Anissa began discussing repairs to the docks out back, but Kathy's thoughts kept circling back to the missing shotgun and the fact that Ronnie Collins had been violent in the past. Was it possible he could summon up that kind of rage on Lucinda's behalf once again?

29

*A*nissa left a little after eight, and Tori and Kathy retired to their shared office once again.

"I've been thinking a lot about Rick Shepherd," Tori said, pulling up a Google search box on her computer. "I didn't like the way he threatened me. I wonder if he's been in trouble in the past."

"I thought you looked him up right after you first met him," Kathy said.

"I did, but I didn't dig very deep." She typed in the businessman's name and hit the enter key. Seconds later, she got a lot of hits, but not many of them referred to the local Rick Shepherd. She narrowed down the parameters: Rick Shepherd, Ward County, New York. Bingo! Rick Shepherd Enterprises came up first. She ignored those links and concentrated on the more pertinent ones.

One was a story from the Rochester newspaper—a rags-to-riches kind of tale. Except that during the "rags" portion of Shepherd's life, he'd been arrested for petit larceny on more than one occasion, as well as domestic abuse. But according to the account, he'd found success in real estate and had been a model citizen ever since.

"Well, he wasn't displaying that kind of moral character when he threatened me," Tori said with chagrin.

The phone rang. Tori glanced at the caller ID and frowned. "Speak of the devil."

"Rick Shepherd?" Kathy asked, aghast.

"Apparently."

"Are you going to answer it?"

"No way."

They let the answering machine take it.

"Ms. Cannon—Rick Shepherd here. I've given you plenty of time to sign that proposal. You won't get a better deal from anyone else. Sign now. I wouldn't want to see Cannon's Bait and Tackle suffer a terrible fate."

The connection was broken.

"Well, that was stupid," Kathy said. "The answering machine just recorded the message, which is absolute proof he's a threat."

"I wonder how long it will take before he realizes that."

"My guess is not long. We've got to record it and get it on the computer—and better yet, on the cloud, in case he realizes we're not as stupid as he is and have recorded it and are keeping a sound file."

"What's the easiest way?" Tori asked.

Kathy pulled out her cell phone. "I'll take a video of you playing the message. The machine gives the time and date, right? And when we're done, I'll upload it to the net."

"Okay." Kathy held her phone in a horizontal position. "I'll say 'go' and then hit the record button. Give it an extra second or two before you do anything."

Tori nodded.

"Go!"

Tori wished she'd taken time to see how her hair looked

before she agreed, but then hit the answering machine playback.

"Sunday. Eight twenty-seven PM," said the flat, electronic voice of the answering machine, and then Shepherd's threat rolled around again. When it finished, Tori hit the save button, Kathy hit the video end icon, and all was well.

"I'll save this right now. It might be months before you'd need to produce it, but I don't think it would hurt for you to leave Detective Osborn another message."

"Why him? He isn't going to be interested in this kind of a threat."

"Well, then just call the Sheriff's Department. It's not an emergency, so you don't need to call nine one one," Kathy advised.

Tori hesitated. Was the Sheriff's Department's dispatcher going to take her seriously?

A big bad man threatened to ruin my bait and tackle shop if I don't cut him in for a majority of the profits on the resurrection of my little motel.

Yeah, she could almost hear the dispatcher yawn from boredom.

"I'll call Detective Osborn and leave a message," she decided. "He'll probably just pass it along down the hierarchy, but that will be his decision—not mine."

Kathy shrugged. "Okay. And while you do that, I'll go make sure all the doors and windows are locked. That man scares me."

"You and me both," Tori said as she plucked Osborn's card from her desk drawer once again.

Tori made her call and left a message, hanging up the phone just as Kathy reentered the room. "Um, what kind of a car does Rick Shepherd drive."

"I think it's a Mercedes. It looked expensive."

"Black?"

"Yeah."

"Um ... I think he might be parked by the side of The Lotus Lodge."

"What?" Tori said and practically exploded out of her office chair.

"I turned off the light in the kitchen so we could see better. Come on," Kathy said in a low voice—as if someone might be listening.

The women crept into the kitchen and gazed through the window in the back door. Suddenly that window looked like it could be a big liability should someone decide to smash it. The lock was only inches from its bottom. If broken, all someone would have to do is reach around and unlock the deadbolt.

Again, Anissa's words came back to haunt Tori.

Honey, if someone is determined to get inside, locks won't keep them out.

Just how determined would Rick Shepherd be?

KATHY AND TORI watched as a figure dressed in black emerged from the corner of The Lotus Lodge, holding what might have been a baseball bat ... except baseball bats are shorter and more stout than the item held in the dark form's hand. Something that looked an awful like—

"Tell me that's not a shotgun," Kathy said with a tremor in her voice.

"Or a rifle?" Tori asked, sounding just as scared.

"Nobody in their right might would threaten you with a gun just to strike a deal for a piece of The Lotus Lodge ... would they?"

"I have a feeling we're about to find out."

Kathy quickly reached for the light switch that suddenly bathed the front of the house in white light.

The figure stopped dead.

It *was* Rick Shepherd.

And he *was* holding a shotgun.

"What do we do?"

"Get on the phone and call nine one one!" Kathy hissed, and Tori rushed to the kitchen wall phone. "There's no dial tone!"

"He must have cut the wires. Get one of the cell phones!"

Tori ran for the office, leaving Kathy to stand guard in the kitchen. But there were no weapons at hand. Grabbing a large knife was a bad idea. It could be turned against them—and Kathy hated the sight of blood. She could handle it on a piece of raw meat; from a cut—or worse, a stab wound—not so much. Instead, she came up with the rolling pin Tori had left out earlier in the day. Fat lot of good it would do against a shotgun, but she needed some kind of reassurance.

By the time she got back to the door, Shepherd was halfway to the house.

"Tori!"

Tori came racing back to the darkened kitchen, cell phone in hand. "Yes, that's the address. Hurry! No, I won't keep calm—there's a man with a shotgun coming toward my door."

"We'd better get out of here," Kathy yelled, just as the butt of the shotgun came through the window with a shattering crash.

"Don't move!" Shepherd ordered as he fumbled to unlock the door. "And drop that phone!"

"There's a Sheriff's cruiser on the way!" Tori yelled back.

Shepherd entered the kitchen and flipped on the light switch. "Yeah, well I've been listening to the police scanner and the nearest cruiser is halfway across the county. They won't be here for at least half an hour, and by then we'll have our stories straight, won't we ladies?"

"Stories?" Kathy asked.

"Yes, how this was all a misunderstanding." He shoved the barrel of the shotgun toward Kathy, indicating she should put the rolling pin down. She set it on the counter and took a step closer to her friend.

Tori leaned forward, squinting at the shotgun Shepherd held. "Hey, that looks like my Gramp's gun."

Shepherd's grin was lopsided. "Well, I'll be damned."

I wish, Kathy thought.

"You broke into my house on Saturday night!" Tori accused the man in black.

"Entered, but I'm not the one who broke in. That was Lucinda Bloomfield's toady, Collins."

"That wasn't much of a stretch," Kathy said, considering what he'd taken. "But it was *you* who ransacked our office and bedrooms."

Shepherd feigned innocence. "Who me?"

"Lucinda Bloomfield may have sent her employee, but she wouldn't have had him trash our home," Tori said. She seemed determined to defend the woman.

"She's no saint," Shepherd said grimly. "I've known her too long—witnessed what she's capable of."

"And you're better?" Kathy charged.

"We were cut from the same cloth. Now, where's that agreement I sent you?" he demanded.

Tori raised her head so that her chin jutted out. "I shredded it."

That would be some feat since they didn't possess a shredder.

"Liar. But that's immaterial. I have another copy." Holding the shotgun propped under his right arm, index finger wrapped around the trigger, Shepherd reached into his jacket and withdrew a sheaf of tri-folded pages. He tossed them in Tori's direction. "Sign. And then we'll attend to that message I left on your voice mail."

"No."

A silhouette appeared behind Shepherd.

Keep him talking, Kathy silently implored of her friend.

"If we're going to go into business together, the terms of the agreement have to change."

"No change," Shepherd said. "Now pick it up and sign it."

Tori picked up the papers. "I don't have a pen."

"I do."

Again, Shepherd dipped into his jacket and withdrew a ball-point pen. He tossed it to Tori, who missed catching it. Kathy bent to pick it up. The casing was black, and in gold lettering it said *Shepherd Enterprises, Inc.* She handed it to Tori.

"Sign it!" Shepherd thundered.

Tori's gaze dipped from the barrel of the shotgun then rose to take in Shepherd's face.

Suddenly the screen door was ripped open. The shotgun flew to the right and exploded with a deafening roar, plaster raining down from the gaping hole in the ceiling. Before Shepherd could turn, a man with a baseball cap pounced, knocking Shepherd against the counter. Kathy swung the rolling pin, smashing it against Shepherd's left ear. He went down with a wail that could curl hair and Kathy found herself looking to Ronnie Collins's brown eyes.

"Sorry to burst in on you ladies like this, but I thought you might need a helping hand."

30

"Now let me get this straight," Detective Osborn said, staring straight at Tori. "You say Collins broke into your house, but that it was Shepherd who trashed it."

"That's right."

Shepherd had been taken away by ambulance to the nearest hospital—not all that close in rural Ward County—and with a Sheriff's Department escort. The deputies would stick with him until it was figured out what was what and who did what to whom. At that moment, Osborn looked totally perplexed.

"And why did you show up here tonight?" he asked Collins.

"I'd just left The Bay Bar and was headed home up Resort Road when I saw Shepherd get out of his car and carrying what looked like a shotgun. I waited in the shadows until I saw him break the window on the front door. I was afraid for the ladies here, and thought I should make it my business to be sure they were safe."

Just then, a knock sounded and they looked around to see Avery Simons, Lucinda Bloomfield's property manager, standing there looking in. "I'm just a delivery boy. I've come to present an envelope."

"Where's your employer?" Osborn demanded, taking possession of said item.

"Home in bed. Collins," he nodded toward his co-worker, "asked me to bring this here."

"Is that true?" Osborn demanded.

"Yes. I called him and asked him to bring it after we subdued Shepherd."

"That had to be more than an hour ago," Osborn said, sounding annoyed.

"I didn't get the message right away. I was otherwise occupied." Simons didn't mention what he'd been paying so much attention to and Tori was just as glad.

Osborn opened the envelope and glanced at the contents. "So?"

"So," Kathy said, picking up the narration. "When I found that piece of paper, hidden in a pile of newspapers, I thought the list of names and numbers might have some special significance."

"But that wasn't the case," Collins said smoothly. Despite his redneck façade of camouflage jacket, grungy jeans, and a Red Wings ball cap, his diction belied his appearance. "If you look on the other side of the page, you'll see it has far greater meaning."

Osborn's gaze darted back and forth for long seconds. Finally, he looked up. "I don't get it."

"It's pretty obvious to me that Mark Charles—or let's call him by his real name: Charlie Marks—was blackmailing Shepherd, and anybody who's anybody knows his less-than-stellar reputation. That piece of paper is proof that Shepherd is in bed with County Commissioner Oran Blanchard and getting special favors as far as developing land deals. My guess is that Charlie was mowing the lawn at one of Shepherd's properties and realized his boss was in cahoots with Blanchard and that it was clear

Shepherd was getting advance notice on the Palmer Packing site that was up for sale. That kind of information put him way ahead of the other developers bidding on the job—and we all know who came in with the winning proposal."

"Pure supposition on your part," Osborn grunted.

"I don't know about that," Tori said. "Ms. Bloomfield once told us that she hears what goes down in Ward County. I don't doubt that for a second," she said with a glance in Collins's direction. He'd sure spied on them every time they'd been in The Bay Bar during the past week.

"Get on with your story," Osborn ordered.

"Somehow Charlie came across that memo. He knew it was important, which is why he kept it. It might only be a copy, but it was initialed by county councilmen Duncan Harris, and it's obvious that there'd be a big payoff for someone on the town council. A lot of money was at stake and Charlie Marks probably saw it as a way to shake down a creep like Shepherd and maybe get out of Ward County once again. He sure was living rough."

"And you know that because?"

Collins sighed. "We talked. It wasn't a pleasant conversation."

"When was this?"

"Last November."

"And how did that conversation go?" Osborn demanded.

"I told him if he ever came near my employer, he'd be sorry."

"So why shouldn't I believe you shot the bastard?" Osborn asked.

"Because I'm telling you I didn't. I don't own a gun, and I've never fired one. Hell, man, I was shot by a lowlife and that's not something I'd inflict on another human being. Except for that one incident up on Lotus Point, I have a clean reputation. Charlie Marks didn't, and neither does Shepherd."

Osborn didn't look impressed. "Go on."

"Charlie told me it was a big mistake when he returned to the area and that he was getting the hell out of Ward County—just as soon as he got paid from a big deal businessman."

"And you figure that was Shepherd."

"That memo proves it," Collins said. "Shepherd isn't one to be blackmailed. What's killing off a penny ante nobody like Mark Charles to him? It was best to shut him up for good."

Osborn paced the confines of the kitchen. "What about the missing Valentine's Day card?"

"I don't know what you mean?"

"According to Ms. Cannon here, that's the reason you broke into the house."

Collins's gaze shifted to the floor. "It was the proof about Charlie Marks I was interested in."

"How did you even know it was here?" Osborn asked, his gaze narrowing.

Collins said nothing.

"Shepherd practically admitted that he ransacked my house," Tori said. "And I have it all on video. Or at least audio."

"What do you mean?" Osborn asked.

Tori brought her cell phone to life. The picture was that of the kitchen ceiling, but everyone listened as Tori replayed the conversation that led up to Kathy knocking Shepherd out.

"I'll need a copy of that for evidence," Osborn said when Tori switched off the playback.

"I'll be happy to email you one."

"Do you want to press charges against him?" Osborn said, shifting his gaze to Collins.

"Do I have to make up my mind right this minute?" Tori asked.

"No. But the sooner the better."

She looked at Collins. "I had to pay for a new window and its installation. My feeling of safety in my home has been damaged, which is far more disturbing to me."

Still, Collins said nothing.

Tori let out a breath. "I'll let you know in a couple of days, Detective."

He nodded.

"Is it okay if I leave now?" Simons asked. He'd remained silent through the entire discussion.

"Sure."

"What about me?" Collins asked.

"I don't suppose you're going to make yourself scarce in the next couple of days."

"I've got a job and other obligations in Ward County. I'm not going anywhere," Collins said, his tone hard.

"Good. Show up at my office tomorrow at ten to make a formal statement."

"Thanks."

"Come on, Ron. I'll give you a lift back to the house," Simons said.

Tori and Kathy glanced askance at each other. Collins lived in the mansion. Was he going back to warm Lucinda Bloomfield's bed—or had Simons been doing that when he'd been otherwise occupied earlier that evening? They'd probably never know.

They watched the two Bloomfield employees leave.

"What about my front door, Detective?"

"Yeah, we can't sleep knowing just anybody could get in," Kathy asserted.

"Don't you have some wood around you can cover it with? Otherwise, I can call the emergency response repair guys, but it could be a couple of hours before they show up—and it'll cost you."

Tori sighed. "Maybe Anissa hasn't gone to bed yet."

"I'll call her," Kathy said. She nodded at Osborn. "I'll be sending you my video of the phone call of Shepherd threatening Tori."

"You do that, Ms. Grant."

Kathy left the room to make her call.

"How much longer will you and your team be here?" Tori asked the detective.

He shrugged. "We can probably wrap this up in half an hour."

"Good. Because I want to sweep up the mess in this kitchen. I suppose I'll have to pay for the repair to the ceiling, too."

"Your insurance should pay for that."

"And we all know how fast they cut checks for stuff like that."

"Better the ceiling got shot instead of you and your roommate."

He was right about that.

Tori's ringtone sounded and she plucked her phone from her jeans pocket. She recognized the number right away. "Gramps?"

"I've been trying to get you at the house number for hours. Why didn't you call me? It's Sunday night—you always call on Sunday night."

"Well," Tori said, turning away and walking into her bedroom. "We had a little trouble at the compound tonight," she admitted. "The phone line got cut and ... it's a really long story, Gramps, and I'm not sure I'm up to telling it tonight."

"Don't tell me you girls have once again been poking around in things that don't concern you," he chided her.

"Well, we figured out who killed Mark Charles—or Charlie Marks."

"You're supposed to let the Sheriff's Department do that."

"I know Gramps. I know."

"All right. You can tell me all about it tomorrow. But there's another reason I called."

"Oh?"

"Yeah," Herb said, sounding rather cowed. "Irene and me have been talking about The Lotus Lodge."

Tori perked up. She and Irene had never been best buddies, but there was no doubt when it came to The Lotus Lodge, Irene was definitely in her corner. For some reason, Irene had it in her head that the little motel should never have closed. She'd helped Tori's grandmother, Josie, accumulate linens and other items to be used should it ever reopen. Tori had kept all of that stuff in protective totes just on the chance that her dream of seeing The Lotus Lodge resurrected ever came true.

"Talking how?" Tori asked.

"Well, first off, she reminded me that it was you who paid for the lottery ticket that brought me all the money for my new life." Since Irene was now shacking up with her grandfather, he might have said "our" to be technically correct, but what he said was true.

"Unlike the rest of the family, most of who are no longer speaking to me, you never asked me for a dime. You never once brought up the fact that I didn't buy that ticket. And you and Kathy worked your tails off last summer to bring the bait shop back to life and in the black."

"I did it for myself, Gramps. I couldn't let it die. I loved it and being here on Lotus Bay too much to see that happen."

"Well, I don't consider that a selfish motive. And because of that, if reopening that money pit of a motel is what you really want, then I'm going to help you do that by financing the restoration. I don't want you taking money from strangers or getting yourself in over your head with loans and stuff. That motel was a family business, and that's the way I want it to stay."

"I don't know what to say, Gramps, except thank you," Tori

managed, tears leaking from her eyes. "And please thank Irene, too."

"I'll do that, honey."

"And please—tell me why Irene has always wanted The Lotus Lodge to reopen. It doesn't make sense to me."

"Aw, that crazy woman is a big bag of sentimental mush."

"What do you mean?"

"Our second summer, your grandma sprained her ankle real bad. She could barely walk from the Fourth of July right through 'til Labor Day. It was make-it or break-it time for the entire season. We had to hire help—and Irene took the job. It was the first job she ever had, and ever since she's had a really soft spot for The Lotus Lodge. It about broke her heart when we had to close it down. And of course, she and your grandma were best friends for all those years—right up until the day Josie died."

"I'm glad Grandma had such a true friend."

"Yeah, I'm glad of that, too," Herb said, and Tori could hear the affection in his voice for his new love. He cleared his throat. "Nothing much can happen this year. I mean—you can't get it up and running in five weeks. But what you can do is make plans. Then at the end of the season, maybe we can make some upgrades and get the place buttoned up for the winter, and then come March when the weather breaks, get it finished up in time for next year. What do you say?"

"I think that sounds fantastic," Tori said, wiping fresh tears from her eyes.

"Good, good. I was thinking maybe we could help Anissa out by having her act as our contractor. What do you say?"

"I think she'd be thrilled to have a steady job."

"Good, good. Okay, we'll talk more about this when you call tomorrow. But not too early. Irene and me are heading for this great little diner that serves pancakes almost as good as your grandma used to make. And get this, it's called Josie's." He laughed. "It seems like your grandma's still taking care of us. What do you think?"

"I'll bet she's smiling down on us right now."

Herb laughed again. "Okay, now don't forget to call me."

"I won't, Gramps. I love you."

"I love you, too, honey. Good night."

"Good night."

Tori tapped the end call icon and stared at her phone, unable to believe how her life had suddenly turned around—especially when just a few hours before she'd been frightened that her life might just end.

Kathy poked her head inside the room. "Anissa's here to board up the window. Hey, are you okay?"

Tori faced her. "Okay? I'm better than okay. I'm fantastic. And have I got a story to tell the two of you."

"I don't know about you, but after what we've been through tonight, I'm going to crack open another bottle of wine and I may just finish it off. Do you want to join me?"

"Yes, because I've sure got an awful lot to celebrate."

31

*I*t was probably far too early to plant flowers in front of Swans Nest since the threat of frost was always possible right up until Memorial Day, but Kathy couldn't help herself. The dual urns that sat on the front porch were probably safe from freezing thanks to being covered, and she could always drag them closer to the house should the temperatures dip into the low thirties, but she could handle that. And the pansies she'd just installed along the front walk were hardy little plants. She had some old sheets she could cover them with if the need arose. Just looking at their cheerful little faces in a myriad of colors had caused her to burst into song. She was just happy no one was around to hear her sing.

As she peeled off her thin gardening gloves, a truck pulled into the lot. "Are you ready for the big day?" Tori called as she got out of the cab with a potted plant. She'd had a teaching job that morning, but was now free for the rest of the weekend.

Kathy smiled, and a shiver of excitement ran down her back. "My guests will be arriving in a little over two hours. I'm as nervous as all get out."

Tori waved a hand in dismissal. "They don't know how lucky

they are to be spending the weekend in such a beautifully restored home."

Kathy laughed. "I hope I don't bore them with my scrapbooks chronicling the work, but I do think at least some of my guests would love to take that journey." She nodded toward the faux orchid in Tori's hands. "What have you got there?"

"It's a house-warming gift. It's not real," she said unnecessarily, "but it looks it. And I figured it would look pretty somewhere in your house. You won't have to water it so you can't kill it, and it'll look nice for years." She handed it to Kathy.

"Thanks."

The sound of an approaching engine caused them to look up and then Anissa's pickup pulled into the parking space next to Tori's truck. She got out. "Boy howdy does this little parking area look sharp. When did the lines get painted?"

"Yesterday afternoon," Kathy said.

Anissa laughed. "I didn't see them because I've been working east of here for the past couple of days." She crossed her arms and took in Swans Nest. "What a pretty B and B. We sure did her proud."

"I'll say," Tori echoed. "A year ago this place was a dump and now...I can't believe the transformation. And next year, we'll be standing in front of the refurbished Lotus Lodge and feeling just as happy."

"You got that right," Kathy agreed.

Movement from her left caused Kathy to turn, and she saw Noreen hurrying over to join them. "It's the big day!" she called.

Kathy felt ready to burst with pride. "For so long it seemed like this would never happen."

Noreen blushed. "I have a little housewarming gift for you."

"Aw, you didn't need to do that," Kathy said automatically.

"Yes, I did." Noreen sobered. "You acted in good faith when you took in my overflow guests, and they treated you terribly by destroying your pretty room. I felt just awful about that, but worse was knowing that insurance wouldn't handle the damage. She reached into the pocket of her bib apron. "I'm sorry it took so long, but after a lot of detective work—and cutting off the people who vouched for those louts—I was able to get them to cough up what I hope will pay for the damage."

Kathy accepted the check, which had been cut from The Bay Bar's account. "Oh, I'm not sure I can—"

"Yes, you can take it. I promise you, this money isn't from Paul and me—although if we hadn't tracked the guy down, it would have been. They paid us in cash. I put it in the bank and wrote the check."

"Thank you, Noreen. You and Paul are good neighbors."

Noreen smiled. "And we may be even better ones."

"In what way?" Tori asked.

"Well, since Kathy has turned this former wreck into a gem, and what with The Lotus Lodge going to reopen, Paul and I have decided that we're going to turn the floor over the bar into a couple more rooms for fishermen."

Kathy could see from Tori's expression that it wasn't exactly good news, as she intended to rent Lotus Lodge rooms to fishermen, too.

"Don't worry, Tori. I was thinking that with all the new business at this end of the bay, we'll be turning away business. You and I can trade overflow—but we'll insist on reservations and vetting."

"If you say so," Tori said sounding unconvinced.

"But having people staying above the bar means we'll be turning our jukebox down even earlier, Kath. That'll give your honeymooners a much more quiet guest experience."

Kathy wasn't about to argue with that new arrangement.

"When do you think you'll open your rooms?" Anissa asked. "How soon can you start working on them?"

"I'll check my schedule and get back to you," Anissa said and grinned.

Just then, a vintage silver Town Car pulled into the small lot. Ronnie Collins exited the driver's door, walked around to the back of the car and opened the right side passenger door, offering his hand and helping Lucinda Bloomfield from the car, which must have belonged to her late father. Collins shut the door but stood by the car as Lucinda approached the other women.

She was dressed in a peach linen suit and holding a bouquet of red roses and baby's breath. "Good afternoon," she said. "I hope I'm not disturbing you."

"Not at all," Kathy said. "I don't think you know our friend Noreen Dancy. She's co-owner of The Bay Bar."

"How do you do," Lucinda asked and offered her hand.

Noreen shook it but seemed tongue-tied.

Lucinda turned back to Kathy, whose gaze was riveted on the roses. "I understand you'll be opening Swans Nest this weekend."

"That's right. My first official guests will be arriving in just a little while."

"I wanted to wish you good luck."

"Thank you."

Lucinda didn't offer the roses. Instead, she turned to Tori. "I hope you'll accept these flowers as a gesture of friendship."

Tori's eyes narrowed as she scrutinized Lucinda's face. "What for?"

Lucinda seemed to hesitate. "You could have made things very difficult for Mr. Collins."

Tori shrugged. "The fact that you sent down a team of people to replace the door and add security lighting around the house was very thoughtful. I hope you received my thank you card."

"Yes, I did. It was much appreciated. But I wanted to thank you in person. You didn't press the issue of the ... the other card. You saved me a lot of heartache with that gesture and I wanted you to know how grateful I am."

"I'm glad I could be of help," Tori said and accepted the flowers.

"Perhaps we'll have tea again soon," Lucinda said.

"I'd enjoy that," Tori replied.

Lucinda nodded and took in the group. "Ladies."

Everyone gave her a wave and, with dignity, Lucinda walked back to the car and allowed Collins to help her into the back seat. They watched as the big car backed onto the highway and then headed toward Resort Road.

"Well, that was unexpected," Anissa said.

"It sure was," Tori agreed.

"For a minute there, I thought *I* was going to get the roses," Kathy said, feeling just a little hurt.

"You and me both," Tori said. "I hope you don't mind, but I intend to keep them."

"They'll look pretty on the kitchen table."

"Sounds like we all have reason to celebrate," Anissa said.

"And I want to treat you ladies to supper at The Bay Bar. I'm cooking up beer-battered haddock tonight. Are you game?" Noreen asked.

"I never say no to free food," Anissa said and laughed.

"Me, neither," Tori said.

"I'm not about to buck the tradition. But first I've got a batch of cookies to bake before my guests arrive."

"What's the recipe this time?" Anissa asked.

"Chocolate chip oatmeal."

"My favorite," Tori said.

"I'll make a double batch so we can all have some for dessert."

"How about you ladies come on over to the bar around seven?"

"Perfect. Meanwhile, I'll go put these roses in water," Tori said.

"And I've got a plugged kitchen sink to fix over at Willow Point," Anissa chimed in.

"Okay. See you then," Noreen said and give them a wave before heading back to the bar.

Tori and Anissa got in their trucks, honked their horns in salute, and pulled out of the lot.

Kathy waved as well, then turned and entered Swans Nest, enjoying what was turning out to be the best day of her life.

ABOUT THE AUTHOR

The immensely popular Booktown Mystery series is what put Lorraine Bartlett's pen name Lorna Barrett on the New York Times Bestseller list, but it's her talent—whether writing as Lorna, or L.L. Bartlett, or Lorraine Bartlett—that keeps her there. This multi-published, Agatha-nominated author pens the exciting Jeff Resnick Mysteries as well as the acclaimed Victoria Square Mystery series, Tales of Telenia adventure-fantasy saga, and now the Lotus Bay Mysteries, and has many short stories and novellas to her name(s). Check out the descriptions and links to all her works, and sign up for her emailed newsletter here: http://www.LLBartlett.com

If you enjoyed *A REEL CATCH*, please consider reviewing it on your favorite online review site. Thank you!

Find me on these other sites:
www.lorrainebartlett.com

An Unexpected Visitor

Grape Expectations

Tales of Telenia

(adventure-fantasy)

THRESHOLD

JOURNEY

TREACHERY (2019)

Short Stories

Love & Murder: A Bargain-Priced Collection of Short Stories

Happy Holidays? (A Collection of Christmas Stories)

An Unconditional Love

Love Heals

Blue Christmas

Prisoner of Love

We're So Sorry, Uncle Albert

Writing as L.L. Bartlett

The Jeff Resnick Mysteries

Murder On The Mind

Dead In Red

Room At The Inn

Cheated By Death

Bound By Suggestion

Dark Waters

Shattered Spirits

A Killer Edition